T0390893

♥ KILL THE LAX BRO ♥

KILL THE LAX BRO

CHARLOTTE LILLIE BALOGH

DELACORTE PRESS

Delacorte Press
An imprint of Random House Children's Books
A division of Penguin Random House LLC
1745 Broadway, New York, NY 10019
penguinrandomhouse.com
GetUnderlined.com

Text copyright © 2025 by Charlotte Lillie Balogh
Jacket photograph copyright © 2025 by Christine Blackburne

Penguin Random House values and supports copyright. Copyright fuels creativity, encourages diverse voices, promotes free speech, and creates a vibrant culture. Thank you for buying an authorized edition of this book and for complying with copyright laws by not reproducing, scanning, or distributing any part of it in any form without permission. You are supporting writers and allowing Penguin Random House to continue to publish books for every reader. Please note that no part of this book may be used or reproduced in any manner for the purpose of training artificial intelligence technologies or systems.

Delacorte Press is a registered trademark and the colophon is a trademark of Penguin Random House LLC.

Editor: Kelsey Horton
Cover Designer: Casey Moses
Interior Designer: Cathy Bobak
Production Editor: Colleen Fellingham
Managing Editor: Tamar Schwartz
Production Manager: Liz Sutton

Library of Congress Cataloging-in-Publication Data
Names: Balogh, Charlotte (Charlotte Lillie), author.
Title: Kill the lax bro / Charlotte Balogh.
Description: New York : Delacorte Press, 2025. | Audience term: Teenagers | Audience: Ages 12 and up | Audience: Grades 7–9 | Summary: Every type of student at Hancock High is a suspect when Troy Richards, the school's star lacrosse player, is found dead on the night before graduation.
Identifiers: LCCN 2024042636 | ISBN 978-0-593-89927-4 (hardcover) | ISBN 978-0-593-89929-8 (ebook)
Subjects: CYAC: Mystery and detective stories. | High schools—Fiction. | Schools—Fiction. | LCGFT: Novels.
Classification: LCC PZ7.1.B3626 Ki 2025 | DDC [Fic]—dc23

The text of this book is set in 11-point Warnock Pro.

Manufactured in the United States of America
10 9 8 7 6 5 4 3 2 1

The authorized representative in the EU for product safety and compliance is Penguin Random House Ireland, Morrison Chambers, 32 Nassau Street, Dublin D02 YH68, Ireland, https://eu-contact.penguin.ie.

Random House Children's Books supports the First Amendment and celebrates the right to read.

for the boys who broke my heart
and the girls who'd murder on my behalf

♥

glossary of slang

Around the world: A trick shot thrown behind the shoulder of your dominant/shooting hand. But don't get cocky, kiddies.

Bar down: A shot that rebounds off the goal at an angle. The perfect angle. Unless you miss.

Bucket: Your helmet, aka your lid, aka the only thing standing between you and a night in the ER.

Cage: The goal.

Check: When one player strikes another. *Hard.* Check someone hard enough, and you'll be fouled by even the sleepiest referees. So . . . don't get caught.

Flow: Any laxer's most prized possession—their long, unruly, sometimes curly, always flowing hair, aka lettuce, aka cabbage.

Goon squad: The kids on the bench who never, ever play. Ever.

Ice pick: When one player checks another by stabbing them with the pointy end of their stick. And yes—*literally*.

Lax: Aka lacrosse. The oldest sport in North America, which was colonized by your favorite chinos-wearing Chad.

Murder pass: Oh, don't worry. You'll find out soon enough . . .

prologue

It's the kind of place that always smells the same. No matter how long we're gone, and no matter how hard we've tried to stay away. Daffodils, cheap booze, gasoline. Reasons to live. Reasons to die. Metaphors, and monotony, not to mention whatever kind of hellish fertilizer the janitor dumped in the flower beds this morning. It's not much, if it's even anything at all.

But hey, as the poets say—*It's high school.*

Tonight the parking lot is full. Half with beloved secondhand cars, half with the newest-model BMW on loan from Maxwell Motors. But what else would we expect? Hilary Maxwell may have graduated last year, but everyone knows that her dad, Max Maxwell, and his dealership run this town. When we move close, closer, and closest, we can see a smattering of bumper stickers, each one slapped into place like a Band-Aid from Mom to help us feel better: EAT MY SHORTS, CLASS OF 1999, and the instant classic I KISSED A BACKSTREET BOY.

Behind the school is a patchwork of athletic fields, one for every sports team our public education system can afford. To the north is a baseball diamond; to the south a tennis court. The lacrosse turf sits at the center.

Dead center, if we're feeling cute.

Now we are close enough to hear it.

Them.

There is a dance party happening in the cafeteria, the first and last of the spring semester. The warble of an almost mournful, uniquely familiar girl group echoes outside the building, over the cars, and all the way to the rotary at the end of the street. And it's nice, if you're into that kind of thing. But between the blasting music and the dancing bodies, the school is like a living, breathing, throbbing creature. The walls expand and contract with the bassline, even as the darkened windows look out without actually seeing or being seen.

Well . . . all except one.

Looks like someone left a light on in the chemistry lab.

Interesting.

Closer still and we can finally see the front of the school. A sun-bleached marquee plopped at the entrance. On any other day, it is plastered with babysitter ads and glee club posters. However, tonight it has been cleared off to remind everyone of the single most important night of the year. If not the rest of our pitiful little lives.

Tonight.

spring lock-in

june 1999

1

...baby one more time

JENNIFER LEE

The bravest couples slow dance—but right now, there aren't many.

Not this early in the night.

The cafeteria is dotted with denim jackets, denim overalls, and brightly colored slap bracelets, and parent chaperones stand guard at the exits. I don't know why they bother. Hancock High held its first lock-in nearly a decade ago, right after a group of seniors died in a drunk driving accident. Now, in their memory—and in an effort to protect the current students from their own bad decisions—the night before graduation all students, teachers, and overly involved parents are—you guessed it—*locked into* the school overnight. It's part dance, part fundraiser, part theater, and every lock-in begins with the drama club staging a car accident involving real cars and fake blood. Just to really send the message home.

That said, with the entire student body packed in like sardines, and someone—somewhere—guaranteed to sneak in cheap booze, everyone knows it will be a night to remember.

Like the Stanford prison experiment—but hornier.

Who'd be caught dead anywhere else?

The music warps to a synthy Ace of Base bop, and the makeshift dance floor swells with bodies. In the daytime, the cafeteria is crowded from wall to wall with circular plastic tables. But in honor of tonight's festivities, the tables have been folded up against the windows to make space. Careful to dodge elbows, I hustle across the room and shimmy between two halved tables—where I'm startled to find I'm not the only one looking for a hiding place.

"Oops! Hi, Naomi."

Naomi King blinks at me from behind an oversized pair of granny glasses. Silent. Although that's not unusual for her. Usually, I'll see Naomi in the hallway between classes, alone and walking alarmingly fast, with her face buried in an Anne Rice novel. Her thick hair is box-braided into pigtails, and her baby-pink overalls have a telltale smudge of sugar at the knee, most likely from when she was working the bake sale earlier tonight. I don't know a ton of freshmen by name, but Naomi's older sister, Melissa King, was an icon—homecoming queen, student senate vice president, Most Likely to Change the World, Best Smile—and Mel is currently on a full ride at Boston University.

"Scram, dweeb!"

I turn to see the Stern twins standing behind me protectively, each one a carbon copy of the other. The three of us are dressed in matching tube tops—Chloe in blue, Zoey in pink. I'm in black. Naomi disappears with a literal squeak, and even I'll admit that I'm grateful for the rescue. The twins beckon for me to follow, and I realize they've managed to crack a window without our chaperones noticing. No small feat. They pass a joint from one manicured hand to the next, and we take turns exhaling through the gap.

"Don't be such a hog, Chloe!"

"Hog? As if!"

I giggle and take a hit when Chloe offers it—and Zoey gives me her watermelon lip gloss to apply when I'm done. The twins are in the grade above me, but this year I effectively became the leader of our little trio. Although it could just be due to the fact that I'm three inches taller.

"Look who it is!"

We turn in unison, the motion just as synchronized as our outfits.

Andrew Garcia is as classically handsome as a guy can be. Tall and lean, long hair, thick eyebrows—one with his trademark scar down the center—and a smile that has curved many a final exam grade. Like the twins, Andrew is a junior. But he's also one of those old-soul types who was held back after kindergarten and now gets along with everyone as a result. Like me, Andrew avoids the dance floor—shy, but on a mission.

"Andrew! Can't believe you came."

"Me neither." He smiles that smile. "Although I hear getting out is the hard part."

Chloe offers Andrew a hit, but he declines. Despite what you might expect, Andrew's never been one for the party scene, and I've always liked that about him.

Even after everything that happened this semester.

"Relax, stud." Zoey nudges him with her Keds. "It's not like you're on the team anymore. Live a little, yeah?"

Instead of responding, Andrew looks away—but this time I don't copy him. I don't need to, to know what he's looking for: his team.

The team.

Here at Hancock, people only go to the football games to watch the cheerleaders drop other cheerleaders. Track and field had a bit of a renaissance, sure, but don't get me started on soccer. Because for us, it's always been the boys varsity lacrosse team at the center of our small-town universe. Each spring, the boys make headlines in the school, town, and state papers, and tonight, like always, they are wearing their electric-blue practice jerseys—plus a girl on each arm.

"Zoey, be nice," Chloe chides. She flicks her twin on the boob.

"What? He's not. Troy Richards saw to that—"

"Zoey!"

Andrew settles for a shrug. Suddenly, he reaches for the blunt, his hand lingering in mine. "Have you seen Sassi?" he asks.

"I thought I saw her drinking with the seniors," Chloe offers. "Moose snuck in a keg."

"Ha! Sassi DeLuca? I seriously doubt that—"

"Why? Is everything okay?"

Andrew nods and steps closer, his mouth brushing my ear. The music changes again, and I only catch a few words. But it's enough.

"... somewhere? To talk?"

I blush—and Zoey and Chloe share a look.

I let Andrew take my hand, and we slip out of the cafeteria relatively undetected. With my height, I'm usually hunched over when I'm standing around the guys my age—physically trying to fit into an unseen mold before I realize what I'm doing, or why, or how I'm doing it. But Andrew and I are the exact same height, and with him I stand tall. In seconds, we fall into an easy rhythm, and we walk side by side through the school.

The entire first floor has been decorated with balloons and streamers in the red, white, and bright blue colors of our school, and each classroom we pass has a different activity meant to keep people awake for the duration of the twelve-hour lock-in. There's face painting, balloon darts, an airbrush station and temporary tattoos, caricatures courtesy of someone's dad's midlife crisis, a cash grab machine, and even a carnival-style fishbowl toss—with real fish as prizes. Last year there was also a dunk tank, but that was quickly discontinued after a certain lax bro peed in it on a dare. Not that I'm naming any names.

I nod when Andrew indicates the south-side stairwell, and once inside, I push him to the wall—"talking" pretty passionately. Even by my standards. Andrew's mouth tastes sweet and sour, like fake cherries and long summers at my parents' place on Cape Cod. But—

"Jennifer . . . ?"

Oops.

I bring Andrew's hands to my waist as the fluorescents zip-zap on above us, and I shiver as his thumb traces the edge of my silk top. For a moment, Andrew forgets whatever he was going to ask. Or two moments—almost three. When he does pull away, I can't tell which of us regrets it more.

Then—gradually—it dawns on me.

"Wait. Did you actually want to *talk*?"

"Yeah. It's about Troy—"

"*Yo!* Get a room, fartknockers!"

We look up.

Tatum Stein is perched in the window above us, a cigarette in her teeth and her Doc Martens on the railing for balance. As far as I know, no one in our school, or in the entire town of Hancock, likes Tatum Stein. Also, no one knows how old she is. Tatum was a senior when I was a freshman, and I honestly think I'll be graduating before she does. Tatum is single-handedly responsible for supplying people at our school with their drug of choice—uppers, downers, pills, and powders. Not to mention booze—and lots of it. Last fall, Principal Clancy conducted a locker search the day before Halloween, and there's a rumor that Tatum only avoided expulsion by hiding her stash in her vagina.

"What are you doing here, Tatum?"

Tatum draws a dick on the glass with her pinkie.

"Troy Richards stood me up. Again," she mutters, waving a telltale plastic baggy in the air. "I saw your boyfriend earlier for a delivery, and he told me to wait here for my payout."

Boyfriend.

The word lances through me like an electric shock—just like Tatum knew it would. She snorts at my obvious reaction and flicks her cigarette, letting the ash fall on Andrew. He scowls, shakes out his flow, and gestures upstairs to the next level. Technically, no one is supposed to leave the first floor during the lock-in, especially not without telling a chaperone first. But that doesn't stop him.

"Tell Troy I say hello!" Tatum calls after us, bitter.

We let the door slam shut in answer.

Alone again, Andrew and I stand awkwardly outside the library. Here, the hullabaloo from the cafeteria is muted, and unlike downstairs, all the lights on the third floor are off. I can barely see his face in the darkness.

"You okay?"

Andrew takes my hand, and—not for the first time—I'm surprised by how soft his skin is. Because the way the varsity boys act on the field, I always thought their hands would be Swiss-cheesed. But he proved me wrong the first time we kissed.

Troy Richards, that is, not Andrew.

"That was awkward," I murmur.

"Yeah. That's one word for it."

My heart is still pounding in both ears from the kiss. At least, I tell myself that's the reason. Because of that, I don't automatically recognize the sound of footsteps. When I do, I tug Andrew behind a set of bulky trash bins.

"Who is it?" Andrew hisses.

I shush him quiet.

Peeking around the bins, I see what Andrew can't—Sassi DeLuca. Hancock's perfect little Polly Pocket come to life, with twice the beauty and brains. Regardless of the weather, Sassi always seems to be wearing the same crimson Harvard sweatshirt—as if she needs to remind the rest of us how big and bright her future is. She glides by in her platform sandals without noticing us, her ponytail obnoxiously high, with zero clue that her timing is the absolute worst. Glad to know some things never change.

But where the heck is she coming from?

"It's no one," I lie, glancing at Andrew. "Can we go somewhere? To . . . talk . . . in private?"

Andrew hesitates, clearly thinking hard about something, then bobs his head up and down in agreement.

"Follow me."

Again, Andrew takes me by the hand, but this time we're not going far. He steers me to the last classroom on the left—closest to the stairwell—and with the door ajar I recognize the offices for the *Howler*, Hancock High's unsung yearbook publication.

I stop Andrew before he can turn on the light.

"Wait. Just . . . two more minutes?" I say. Andrew is about to hesitate, but I pull him farther into the room. Then my arms. We stumble through a circle of chairs, laughing—until my back bumps into something.

Something cold.

Something solid.

Something . . . big.

"Holy shit."

Andrew, ashen, gawks at the something over my shoulder, and I turn around as quickly as I dare. Because at a glance, it looks like there is a lopsided piñata hanging from the ceiling fan.

A very human-shaped, very human-sized piñata.

"Jennifer . . ."

I step to the side for a better view, and the milky blue-white light from the hallway falls inside, across the floor, and over the bloody lacrosse jersey directly in front of us—the last name RICHARDS is as clear as day.

"It's Troy," Andrew finishes.

And I scream.

january

2

all the young dudes

ANDREW GARCIA

Someone is screaming in the cafeteria, and I hear them before I see them.

Then again . . . everyone in the building must.

Today, Monday, was our first day back from winter break, and the spirit committee is wasting zero time getting things ready for the new semester. At the moment, the Stern twins are sprawled out in front of the vending machines, hard at work and hardly working. Stretched on the linoleum between them is a massive paper banner with the words CONGRATS CLASS OF '99 sketched in pencil, and Chloe and Zoey are in the process of painting them over with bubble letters. But so far, they've only finished the first *C*.

And Chloe has blood-red paint spilled on her jeans.

"You ruined my flares!"

"*Pfft*. You didn't need me for that—"

Chloe or Zoey lunges at her twin. I gotta admit, I can't always tell the difference. Every head in the cafeteria turns to watch, and I'm careful to avoid their tangled limbs on my way to the back of the room. Like always, my boys have pushed three tables together in our corner closest to the emergency exit. The varsity players sit against the windows with their feet on the tabletops, and junior varsity sits below them. Freshmen know to remain standing.

Because even if classes are over for normal people, for us, the day is only getting started.

"Garcia!"

As soon as I'm within reach, Moose grabs me for a one-arm hug. Then a headlock. He might be younger than me, but Moose is already twice my size, which is part of the reason he's the top-ranked goalie in our region and no one bothers with his real name. The other reason is that he's just dumb enough to enjoy getting hit with a ball moving seventy-five miles per hour.

"I gotta question for you, stud," Moose says. He flexes his arm, and his newest bruises and battle scars leap to attention an inch away from my nose. Each one holds a story of one game or another from his lacrosse career, in most cases a victory.

"Fire away."

"Fuck, Marry, Kill . . . ?" Moose pauses for emphasis, waggling a finger in front of my eyes. "Demi Moore in *Ghost* . . . ?"

"Okay."

"Demi Moore in *The Hunchback of Notre Dame* . . . ?"

"Okay."

"Or . . . Principal Clancy?"

I snort and try to shove him off me. No dice.

"C'mon, Moose," I tease, "this is a safe space! You can just come out and say that cartoons really do it for you. No one will judge you any more than we do already."

The varsity boys hoot and holler, and I grin when Moose lets go, knocking off my Red Sox cap in the process. Like me, like all of us, Moose is wearing his blue practice jersey, and he holds a hand over his heart, where the familiar image of Hootie, Hancock High's owl mascot, has his wings spread wide. But the longer he stares at my face without my hat to cover it, the more Moose's expression falters, and a genuine horror flickers in.

Here we go . . .

"Whoa. Jesus *fuck,* Andrew. What happened to you?"

I bristle, resisting the urge to turn away. Judging by the hum that zigzags around our tables, the others are all noticing it too. "It" being the fat black eye on the left side of my face. I don't know what I was expecting the bump to be like when I woke up today; it's not like I thought it would look any better than it did this weekend. But I didn't think it'd be this bad.

I guess part of me . . . a very big part of me . . . was hoping to ignore it.

"I'm just trying to catch up with Todd," I tease. I lie.

And . . . it's over.

Behind Moose, Todd Gordon punches both fists in the air. Todd's another junior, and his first year on the team he set the school record for most concussions in a single season. Not that anyone is trying to take the title away from him.

Moose leans in to examine my bruise, a little in awe.

"Shit, man. Did it happen at the Maxwell party?" he asks. I nod, and Moose steamrolls ahead, filling in the blanks for himself. "You don't have anything to be embarrassed about, my guy. Saturday was crazy. Casey got so drunk he peed himself on Hilary's couch."

Daniel Casey, the best defender on junior varsity, pipes up, defensive as always.

"Shut up, Moose!"

"You shut up!"

"No, *you* shut up!"

"No—"

"Everyone ready to go?" I interrupt.

It's more of a challenge than a question, and my boys respond by drumming their knuckles on the table. After this semester, I'm next in line for varsity captain, and moments like this remind me that very soon I'll be the one in charge. Everyone in the cafeteria turns away from the Stern twins to look at us, even the people who typically pretend not to be looking at us. But I've been on the team long enough that I'm used to the attention.

And like the rest of my boys . . . I love it.

"Hell yeah!"

"Let's *goooooo!*"

"Born ready!"

"Made ready!"

"I gotta pooooop!" Moose adds.

I grin and do a quick head count, but I already know who's missing. I'm sure we all do. "Where's Troy?" I ask everyone and no one in particular. Nobody seems to know, and I check the clock above the vending machines. It's not like Troy to be late.

Well . . . not for something as important as practice.

"He'll know where to find us," I say, adjusting my backpack. "Let's bounce, boys."

Moose claps me on the back with enough brute force that I

stumble, and I muster another smile before leading our squad out of the cafeteria.

Our locker room is in the basement of the school, and Moose slides down the railing of the stairwell on his butt. Inside, the air is twenty degrees warmer, and muggy, which we've always blamed on the communal showers and Hancock's infamously shit water pressure. That said, my muscles immediately relax in the perpetual humidity, and I let my bag fall off my shoulder.

"Garcia! Do you know what we're doing today for warm-up?" Todd asks.

"Suicides," I answer, and I smile so big at the groan from the aisle next to me that the skin around my black eye twinges. "Save it for the turf, boys..."

My locker is the same one that I've been using since freshman year. It's sandwiched between Troy's and a guy named Parker Reid's. He's a senior, like Troy, and a casual nudist, like no one else I've ever had the pleasure of knowing. None of our lockers actually lock, thanks to Principal Clancy's predecessor, but it's not like anyone on our team has something to hide. I grab my lacrosse stick from where it's stashed and chuck my school stuff in its place, catching a glimpse of the newspaper article that I stuck up last fall. Splashed across the top is a photo of Troy and me from last season, hugging in the center of the field at regionals. Winning.

Suddenly, someone tugs on my jersey. I don't bother turning.

"One sec, Moose..."

"Um... Andrew?"

Startled by the high-pitched and distinctly not-Moose voice, I spin around. My confusion only skyrockets when I see a girl standing behind me, a freshman wearing a ridiculous-looking pair of glasses and pink overalls. At least, I assume she's a freshman. I don't know who the hell she is.

Even if there's something about her that's almost . . . familiar.

"Um . . . hi?"

"Hi," the girl chirps. And then says . . . nothing else. Moose, Todd, and our entire starting lineup walk by at the exact same moment, and they all make kissy noises as they go.

"Garcia's got a girlfriend!"

"K-I-S-S-I-N-G . . ."

"Sorry. Who are you?" I ask, not knowing what else to say. Out of habit, I roll my lacrosse stick forward and back in my hands. There are three different types of stick you can choose from, each one a different length depending on what position you play. Attack and middie. Defense. Goalie. Because I'm on attack, I have a shortie.

"Naomi." She says her name like I should know it. Which I don't.

"Okay . . . what are you doing in the boys' locker room, Naomi?"

Naomi hesitates, as if just realizing where we are. Parker Reid seizes his moment to strut between us in nothing but his birthday suit, and Naomi backs into the lockers to give him as much room as possible. But to her credit, she keeps her eyes on me. The attention makes my skin flush hot.

Not in a good way.

"I called your name on the stairs, but you didn't hear me."

"Well. You have my attention now," I say, hooking my stick behind my neck, milkmaid style. "Is there something I can do for you, Naomi? I kinda need to get—"

"I saw Troy in Principal Clancy's office."

"What?" I frown. "Is he okay?"

Naomi shakes her head, her glasses sliding down her nose in the process. But before she can elaborate, the PA system goes off, answering the question for both of us:

"Andrew Garcia to the principal's office . . . Andrew Garcia . . ."

3

lovefool

SASSI DeLUCA

Kyle Hennessy kisses like he debates for Model UN.

Things start off strong, passionate, and with a clear sense of purpose. But whatever thesis he was working with gets lost in a botched attempt at creativity. Ugh. Without breaking contact, I open one eye, then not-so-subtly the next, and am instantly reminded why people don't kiss with their eyes open. Kyle is so, so freakin' close that I can see his eye boogers. Lip-locked, I look away from him to avoid going cross-eyed. In addition to a chalkboard with the spread for our final issue, the yearbook office is filled with a long bank of computers, and the even row of monitors suddenly reminds me of teeth.

Which totally has nothing to do with how Kyle is gnawing on my lip.

Ow?

I sigh through my nose, but Kyle only takes it as a sign of encouragement. His tongue changes directions, then changes again double-time, and he uses both hands to ease me up and onto the fax machine. Which beeps.

Glad at least one of us is turned on.

"Hey," Kyle says, breaking away. He searches my face. And based on the smile, he must find whatever it is he's looking for. Most people do.

"Hey," I echo. I check the clock as casually as possible. I've already missed the last bus of the day, which means I'm going to have to walk home. I sigh and give Kyle another up-down. If I asked him to jump, odds are he'd make it to the roof of the school in a single leap. And sure, we'd have fun. Just like we did when we were the last people to leave Hilary Maxwell's New Year's Eve party. Because, I mean, Kyle's that guy. He's fun. Happy. Actually, he's perfect.

He's just not Troy Richards.

"You are . . . so cool."

"Okay."

"And so pretty."

"Oh . . . kay?"

Kyle waits to see if I'll return either compliment. Which I don't. Instead, I wrap my fingers in his lacrosse jersey and tug him closer, but Kyle surprises me and resists.

"I mean it, Sassi. You do so much. You're so kind . . . so thoughtful . . . so funny. I'm the luckiest dude in the world . . ."

Kyle leans in again and I fight the urge to snort. Eyes closed, lips puckered, he looks an awful lot like a dead blowfish.

"You're not like other girls."

This time I swerve before Kyle's lips reach mine.

"What do you mean?"

"What do *you* mean, what do I mean?"

"*Not like other girls*," I repeat. "Why wouldn't I want to be like other girls? Is there something wrong with being like other girls? Who are these girls that it's so bad to be like?"

"Hang on, Sass. I didn't mean to start some kind of feminist thing—"

Welp.

Cock sufficiently blocked, I groan and hop down from the fax machine. Kyle isn't the first guy at Hancock to ruin a hookup. And even if I don't have the time to undo his eighteen years of accidental misogyny, I do have standards. Dressed down in checkerboard shorts and an intentionally mismatched flannel that is unbuttoned over his jersey, Kylie looks equal parts *Fresh Prince* heartthrob and lost puppy. He might as well have his own theme song.

Perish the thought.

Kyle gapes at me as I pull my skort back into place.

"Sorry, Sass. I don't get why you're mad . . . but I am sorry."

"Whatever, Kyle. I should have known you'd be just as dumb as every other lax bro at this school." I shake my head. "Seriously. Maybe I was wrong. Maybe you're just like Troy after all."

"Sassi—"

"I need to pee," I snap. "And *you're* late for practice."

I storm out before Kyle can start debating for real. My feet lead me downstairs, beyond the library, toward the cafeteria, and the *slip-slap* of my sandals is the only sound in the otherwise desolate hallway. It would seem that everyone else has somewhere to be, be it drama practice or golf club or whatever else kids are doing to boost their résumés these days.

Or at the very least, they have someone to be with.

Outside Principal Clancy's office is a massive trophy case, a gold-and-silver plastic homage to everyone unlucky enough to peak in high school. At the front is a black-and-white picture of the 1975 boys lacrosse team, the triumphant state champions piled in and around a sports car with a massive double-decker trophy balanced on the roof. But my favorite photo is a smaller printout of the girls volleyball team from several years later, because unlike the other athletes standing in regimented side-by-side formation, someone among them must have suggested taking a jumping photo. Their perms have been frozen in time ever since.

I stop to check my reflection in the glass. My sweatshirt is still rumpled, and I tug on the bottom until the stitched Harvard crest lies flat across my chest. Perfect. Sighing, I yank the lime-green scrunchie out of my hair, which is long like my mom's, pin-straight like my stepmom's, and Campbell's tomato soup red like my dad's, and flip my head over to redo my ponytail.

But now I see him.

Andrew Garcia storms out of Clancy's office like a good old-fashioned nor'easter, slamming the door behind him. Andrew is one of those special boys who have a reputation for their lack of reputation. He's average in almost every sense of the word: a junior and a B/B– student. If he's trying. In fact, the most standout thing about him is that he's been Troy Richard's lackey for years. Some people might even call them best friends.

Me?

I don't believe in that kind of thing.

I can hear Principal Clancy shouting something at Andrew

from her office, and I'm more than a little surprised that the glass panel in the door doesn't shatter. Even though I'm not the one in trouble, my blood kicks up speed.

"Wowie," I call, still upside down. "What happened to you?"

A flash of something I don't recognize crosses Andrew's face. And for a second, I wish I could take it back. Andrew and I have lived next door to each other our entire lives, meaning that, unlike the other lax bros at our school, I knew him before he became a lax bro. And I'm almost willing to believe he still has a soul.

But the moment passes.

Instead of responding, Andrew marches away without acknowledging me, and I rise as quickly as I can. But by the time I'm right-side up, the hallway is empty. Although I guess Andrew's speed shouldn't surprise me, especially considering that he's the only guy who's ever been recruited to the varsity lacrosse team as a freshman.

Besides, whatever Andrew and Principal Clancy were shouting about, maybe it was nothing.

Maybe.

But I've never been wrong before.

4

whatta man

ANDREW GARCIA

The cafeteria is deathly silent.

Troy was gone by the time I got to the front office, but Principal Clancy kept me for over an hour. An excruciating, mind-numbing, dumpster fire of an hour, during which I entirely forgot about the Stern twins and their banner. However, as I cut through the cafeteria, I nearly step right on them, and I realize that the girls have only made it as far as painting *CONGRAT*. For one precious moment, the twins are too busy to notice that it's me. When they do, their eyes tick from my face to the cardboard box in my hands, my helmet, jockstrap, lucky Nalgene, and a trophy from last spring hastily piled inside.

"Where's Jennifer?" I ask. My voice comes out hoarse, and for a panicked moment I wonder if I'm going to cry.

But Zoey and Chloe simply mistake my tone for anger, and they point through the windows to the parking lot.

"Thanks."

"Hey . . . Andrew? Everything okay . . . ?"

I ignore Zoey or Chloe and march across the cafeteria. Once

I'm outside, the walk to the lot is mostly uphill, and between that and the rank smell of mulch, for a split second I stop breathing.

Until . . . I see her.

Jennifer Lee is sitting on the back of an open convertible, her chin tilted toward the pale January sky and an unlit joint in her hand. It's been unusually warm this winter, but today her breath hangs in the air like cut-paper snowflakes. Jennifer is wearing an oversized varsity letter jacket with a black dress, black tights, and black loafers, but the dark colors have the opposite effect of what they are supposed to and only make the rest of her look softer. Unlike on most days, her hair is down around her shoulders, not exactly curling but floating around her cheekbones. I slow down when I get closer.

There's something about her that looks a little . . . sad.

"Jennifer . . ."

She jerks forward at the sound of my voice and swings both feet over the side of the convertible to stand. Her eyes go wide when she takes in my appearance, and I prickle as her attention lingers on my black eye.

Based on her reaction, I have to believe it looks even worse than the last time she saw it.

"No."

"Jenn—"

"No, Andrew. I'm not allowed to talk to you. Not here."

"Jennifer, we need to—"

"*No!*"

I'm more than a little surprised when she shoves me with both hands, and I am genuinely surprised by how strong she is. But a second later, I realize she's only preventing me from getting nailed by an asshole on a skateboard. Tatum Stein zips between us fast as hell, and I drop my box, causing the trophy inside to snap at the neck. I can't help but wince.

"Watch it, Tatum!" Jennifer shouts.

"Blow me, princess!"

Jennifer flips Tatum the bird, and even though she doesn't look back at us, Tatum returns the gesture with both hands. The girl might be five foot one, but she's fucking fierce.

"God, what a jerk . . ."

I grunt in agreement and start to pick up my belongings. Because as much as Tatum annoys me, I have way more important things to worry about right now. The dismembered trophy head has bounced somewhere under the convertible, and I crawl on my knees to reach for it. After a pathetic beat Jennifer joins me, but I don't know if that makes me feel better or worse.

Never mind . . . it's worse.

"What are you doing with all this junk?"

"Troy got me kicked off the team, Jenn. I'm done."

Jennifer balks. When she speaks again, her voice is quieter, and I drop mine to match. You would think we were whispering at a corner table in the library, not scrambling across the asphalt on our hands and knees.

"*What?* Why the hell would he do that?"

"He told Principal Clancy that I got wasted on New Year's Eve and started a fight," I say, shoving my jockstrap into the box with far more force than necessary. "And after what happened at Hilary's . . . something tells me Troy just wants me as far away as possible."

"Andrew . . ."

Jennifer's gaze goes from my black eye to my scar.

I've had the mark through my left eyebrow ever since fifth

grade. Now it looks more like a bald spot. One summer, Troy's dad made it his mission to teach the two of us how to fish on our own. But the first and last time Troy cast his rod, the lure landed squarely in my eyebrow. When Mr. Richards drove me home, I tried to soften the blow by wearing Troy's Red Sox cap. My mom was still horrified, of course, and after a quick trip to the ER she said I would always be connected to Troy by that invisible fishing line.

I spot the missing trophy head, and Jennifer and I grab for it at the same time. She giggles despite herself. Her eyes are a dark brown, with light parts at the center. She used to wear glasses when we were in elementary school, and no one knew how pretty her eyes were. But when you're close enough, like we are right now, you can see just how many different colors are in them. Almost like my bruise.

"Jennifer . . . you need to tell people what really happened at Hilary's."

Her laugh fades as quickly as it started.

"Jennifer, *please*—"

"You know I can't do that."

"No. I actually don't," I mutter, doing my best and worst to keep my face expressionless. When I frown, the bruise hurts even more. I ball my hands into fists, pressing the decapitated trophy into my palm until it stings.

"Hey, gang!"

Jennifer and I look up.

Troy Richards stands behind us, watching us, with one hand curled into a casual fist. The man, the myth, the asshole, the living New England legend. You can barely tell that he just finished a grueling warm-up with the boys and will be ready for another if you give him ten minutes. Tops. His pits stains are a badge of honor, and his honey-blond hair floofs in the wind like one of those ridiculous Calvin Klein commercials that only come on TV at three a.m. I'm more than a little surprised to see him, sure. But I'm not surprised that he's wearing his blue practice jersey.

Which is number one . . . obviously.

"Hi, babe," Jennifer murmurs. "Shouldn't you be at practice?"

"Coach Mancini and I gave the boys the rest of the afternoon off," Troy says, unsmiling. He takes Jennifer by the hand, his eyes never leaving mine. "We just got some pretty rough news from Clancy. Figure they need time to process."

"What are you playing at, Troy—"

"*Me?* Nothing. But if I catch you talking to my girl again, Garcia? You'll wish you were dead."

"Leave him al—"

"Don't. Start," Troy interrupts, suddenly way louder than necessary. "After what he did to me?"

It's like I've been gut-punched.

We have an audience forming in the parking lot, skeptics and lookie-loos alike, and among them I spot Tatum. Troy must know that people are listening. Actually, I bet he wants them to. Tatum stares the longest, and when she catches my gaze she pulls her neon windbreaker over her head, scuttling away like a hermit crab.

"Can we just go? Babe?" says Jennifer, always the peacemaker. Even, or especially, now. "Please?"

Troy huffs his hair out of his face. The two of them climb into his convertible, Troy at the wheel, and he throws the car into reverse.

He also manages to steamroll my cardboard box into a pancake with unbelievable precision.

"Garcia! Almost forgot . . . I need that number. Now."

I steel myself.

And slowly . . . finally . . . I strip off my jersey.

All the uniforms on our team are passed down from seniors to freshmen at the beginning of the school year. We wear our practice jerseys every day to class, and it's a longstanding tradition to save our iconic white uniforms for actual games. It's also a tradition to wait to wash our jerseys until the first pep rally of the year, which means mine still smells like last season. We set an undefeated spring record due in large part to me and Troy and our seamless work as attackmen. For a moment, the bleary winter sunlight is distorted through the fabric, and it reminds me of one of those tchotchke kaleidoscopes I used to play with as a kid. As soon as my head is free, I'm greeted by the unforgiving January air, and I shudder despite my best efforts to seem unbothered.

Someone, probably Tatum, wolf whistles at me from across the lot.

"Drop fucking dead, Richards," I growl.

I chuck my jersey into the convertible as Troy floors it. To her credit, Jennifer doesn't look back.

Well . . . maybe just a little.

5

friday i'm in love

TATUM STEIN

In my time as a Hancock Howler, there's been a handful of adults who wanted to help me stop smoking. Teachers. Aides. Substitutes. Principal Clancy. Principal Motta. Plus one senile school nurse with a god complex and a weakness for strawberry hard candies. Some were creative, others patient, and by the end of my first senior year I'd already sat through too many D.A.R.E. classes to count. But it was Nurse Whitter who made it her mission to get me to quit before I graduated, warning me that if I didn't, no boy would want to kiss me. When that didn't work, good ol' Nurse Whitter and I started sharing her cigarettes at lunch break. As it happens, Nurse Whitter died two years ago, and now I'm everyone's favorite super-super-supersenior. I still smoke too, but only because I have to.

I do it to remind myself I'm still breathing.

"Hey! Tony Hawk-a-Loogie!"

I groan and throw down my heel, skidding to an awkward stop roughly two feet farther than I wanted. There aren't many people in the building this early on a Friday, and I shuffle back the way I came with my board still under one foot. Yeah, it's not exactly glamorous. But it works. I yank off my headphones connected to the Walkman at my hip, stubbing out my cigarette with my Docs for good measure.

The Stern twins are stationed on opposite sides of the library doors, struggling to hang one of the many grotesque banners they've been working on this week with nothing more than Scotch tape and blind optimism. While Chloe finishes her side, Zoey paws through her tacky crocodile shoulder bag. There is a tray of red paint on the ground, presumably for touch-ups, and even I don't have the heart to tell them the banner is already crooked.

"Zoey, take a chill pill. Did you ask Troy if he's seen it?"

Zoey holds a finger to her lips as I get closer.

"Chloe! Don't go there!"

"What?"

She points at me. Subtle. I smile and take a mystery-flavored Dum-Dum out of the front pocket of my windbreaker.

"Rise and grind, ladies."

"Ugh. Hi. Have you seen Zoey's wallet?"

"What? *Psh.* Me? Why?"

"Because you, *psh,* you are a klepto with daddy issues who has a nasty habit of finding lost things."

I gasp and hold the Dum-Dum to my heart.

"Please. *Reformed* klepto with daddy issues—"

"Whatever. Can you help us find it?"

"Why should I? Your supreme leader Troy Richards owes me both your weights in gold."

"Pretty please?" Chloe pouts. Once she realizes I have no intention of changing my mind, the brat stomps her foot like an even brattier toddler. "Pretty, pretty, *pretty* . . . ?"

I check the time on my watch. It was a gift from my youngest half sister, one of two younger half sisters, and it has an off-brand Cinderella on the face. It's a little janky, sure, but the thought was there.

"Sorry, gals." I crunch into my lollipop, the candy sticking to my molars like a bad radio jingle. "Can't be late for homeroom. But, bit of free advice? It's always in the last place you look."

"Yeah . . . no duh."

I salute them and skate off, restarting my Walkman as I go. I kick my board faster and faster, and the hallway devolves into an early-morning blur of animal print and frosted tips. But for the time being, everyone ignores me. Which is fine. Preferred, actually. Until I plow into some buzzkill in a Pink Floyd T-shirt.

Andrew Garcia, the all-American wet dream.

"Tatum! You mind? I'm already running late—"

"*Woooowieeee!*" I whistle, jumping off my board. "What crawled up your shorts?"

"No one."

I raise an eyebrow.

"Nothing," Andrew corrects himself.

I smirk. I hold up my hands, making a frame with my thumbs and pointer fingers, and scan the crowd in the direction that he was daydreaming. Troy Richards and Jennifer Lee are walking to class in front of us, his hand in her back pocket. But it's not flirty; it's casual, territorial. Maybe flirty and casual are the same. Either way, Andrew is staring daggers and spades and butcher knives at the obvious shoo-ins for this year's prom king and queen.

"Busted."

"Do you annoy everyone, or is it just my lucky week?"

Andrew mutters, effectively answering my question with his own. He starts walking away without waiting for an answer.

"Eh... everyone."

I drop my hands, scoop up my board, and trot after him. As Andrew and I head down the hallway, I notice that not only are people watching him, which I've come to expect after the news of his suspension broke on Monday, but a few are staring openly at me. Bemused. By now, a dozen rumors of his untimely demise have more than made the rounds, in school and in town. Still, it isn't until we pass two freshmen girls literally whispering behind their hands that Andrew notices it too.

"You probably shouldn't be seen with me," he mutters.

"You know me—I love a scandal."

At the end of the hallway, Jennifer whispers something to Troy. They both laugh.

"Wanna make a bet?" I ask.

"Not really, no."

"Five bucks says they break up before Valentine's Day. Troy isn't going to keep a sophomore around very long. No offense."

"Why are you even talking to me?" Andrew mutters. "No one else is."

I point to his Pink Floyd shirt, and Andrew looks down as if realizing for the first time how public his public shaming really is.

"Hey. I don't know what happened between you kids, but you don't have to protect Troy anymore," I say, jumping back on my board and rolling alongside Andrew as he walks toward his homeroom. "You're one of us now. Trust me, we mortal folk? We all hate Troy! No offense. It was only a matter of time before he dropped you like a steaming hot deuce."

"Yeah, right. Name one other person who—"

"Lauren Perez," I interrupt, counting the names on my fingers. "Matt Shelley. Grace Tam. And don't forget the shit he pulled on the eighth-grade field trip! Sarah Thompson is still banned from the zoo. For life."

"So?"

"*So?*" I make a face. "Haven't you realized that Troy Richards is behind every rotten thing that happens to people at this school? During last semester's student senate elections, he got all the lax bros to write in, and I quote, *Kylie's boobs* as their final vote—"

"That was supposed to be funny—"

"It wasn't to Kylie, or her boobs." I punch him on the arm. "Troy's the reason the girls swim team disbanded. And where do you *think* Geneva Poch's pet hamster went?"

"The microwave thing is a lie—"

"Whatever, dude. I'll believe it when the teacher's lounge stops smelling the way it does. Besides, you can't tell me you've forgotten when Troy was in fifth grade and told poor little Stan Hargus that drinking soap would allow him to burp bubbles. Poison control couldn't arrive fast enough! Seriously, Andrew. You guys have been close for years, which means you're either even stupider than I thought, or complicit." I shrug. "I don't know which is worse."

Andrew wilts but doesn't deny it.

"What has Troy done to you?"

The question is so absurd that I could laugh. So I do.

"What's so funny?" Andrew asks, his already shaky confidence faltering. He chews on his bottom lip until it looks like he's sucking on a Warhead.

Ugly truth is, I got to know Troy for the same reason I know most people in this sad-sack town. He needed something. Not to brag, but also, to brag, it's an open secret that I have connections others don't. I grew my business over time, and as a scrawny tyke, I started out collecting tennis balls behind the Hancock Country Club and selling them at double the cost to the wall ball nerds at recess. The only reason I graduated to moving drugs was because my sisters wanted an Easy-Bake Oven for Hanukkah and my dad got caught selling to an undercover cop. He never wanted me to follow in his footsteps, but once he was arrested, I realized there's no easier place to make money than a three-story cement box filled with hundreds of kids who have undiagnosed ADD, ADHD, OCD, and boredom. The first time Troy reached out to me I thought he was just another douchebro who liked to get crossed in the offseason and binge Sunday-morning cartoons. But after a few months, I learned that Troy was splitting his blunts with tobacco to make the stash last longer and selling the extra behind my back. When I confronted him, Troy just smiled and informed me that if I made a scene, he and all his bros would parade into Principal Clancy's office and point the collective middle finger at me.

And with that threat hanging over me like a bad fart, I've been supplying the entire lacrosse team at a friends and frenemies discount ever since.

"You really don't know?" I gasp for air, grabbing at my stomach with both hands. Sometimes, when I laugh this hard, I'm prone to hiccupping.

"No . . . I guess not."

The final bell rings, startling the two of us and everyone else killing time in the hallway. I stand up straight, wiping a pretend tear from the very real crinkle at my eye.

"Jeez. Thanks for the laugh, Garcia. It's been real. But I have an appointment with the chess club—"

"Wait, how bad was it? What was it, whatever he did?"

Unhurried, I grin and remove Zoey's faux-leather wallet from where I stashed it in the waistband of my cargo pants. Andrew stares as I extract a spare joint from the innermost pocket, and I put it in my mouth without lighting it. "I'll tell you when you're older," I promise, tossing him the wallet. Then I turn my board in the opposite direction, giving him a salute before I kick off. "Later, bro."

"Yeah . . . later . . ."

6

just a girl

NAOMI KING

I'm sitting in the last stall on the left, playing my Game Boy with one hand and picking my nose with the other. My untouched lunch tray is balanced on top of the industrial-sized TP, my smiley-face fries long cold and scowling. The game *BEEP-BEEP-BEEP*s as I go, and soon, just like that, Mario saves his princess.

"Booyah," I whisper to myself.

Originally, the Game Boy and all its heavy hitters belonged to my sister Mel. *Pokémon, Zelda, Final Fantasy.* On weekends, we'd stay up until two or three a.m. with her sprawled in front of the air-conditioner and me watching her play over her shoulder, both of us chowing down on Cheetos as soon as our parents fell asleep. Mel gave me the Game Boy when she left for BU, but there's a cartridge jammed inside, so this is the only game I can play. By now I've beaten this level enough times that it's easy, and if you die, you can always respawn and pick up where you left off.

The door to the bathroom swings open and shut, and I wait for the sound of a flush before starting the next level.

Our school chops the student body into two lunch blocks, regardless of grade. Hence the creatively named first and second lunches. Even if my sister hadn't warned me before going off to college, it was obvious from day one that only freshmen are desperate enough to eat in the cafeteria. All seniors and juniors have off-campus driving privileges, and most sophomores know someone who knows someone else who is willing to bring back a burger from Five Guys in exchange for an IOU. I was willing to give the lunch ladies and their ambiguous Meatless Mondays a fair shot, but after a few weeks of sitting alone at the peanut-free table, not even Tender Tuesday could convince me to stay.

BEEP-BEEP-BEEEE—

Suddenly, the bathroom door hurtles open, this time with enough force that it makes the TP rattle.

"—*legit* going to strangle you—"

"—not like I meant to do it!"

Curiosity piqued, I look through the stall door. Zoey is scrubbing red paint off both arms, and it looks a little like blood. Her sister flutters at her side.

"We were supposed to save the extra paint for the pep rally!"

"We can always buy more—"

"You did this cuz you're jealous!"

"Me? *Psh!*" Chloe leans into the mirrors, and between the two of them, their spray tans are repeated a dozen times over. "What would I be jealous of?"

"You keep looking for ways to embarrass me! Ever since Troy and I started hanging out—"

"*Hanging out?* Is that what you call it?"

The twins share a look.

And break into furious giggles.

No way! Zoey and Troy?

I frown at the very real possibility that Jennifer Lee's BFF is sleeping with her boyfriend. I mean, it's awful, *and* cliché! Ask anyone at Hancock High and they'll tell you the same thing: Jennifer is the dreamy girl next door; Zoey, the girl from the other side of the tracks. And Chloe is . . . well . . . Zoey's twin. Meanwhile, there's me. Black hair, brown skin, acne, and acne scars. Chapped lips, too. I don't have braces anymore, thanks for your concern, but after wearing my headgear to school just one time in second grade, I might as well.

I shift for a better view, accidentally flushing the motion-sensing toilet under me.

And it's loud.

Really, *really* loud.

PWWWWWSHHH!

I look back at the mirrors, but this time a liquid-eyeliner-lined eyeball is glaring at me through the door crack. What happens next happens faster than fast. Zoey forces the janky stall open and grabs me by my braids. I stumble, grateful that I wasn't actually using the toilet, and try to shield myself with my backpack as she forces me through the door. Outside the bathroom, the hallway is empty.

Even if it wasn't, it's not like anyone is coming to save me.

"Look, freshmeat. I don't know what you *think* you heard"—Zoey seethes, releasing my hair—"but if you don't want the *entire* school to know that you were *spying* on us? You'll forget it. And forget it quickly." She jabs me with a fingernail. "Capisce?"

I nod, too afraid to do anything else.

Triumphant, Chloe pulls Zoey toward the exit. I watch them

go, but just as they're about to disappear, I break. I might not have friends, but I know what a bad one looks like.

"Yeah! I didn't hear anything!"

The twins stop where they are.

"Um . . . duh? I just said that."

"I mean . . . yeah. I *definitely* didn't hear that you're hooking up with Jennifer's boyfriend. Because that would be . . . uh . . ." I lose steam when I realize they are smirking at me. ". . . bad?"

Zoey and Chloe look over my shoulder.

"Speak of the devil."

I spin around.

Troy stands in the hallway behind me. Watching me. He's wearing a bright orange pinnie over his jersey and carrying his lacrosse stick with both hands. He's objectively hot. So hot it's almost aggressive, and so aggressive it's almost hot. With the kind of arms and hands and eyelashes that people like to write fan fiction about.

"'Sup, ladies?"

It's not a real question, and I don't respond. It doesn't take a genius to know he must have heard everything I said.

Even though I'm not in the same grade, I managed to test into a handful of classes with the upperclassmen, including Troy. We were randomly seated next to each other in AP chemistry, and because my sister warned me about him before she graduated, I was surprised to discover how nice he can be. One time I came to class sick, and the next day Troy surprised me with saltines and Gatorade. Another time, he returned from off-campus lunch with a box of scones to split. In return, I pretended not to mind when he asked to look at my homework every once in a while. But when it quickly became *more* than once in a while, I finally learned the best and worst thing about Troy Richards: He's nice to everyone. At first.

Troy's eyes fall on my Game Boy.

"Sweet! What's this?"

He uses his lacrosse stick to smack the Game Boy out of my hands.

"Ow!"

Troy laughs and scoops up the Game Boy, playing catch with himself as if nothing happened. Sicko. To their credit, both Chloe and Zoey look horrified. But neither of them tries to intervene. My hands are bright red and trembling.

"That r-really hurt!"

"Aw, man. R-really *sorry*."

I reach for the Game Boy and Troy twists the stick even farther out of reach. First with his left hand, then his right. *Left. Right. Left. Right.* He's enjoying this.

"Give it back, Troy!"

"Or?"

"Or . . . I'll tell!"

"Right, right. I guess you would." He leans in close. "C'mon, Naomi. You're a smart chick. You know what they call you, right?"

I stand perfectly still. Troy starts to pace around me in slow, slow circles. He lobs the Game Boy into the air and catches it behind his back.

"Dweeb," Zoey offers.

"Creep," Chloe adds.

"Actually, I was thinking of the other one . . ." Troy narrows his eyes. *"Snitch."*

I blink, cradling my hands to my stomach. They're still vibrating from the hit, and the pain begins to pool hot and steady in my fingertips. Despite my best intentions, a single tear leaks out.

When I realized that Troy cheated off me during midterms, I broke and explained everything to our chemistry teacher, Mr. Levitan. He's been at Hancock longer than anyone else I know, and I thought that might make him immune to Troy's charms. However, Troy simply denied everything and asked to retake the midterm to prove his innocence, somehow pulling off a near-perfect score in the process. I realized then that Troy hadn't been cheating off me because he *couldn't* do the work but because he didn't *want* to, and for him the power trip was the fun part. Afterward, Mr. Levitan told me that the only thing he takes more seriously than a cheating accusation is a *false* accusation, and I got a strike on my academic record. Making matters worse, Troy started telling everyone who would listen that I had a crush on him, and that I had reported him because I was jealous of him and Jennifer.

I still don't know which is worse, the lies or the truth.

"So say whatever, to *whoever*," Troy continues. I can tell by the wild look in his eye that he's not just talking about the Game Boy. "No one will believe you! Am I wrong?"

Zoey and Chloe shake their heads.

Troy steps toward me, towering over me, and when he's close enough I can smell the sweat from his jersey.

"*TROY!*"

I spot Andrew running down the hallway. Toward us. Toward me. There are a handful of other people with him, but unlike Andrew, their only priority seems to be getting a front-row seat.

Despite the ferocity in Andrew's face, it's impossible not to notice that he's looking great in a tight band T-shirt. And apparently, he's looking for a fight.

"Stay in your lane, Garcia—"

"Oh, fuck off." Andrew mocks his tone. *"Richards."*

Andrew shoves Troy away from me. Troy winds up, and it looks like he's about to strike with his lacrosse stick, but he settles for hurling my Game Boy at the wall instead. It misses my head by inches.

I drop to my knees with a pitiful peep.

"Leave her alone."

"Fine. She's all yours," Troy sneers, tossing his hair out of his eyes. "See you in class, Naomi. And make sure to finish our lab on time, okay? You know I hate doing extra credit." He jerks his head to the twins without looking at them. "Girls?"

Troy heads for the parking lot with Zoey and Chloe falling in line, and the trio vanishes through the double doors. Leaving Andrew and me and the dwindling crowd in their wake.

"Naomi . . ."

I ignore him, trying to assemble what's left of my Game Boy.

Andrew takes a knee at my side.

"Hey, leave it," he says, surprisingly gentle. "Are you okay?"

"Why did you do that? You're just going to make it worse. You don't even know me."

"What are you talking about?" Andrew frowns, chewing on the inside of his cheek. "You're Mel's sister, right?"

I nod.

"Mel was my camp counselor a few years ago. Remember?" Andrew explains, his voice dipping from gentle to patronizing. He reaches for my shoulder but then appears to think better of it, letting his hand fall open at his side. "Your parents drove me home once or twice. You still had headgear."

"Oh . . . okay," I manage, not sure what else I'm supposed to say. Andrew sighs in a way that makes me think he doesn't know either.

"We can tell someone about Troy. We should. If you want to."

"When has that ever worked?" I ask, my voice fraying at the edges. Andrew doesn't bother answering my question, but I don't take it personally. Because telling the truth about Troy Richards has never worked for anyone. Never has, never will.

Especially not for me.

"But—"

"No one believes me, Andrew, and they're not going to believe you," I say. "Not when it's Troy Richards. He's untouchable. Even the adults are on his side."

"That's not true—"

The sound that comes out of my mouth frightens both me and Andrew. It's part groan, part sob.

"Don't cry—"

"I'm not *sad*, Andrew," I snap. "I'm furious."

Andrew physically draws back from me, stupefied by the acid in my voice.

"I *hate* Troy Richards and I *hate* this school," I say, rising to my feet. "He has this whole place wrapped around his big toe. And in case you haven't noticed—which, by the way, *you haven't*—I've been putting up with Troy all year. So thanks for the help, really, but I can manage on my own. I always have."

"Naomi—"

I stumble away from Andrew without bothering to explain myself, and I barely notice when a girl in a Harvard sweatshirt breaks from the crowd and shoves a wad of tissues in my hand. But it just makes me feel worse. Angrier, and weaker, too. I wonder what Andrew, or anyone else in this school, sees when he looks at me. Then again, even the answer to that question is obvious. Because at the end of the day, I'm always going to be perfect Mel King's sister. The little sister.

The snitch.

7

semi-charmed life

ANDREW GARCIA

I drop my backpack just inside the front door. There's a candle burning in the downstairs bathroom, and the smell of Christmas and Clorox welcomes me home. It's certifiable proof that my mom is off the deep end.

"Andrew? That you, sweet pea?"

"Yeah, coming."

I grab a hoodie from the closet and fist my hands through the sleeves. Trudging down the hallway, I pass the living room and a wall of photo accolades and medals that have been hung with care over the years. My dad is a salesman and spends most of his time traveling for work, and my mom makes sure to document everything so he can see what we're up to when he's gone.

Elementary school. Waiting at the bus stop with a pint-sized Sassi DeLuca . . .

Middle school. Cheesing on the last day of summer camp with Mel King . . .

High school. Playing lacrosse freshman, sophomore, and

junior years and absolutely dominating alongside our varsity captain . . . and my best friend . . . the one and only . . .

Troy Richards.

I double back for that last one and tip the frame off the wall. It hits the floor but doesn't shatter, so I step on it until it does.

In the kitchen, my mom is chopping vegetables with an elaborate set of Japanese knives. Her newest QVC purchase. She doesn't look over when I enter, but I notice her knife pick up speed. Her straw-colored hair is pulled back from her face with a polka-dot bandana, and her cheeks are Starburst-cherry red from the effort. At first and second glance, most people don't realize the two of us are related, which is always a sore subject around the holidays. I have my dad's dark coloring—and his temper, if you ask my mother. In fifth grade, I remember an idiot on the playground pointing out the distinct line on my arm where my skin changes from dark-dark on top to light-dark underneath. When that wasn't obvious enough, he asked me every mixed kid's favorite question: *What* are you?

At which point Troy punched him in the dick.

"How was your day at school?"

"Fine."

"Did anything interesting happen?"

"Not really."

"You just sat at your desk twiddling your thumbs?"

"Pretty much, yeah."

My mom sighs. "Any big plans for the weekend?"

"Um . . ." I blink. "I'm still grounded, aren't I?"

"Oh, you are. But I'm just checking." She smiles humorlessly and changes knives. Without my dad around, my mom has become an expert at playing both good cop and bad cop in the same conversation. Although I can't always tell which is which. Even now she doesn't make eye contact with me, but she's wearing the same exact expression she's had since Principal Clancy called her on Monday and informed her I was suspended from the team.

Sympathy . . . and humiliation.

Sighing, I hop up onto the counter next to where my mom is working. It's the same place I'd sit when I was little and she'd try to give me cooking lessons, but most of the time I'd just end up licking the spoon or spatula or whatever other utensil we were working with. Once, she tried to teach me how to prepare duck for my dad's birthday, but I didn't have the stomach for handling uncooked meat and ran out of the room in tears. Raw things still make me squirm.

"Fingers. Watch 'em."

I tuck my hands between my knees and my mom aggressively crunches her blade into a fresh stalk. It makes me wince.

"Jeez . . . what are you doing?"

"Chicken pot pie. I think." She checks her cookbook, another QVC purchase. And, if you ask her, Betty Crocker's finest. "Dad and I thought it would be nice to eat in for a change."

"Dad's coming home?"

"Mmhmm."

"But . . . we usually go out to eat when he's here."

My mom turns to rinse her knife in the sink. She doesn't answer me, and that alone is answer enough.

"Mom . . ."

"Andrew," she says, her voice dropping low, "do you think that your father and I expected to start the new year like this? With you off the team? Suspended?"

I flinch at the anger in her voice. Because I'm not sure if it's anger at Clancy, at the entire situation, or at me.

Suddenly, the phone rings, and as objectively stupid and unlikely as it is . . . I want it to be Troy. Saying this last week was a joke . . . promising he'll talk to Principal Clancy . . . offering to pick me up in his dad's car in five.

Hancock is a smaller-than-small-town suburgatory just forty-five minutes outside Boston, and when we were younger, the only thing Troy and I could do for fun was bike to CVS to eat ice cream by the pint and try on discount Halloween costumes until the salesclerks kicked us out. From there, we graduated to sneaking into the woods behind the grocery store, where we would join the older boys lighting bonfires and daring one another to see who could stand closest the longest and pee into the flames. But when Troy got his license, we found freedom driving around listening to his mixtapes and looking for upperclassman parties to crash.

Until eventually, we became the upperclassmen.

My mom answers the phone before the second ring, but a moment later she frowns.

"Who is it?"

"Must have been a wrong number." She shrugs and puts the phone back into place. "What were we talking about?"

"Mom, I can explain the Troy thing—"

"Can you?" She sighs, slamming her knife back into the block. Her eyes are the same dark green as my own, but right now I barely recognize them. "Please. I'm all ears."

I open my mouth to respond but close it just as fast.

Truth is, I should have known something was wrong the moment Naomi told me she saw Troy in Principal Clancy's office.

The only time Clancy dares to open her door is when something really, really bad has happened. A death in the family, a cheating scandal, or maybe even a clogged toilet in the teacher's lounge. At first I was afraid that something had happened to my dad. But once I was sitting across from Principal Clancy, Troy nowhere to be seen, I was too dumbstruck to really hear the charges against me.

Too dumb not to know this is exactly what I should have been expecting after New Year's Eve.

"When did you become like this? Hm?" my mom asks. She sighs when I make no effort to respond. "All week you've been avoiding me. Why won't you talk to me?"

"Mom—"

"Do you know how lucky you are that Troy isn't pressing charges? You're eighteen years old—"

"Me? *Lucky?*" I splutter. I consider reminding her that I'm the one with the black eye, but just like with Principal Clancy, I'm beginning to understand that that alone won't do anything. Naomi's face flashes across my mind's eye, and I realize she was right: Everyone in Hancock is on Troy's side. Even my own mom. "Without lacrosse, I lose . . . everything! My friends, my shot at playing in college, my—"

"Keep up the attitude and you'll lose my respect, too."

That hits hard.

I force myself to stare into my lap, clenching and unclenching my hands into fists. Why isn't my word enough for her? Or anyone else, for that matter? Fine, it might not be the full truth. But if I could only get her to hear me when I say that I didn't—

"Sweet pea?"

I nod, silent. My gaze slides off my mom's heart-shaped face and to the window over the sink. There are two massive rhododendron bushes separating our backyard from the DeLucas', and I could swear that a shadow the size and shape of a full-grown man moves between them.

Until a moment later, when Stanley, my mom's impish tuxedo cat, pops out the other side.

False alarm.

"I know you don't want to talk about it, Andrew . . . but this affects all of us. You, me, your dad, too," my mom continues. She dumps the vegetables into a pan and turns the stove on full blast. "Also, if lacrosse is out of the picture, Dad and I want you to sign up for another club as soon as possible. Any club. Your junior year is too important to waste."

"Lacrosse wasn't just some club—"

"You know what I mean." My mom cuts me off with a flick of her wrist. "Perhaps I'm not being clear, Andrew. You are on thin, thin ice here. I need to know that you're staying busy . . . and staying out of trouble. Got it?"

"Why can't you just believe me?" My voice breaks. "I would never hurt Troy . . . or anyone."

My mom sighs and rests both her hands on mine. They are shockingly cool to the touch. Suddenly, I feel like the little kid sitting on the counter and trying not to cry. Except this time, she might not come rushing after me if I run off.

"Hey. I do believe you, sweet pea. I believe you made a mistake."

"But if Troy hadn't—"

"Hadn't what? Are you saying he deserved it?"

"That's not—no! I mean . . . I don't know. But . . ." I stop myself when I catch her expression. She's not listening, or even seeing me . . . if she ever was.

Troy and I met in kindergarten, before I was held back in school. We instantly became best friends and have remained so ever since, even though we've been in different classes. Troy's mom died the summer before he started second grade, and he became like a second son to my mom. Also her favorite, if you ask her. Anytime his dad had to work late, Troy would spend the night with us—the two of us sneaking downstairs to play video games and my mom pretending not to notice us dozing into our Lucky Charms the next day. There's nothing I can say to change that image in her mind. Besides, I don't know if I want to.

Because up until a few days ago . . . I also thought Troy and I were still best friends.

"Like I was saying," my mom continues. "You. Made. A. Mistake. And now—"

She stops mid-thought, with her mouth hanging open. She's distracted by something in the bushes where I was looking a moment ago.

But like me, she shakes it off.

"And . . . now . . . you need to fix it," she finishes. My mom boops me on the nose and I resist the urge to push her hand away. "Besides, trying something different could be good for you. Maybe the chess club needs some new blood."

I shrug but don't trust myself to respond, and drop my gaze. Defeated.

Until my eyes go to the knife block.

8

that don't impress me much

SASSI DeLUCA

I crank my boom box as loud as it will go to try to drown out the hyenas downstairs. Which I do mean literally. Because based on the telltale sound of drums, my stepmom is about to spend her Friday night watching another *Crocodile Hunter* marathon. When that doesn't work, I resign myself to sitting on the shag carpet directly in front of my speakers. From the floor, it looks like my lava lamps are sucking their goo down in reverse, and I can make the pink zebra stripes on my bed wriggle if I blur my eyes just so.

I redecorated my bedroom in seventh grade in direct protest of the monochromatic color scheme my stepmom enforced when she moved in. Now there are similar and increasingly outrageous animal patterns on my sheets. My curtains. My wallpaper. Seriously, everything.

Even Lisa Frank would be jealous.

"Sassi?"

My stepmom opens the door without knocking. Per usual. Her hair is blown out to Jennifer Aniston perfection, and unlike on the billboards around town that show her iconic pearly whites, Hancock's favorite personal injury attorney is now frowning at me over a mug of green tea. I don't know who she and her knockoff Classique perfume think they're fooling.

"Yes, Deborah?"

"Are you just going to let that boy wait?" she asks, her downturned lips turned even more down than they usually are. "He's been standing in my azaleas for twenty minutes."

"Yes, Deborah."

Deborah sighs and exits, not bothering to shut the door. Once she's gone, I stand and chuck my makeup bag onto the inflatable chair at my bedside.

Whoever it is, I already know he's not worth it.

Kyle stands on the lawn between our house and the Garcias'. Instead of tossing rocks at my window, he's busy fishing decorative seashells out of our nautical-themed garden. We're big on themes here at the DeLuca household, if you couldn't tell.

"Prick," I mutter to myself. I sigh and lean out the window to shout, *"What?"*

"Do you have plans tonight?"

"I'm busy, Kyle."

"Doing what? It's Friday!"

"College stuff," I lie.

Kyle whistles and crosses his arms. "Harvard has you grinding already?"

"Yep," I lie again.

"Cool, cool, cool . . . well . . . I'll see you later?"

"Yep!"

I slam my window matter-of-factly, hiding behind my beaded curtains until Kyle sulks off. My gaze gradually shifts to my own reflection, and between my yellow satin pajamas and the towel twisted like a dollop of soft serve on my head, I barely recognize myself. Because I'm at the window, and because my music is still playing, I don't immediately hear the alert on my computer from a new message notification. For the longest time, my dad and I shared the chunky desktop computer in his attic office, but he agreed to move the beast into my bedroom once I got to high school. When the song changes and my computer beeps again, I move to check my messages. Honestly, I don't know what I'm expecting.

But it's not Andrew Garcia.

LAXative_22: hey

I glare at the Garcia house on the opposite side of the driveway. From what I can tell, the overhead light is off in Andrew's room, and I consider ignoring him, especially given the way he snubbed me outside Principal Clancy's office earlier this week. But I know he can see me. This time of day, Andrew normally would be, should be, headed out with Kyle and the rest of his Neanderthal teammates to find trouble wherever they can. Instead, thanks to Principal Clancy's decision earlier this week, he has nowhere to be but home.

But you know what they say. Curiosity killed the kitty cat.

And I freakin' *hate* cats.

I switch my status from Away to Online.

pinktiaragirl: hi
pinktiaragirl: shouldn't u be out with the boys?
LAXative_22: my mom grounded me
LAXative_22: besides... it's not like the team is talking to me

pinktiaragirl: lucky u
(LAXative_22 is typing...)

It takes Andrew longer to respond than I'd expect, and I plop into my rolling chair with a falsetto sigh. My desk is the only part of my room that's ever messy. Inside the top drawer is a rat's nest of supplies and back-to-school memories, and anything else I don't want Deborah digging out of the trash: extra ribbon, mechanical pencils, half a pack of Hubba Bubba, crazy scissors, a handful of raw almonds, and three spiral notebooks with my half-assed attempts at keeping a diary, all with only the first page filled in. My mom and I used to celebrate the beginning of each semester by bleeding Staples dry, and our favorite thing to do was to close our eyes and sniff-test the scented markers. Grape, orange, lemon, fruit punch, licorice, too. If I asked nicely, I might be able to swing a new pencil box or a Velcro-closing multi-binder, and we always left with a surplus of matching Gelly Roll pens.

My mom taught me at least two things during our afternoon shopping sprees. The first and most important: Appearances are everything. Even with the little things. The second: If you're going to cheat on your husband, don't you dare get caught.

pinktiaragirl: still there?
LAXative_22: yeah
LAXative_22: just thinking
LAXative_22: why did we stop being friends?

It's the simple stupidity of the question that makes me freeze mid-swivel.

Troy and I started dating the spring of our sophomore year. Or at least, I thought we did. Because one day during homeroom,

Chloe told Zoey that *Troy Richards* wanted to ask me out. And I told Zoey to tell Kyle that her sister, Chloe, is an idiot. And that if Troy *did* ask me out, I'd say yes. Next thing I knew, we were at the movies. Not just Troy and me, but all of us. Kyle, Chloe, Zoey. Andrew, too. Andrew and I had started to drift apart at some point in fifth grade when he jumped into sports and I kept both feet firmly on academic soil. But I, like everyone else in school, knew him as Troy's unofficial little brother. Our merry band bought tickets to an afternoon showing of the newest *Jurassic Park* movie, and the twins finagled it so Troy and I sat together. When the lights went down I took a handful of popcorn, and I screamed when I saw rat poop at the bottom. Turns out, Andrew had dumped his box of Buncha Crunch in the bag when no one was looking. Troy thought it was funny, so I did too. And after the movie, Troy kissed me goodbye in front of everyone. It was just like him. Goofy. Showy. Romantic. Confident. From there, it just happened.

He made me laugh.

I met his dad.

He made me a mixtape of songs I pretended to like.

I helped him study for the PSAT.

He surprised me with a trip to Rockport for my birthday.

I went to his lacrosse games.

He said he was in love.

And I thought he meant it.

pinktiaragirl: idk. people change
LAXative_22: really?
LAXative_22: u still have the same wallpaper
That makes me laugh out loud.
LAXative_22: were you at Hilary Maxwell's party?

I frown. With one hand, I begin twirling myself in slow circles, and each time the Garcia house slides by my eyes, I wonder if Andrew is doing the exact same thing. I also wonder what he's wearing.

Then I wonder why I'm wondering that.

Hilary Maxwell has been known for throwing the most outrageous house parties for as long as I can remember. That, and the nose job she denies getting as a birthday gift in eighth grade. But I digress. Mr. and Mrs. Maxwell are the kind of people who'll insist they aren't rich, they're comfy. Although I'm not sure their home movie theater would agree. As far as I know, Hilary has never done anything without her father's emotional and financial support, and for the past four years he's supplied her parties with enough appletinis and peach schnapps to keep the entire school hydrated. This New Year's was Hilary's first back from college, and even though I arrived late, I had just enough time to see the lax bros set off fireworks in her backyard.

I also got roped into a game of spin the bottle. Which explains how Kyle and I ended up in the back of Mrs. Maxwell's walk-in closet.

More or less.

pinktiaragirl: yes
pinktiaragirl: i don't drink, but i'm not a loser
LAXative_22: Troy is saying that i got drunk and jumped him at Hilary's party
LAXative_22: because I was jealous of him and Jennifer
pinktiaragirl: aren't you?
(LAXative_22 is typing...)
pinktiaragirl: sorry, is that supposed to be a secret?

pinktiaragirl: you've been in love with Jennifer ever since I've known you,
pinktiaragirl: way before she and Troy started bumping uglies
LAXative_22: u were the first one to bump anything with Troy
pinktiaragirl: and THAT is crass, Andrew
LAXative_22: listen! i never laid a hand on Troy
pinktiaragirl: shame
pinktiaragirl: but then who gave you the black eye?
LAXative_22: it was an accident ... and i WAS drinking
pinktiaragirl: then shouldn't Jennifer be able to back up your story?
LAXative_22: it's complicated
pinktiaragirl: because?
LAXative_22: because ... we kissed

I'm not sure how I'm supposed to react, so I settle for narrowing my eyes. Demure, selfless, and appropriately judgmental. Because for obvious reasons, I don't condone cheating. Even in cases where my ex-boyfriend is at the short end of the proverbial lacrosse stick.

LAXative_22: you gotta believe me, Sassi
LAXative_22: Troy knows the team is my life, and he wants me to suffer
LAXative_22: i didn't touch him
LAXative_22: and i guess Jennifer still ... loves him?

Ugh.
Love?
Vom.

pinktiaragirl: y are you telling me this?
LAXative_22: because of prom
LAXative_22: i know you hate him as much as i do
pinktiaragirl: PROM?
pinktiaragirl: you think that's why I hate Troy?

Suddenly, I'm not angry. Not even close. Instead, I have the distinct and simple urge to draw blood. I settle for my own, digging my nails into the meat of my palms as hard as I can.

Troy and I had been dating for almost a year by the time girls in our grade started picking out their dresses for junior prom. As for the guys, Eric Ashley was the first to find a date, which he did by streaking around the bases at the girls varsity softball game until Ruth Sherman agreed to go with him. Even Sam Klein got his shit together in time to ask Tessa Pearce, and he did it by setting up one hundred cannolis spelling out the word *PROM* in the middle of the cafeteria. Which was cute, if unhygienic.

But Troy never asked me.

At first I thought he was waiting to do something special. And then I hoped. And then I gave up. When I finally confronted him about it, the day before prom, Troy said he was too busy with lacrosse to ask me. He couldn't even be bothered to make me a sign. And he sure didn't apologize. Because when I said that was a freakin' shitty thing for a boyfriend to do, he said we weren't actually dating. We were just hanging out.

Because, again, he never actually asked me.

On prom night, I still went to preprom with the Stern twins and the rest of the lacrosse team to take group photos. I already had my dress, and my pride, and I didn't want anyone to know just how badly Troy had hurt me. But my plan backfired as soon as I saw him grinding with Kat Hicks on the dance floor.

I can still hear the sound of Mrs. Garcia's camera as she took our photos, all of us standing in a perfect row. It sounded like a machine gun.

But that's not the worst thing Troy has ever done to me.

pinktiaragirl: andrew

pinktiaragirl: my entire life, all i've wanted is to go to Harvard like my mom

pinktiaragirl: study prelaw, move to Boston

pinktiaragirl: it's the only reason I do yearbook

pinktiaragirl: and Model UN

pinktiaragirl: and UNICEF

pinktiaragirl: and violin

(pinktiaragirl is typing...)

LAXative_22: are you done bragging?

pinktiaragirl: TROY GOT IN BECAUSE OF LACROSSE!

This time it's Andrew's turn not to respond, but I don't mind. Again, I wonder what he's doing locked away in his room, and the more I think about it, the more I have the bizarre urge to giggle. Because as different as we are, Andrew and I have something in common. And in telling the truth about Harvard, he's most likely realized it too.

Troy has taken both our futures away from us.

pinktiaragirl: everyone knows that Troy committed to play last fall

pinktiaragirl: but i was waitlisted

pinktiaragirl: ME

pinktiaragirl: do you know how pathetic that is?

LAXative_22: how... is that possible?

pinktiaragirl: turns out Harvard only takes one person from our high school every year
pinktiaragirl: i haven't told ANYONE that person is my ex-boyfriend
pinktiaragirl: so what, he got you kicked off the team?
pinktiaragirl: you still have your senior year, and everything else after that

I settle fully into my chair, the words taking the fight out of me. Not that there's anything worth fighting for. I've kept the truth about Harvard to myself for so long, and I never practiced how I would tell anyone. Let alone Andrew Garcia, my ex-boyfriend's pseudo little brother. I never thought I would be in this situation. I doubt either of us did.

The message Andrew sends next stops me in my tracks.

LAXative_22: you're not the only one who wants Troy Richards dead

Again, I glance to Andrew's window. Suddenly, there is a whistling in my eardrums, and it reminds me of being on an airplane. Ready to descend. I type my response without looking at my keyboard.

pinktiaragirl: what do you mean?
LAXative_22: i mean … i think it's time we do something about it

For the first time in a long time, I'm lost for words. The whistle in my skull heightens to a sonic needling, and I suddenly realize how cold I am in my pajamas.

pinktiaragirl: sorry Andrew
pinktiaragirl: i'm not interested in whatever dick-measuring contest you have in mind
LAXative_22: this isn't about me!

LAXative_22: today I saw Troy with Mel's little sister
LAXative_22: he HIT her
pinktiaragirl: i know, i was there
LAXative_22: and it made me realize that even after graduation... Troy's going to keep hurting people
LAXative_22: unless we teach him a lesson
pinktiaragirl: i'm not saying i would hate to see Troy knocked down a peg or two
pinktiaragirl: but why should i help you?
(LAXative_22 is typing...)

Once again, there is a long delay between messages. And when Andrew's response finally comes through, it only makes me more confused.

LAXative_22: window

Sighing, I throw up my window and lean out over the sill as far as I can. From here, I have a direct view of Andrew's bedroom, and when he sees me he turns on his light. A stray swooping curl falls into his eyes. He really is gorgeous, in his own easy way. My dad always wanted us to date, and from here, if I squint, I can see what my dad sees. A sweetheart. A goofball. The loyal, lovable, literal boy next door.

Before I can shout across the way, Andrew holds up a piece of paper with the word *PLEASE?* written across the center.

It's as much of a promposal as I've ever seen.

right freakin' now

9

we like to party!

JENNIFER LEE

The five of us form a semicircle around Troy's body. No one speaks. No one looks away. At first I wanted to move him—help him—but Andrew didn't let me get close enough to try. Once the initial shock passed, he left to find help—and I expected him to come running back with Principal Clancy. Instead, he brought them.

Naomi King.

Sassi DeLuca.

Tatum Stein.

I stand a few steps back from the others, and I watch the girls with equal parts horror and confusion. At a glance, they have nothing in common—not with each other, and certainly not with Andrew. Even I know this. Everyone must know this. They're all in different grades, different social circles, and I've never seen Tatum speak to anyone without money changing hands. But if that were true, there'd be no reason for Andrew to ask them for help—and the fact that they're here in the first place proves that there's history between them.

Not to mention a literal dead body.

"I'm gonna vom," Sassi mutters.

Tatum turns the lights on, but Naomi quickly turns them off.

"Yeah," Tatum snorts, "because that makes it so much better..."

I can feel Sassi roll her eyes in the dark. She takes a lap around the body, but what she's looking for is anyone's guess.

"Shouldn't we call the cops?" Naomi whispers.

The others ignore her, and I clear my throat, trying to address Andrew as discreetly as possible. "Andrew, what's going on? Why did you bring them here? I thought you were going to get a teacher, or—"

"I trust these girls more than anyone in the world," Andrew interrupts. But his voice is gentle. He moves closer to me and wraps an arm around my shoulders. "Besides . . . it could've been a teacher, for all we know. Everyone hates Troy Richards."

Naomi mumbles something.

"Christ," Tatum groans. "Speak up, dude."

"Leave her alone, *dude*," Sassi throws back.

I shrug out of Andrew's embrace and hastily put myself at the center of the three girls—one hand on Naomi's shoulder and the other in front of Tatum, like I'm a bullfighter. Sassi lowers her perfectly plucked eyebrows in my direction.

"Keep your voices—"

"Hated."

This time, everyone looks at Naomi.

"Everyone hated Troy Richards," she says again.

At that, my attention returns to Troy. With my eyes adjusting to the dark, I can now see that his neck is wrapped in one of the jump ropes that Mr. Warren uses on rainy days in PE, his skin bulging between the plastic beads. For some reason, it reminds me of falling asleep with a hair elastic on my wrist. It's something simple, painful—and easy to avoid. I open my mouth to respond to Naomi, but a sob comes out instead. Andrew opens his arms, and I hurl myself at his broad chest. Naomi pretends not to watch, and I pretend not to know exactly what the look in her eyes means.

"Syntax aside . . ." Sassi exhales. "We're forgetting one teeny-tiny detail."

"What's that, Sassi?"

"It's lock-in night, remember?" She crosses her arms. "We're all freakin' *locked in.*"

The group falls silent. Something new, something heavy, is settling into the space between us. Because—like always—Sassi's right. But I say it first.

"The killer is inside the school."

february

10

the boy is mine

ANDREW GARCIA

Room 313 is a bore at best . . . a closet at worst.

According to legend, the current yearbook office belonged to the Hancock drama department when my parents were in high school, back before the arts budget was slashed by a particularly bloodthirsty superintendent. Then, for many years, the room was a make-out safehouse turned lost and found, before ultimately becoming the headquarters for the *Howler*. Because it's a Saturday, I'm expecting the door to be unlocked, and when it's not, I face-plant into it.

Sassi's voice comes from inside, unhurried and dreamy-sounding.

"Password?"

I hesitate, but she unlocks the door before I can blink the stars out of my eyes. Because in addition to her many other accolades, Sassi is also the *Howler*'s editor in chief.

"You should see your face." She smirks. "Exactly how many people do you expect to show up to this bash?"

"Four."

"Not including us, or total?"

"Erm . . . total?"

Sassi nods to herself, glossed lips pursed.

We've spent the last few weeks brainstorming ideas while walking home from school, and based on the telltale box of Dunkin' Donuts, Sassi was here early to set up an objectively optimistic circle of chairs. She's preparing for war, in her own way. On one wall of the yearbook office is a less than convincing D.A.R.E. poster reminding everyone that DRUGS ARE BAD, and against the other is a graveyard of rolling TV carts. A screen for a projector sags over the blackboard in preemptive defeat.

"What's this?" I ask, following Sassi to a low table by the windows. It looks like I've caught her in the middle of an arts and crafts project, and there are several reels of film curlicued in a pile before her.

"I'm colorizing the Hancock archives," Sassi explains. She grabs one strip and holds it up to the light for me to squint at. "The school initially printed everything in black-and-white, but Clancy asked me to take a crack at an upgrade before I graduate."

"Impressive," I admit, because it does sound impressive. Tedious, too. I return to the center of the room, but when I reach for a jelly doughnut, Sassi promptly swats my hand away.

"Hey!"

"Hey yourself," she tuts, taking a seat. I realize she's stress-chewing on a wad of tropical Hubba Bubba, and she sticks it on the side of her paper cup before sipping. "So? Who else did you invite?"

There it is. The question I've been dreading just as much as I've been looking forward to this meeting. Because even on a good day, Sassi doesn't really do happy. Before I can respond, there's a second knock on the door, and I watch the curiosity melt off her face as I open it.

"Hey, Tatum..."

"Greetings, earthlings."

There are plenty of seats for her to choose from, but Tatum decides to plop down directly next to Sassi. Close enough that their knees knock. And I bet she only does it because she knows it will piss Sassi off. Bored already, Tatum takes a purple pipe out of her windbreaker and begins packing the end.

"What is she doing here?" Sassi hisses at me.

Tatum hoots and folds up her limbs like a soft pretzel. "You surprised?"

"No. *Disappointed?* Maybe."

"I think what Sassi wants to say is that we're happy to have you here," I inject. "Thanks for coming in on a weekend."

"You're welcome."

"As if."

"Sassi—"

"*Andrew.* You can't trust Tatum! No offense."

"None taken." Tatum smirks and reaches for the doughnuts, greedily fishing a fat Boston Kreme out of the box. "Thanks for doing the Dunkin' run, by the way."

"Don't thank me, thank my stepmom," Sassi mutters. But her eyes don't leave my face. "Andrew—"

"Sassi, trust *me.* Tatum and I have been talking, and I really think—"

The three of us jump at another furious knock, and when I open the door to see Naomi, I actually look both ways in case there is someone else with her. But there isn't. Naomi scurries inside, directly under the arm I'm using to prop the door open. Her hoodie is pulled tight over her face, and she's cradling a misshapen brick of tinfoil against her chest.

"Hi, Naomi," I offer. But Naomi stays silent, ignoring me as she enters and sits as far away from us as humanly possible. Then, on second thought, she stands and drops the tinfoil brick next to the doughnuts from Sassi's stepmom.

"Banana bread," Naomi whispers. She sits back down. "I made it last night."

Sassi raises her eyebrows in my direction.

"W-well . . . this is everyone," I stammer, moving to stand in front of the projector. "Seeing as we don't really know each other, I think it might be nice to start with introductions—"

"What is this, AA?" Tatum cuts in. She grabs for Naomi's banana bread, rips off a sizeable chunk, and closes her eyes while she chews.

"You would know," Sassi throws back. I shoot her a look and she pretends to zip her lips shut.

Naomi stands up.

"Um. Hi. I'm Naomi. And . . . um . . . I'm a freshman?"

"Was that a question?" Sassi asks.

"I mean," Tatum adds, "it wasn't a fun fact—"

"Thank you, Naomi," I interrupt. Naomi slouches low in her chair, pulling the drawstrings of her hoodie as tight as she can. My coolness fades when I see her knuckles. The skin has finally started to heal from her run-in with Troy a few weeks ago, but it's clearly going to scar. Neither Sassi or I comment on it, but Tatum lacks the same sense of discretion.

"What happened, noob? Trip on your pigtails?"

Sassi kicks Tatum into standing.

"Okay, okay . . . *hi*. I'm Tatum. I'm a senior. And a Gemini. And . . . I ate my twin in the womb." She snorts when she sees Naomi's horrified expression. "Kidding, bro. I'm a Libra."

Sassi takes her place.

"Sassi DeLuca. Senior." She nods at me. "We're neighbors. And *he* sings in the shower."

"All right, all right. Thanks, Sassi." I sigh, and she curtseys before sitting back down. "That leaves me, then. Andrew, as you already know. It's my junior year. And like all of you . . . I hate Troy Richards."

My eyes go from one girl to the next.

And, I mean . . . if only looks could kill.

"I got it from here, Andrew." Sassi pops back to her feet. She walks across the room and yanks on the projector screen, sending it to the ceiling with a nasty hiss. On the blackboard underneath is a spread of images for the senior tribute, but Sassi takes a bright polka-dot folder from her bag and begins replacing them with new ones.

Tatum forces an obnoxious yawn.

"We're here to talk about Troy Richards," Sassi begins, ignoring Tatum. She takes something small out of her pocket and flicks on a laser pointer, moving a bright red dot from one photo to the next. When I look closer, I see Troy is in every single one.

Troy and the team winning state . . . Troy and me winning best Halloween costume . . . Troy and Hilary Maxwell winning last year's prom king and queen.

Troy . . . Troy . . . Troy . . . winning . . . winning . . . winning.

Next to me, Naomi raises her hand.

"No," Sassi tuts. "No bathroom breaks."

Naomi drops her arm.

"Our plan, *the* plan, is perfect." Sassi gestures to me. "Andrew has allegedly selected everyone in this room because of our expert know-how. And together, we're going to make Troy's final semester at this school just as miserable as he's made our lives."

I take my cue to speak.

"Tatum."

"Aye aye, cap'n."

"Everyone in this school owes you for one thing or another, and that's currency we can cash in on," I say. "Naomi . . ."

Naomi perks up instantly.

"No one pays attention to you. So you'll be our eyes and ears."

She nods. Happy to be included.

"And Sassi."

"Yes, sir."

"You have complete control of the school yearbook—"

Tatum snickers.

"What?" Sassi pouts. "I get that some people think it's dorky—"

"Only some—?"

"Sassi's right. The yearbook has power. And humiliating Troy is going to be the easiest part," I explain. "But if we play our cards right, Sassi can use the *Howler* to immortalize him and his real legacy in its pages. Forever."

This lands for everyone, and I catch Naomi giving the room another once-over.

"What about you?" Tatum asks.

"I—"

"Andrew is our secret weapon," Sassi chimes in, speaking for me. "You know everything about Troy, don't you?"

"Well, I don't know about *everything*—"

"What's his favorite movie?"

"Space Jam."

"Lefty or righty?"

"Righty."

"Favorite food?"

"Gushers."

"*Least* favorite color?"

"All right, all right, point made." I frown. I hold out my hand and Sassi innocently passes me her laser pointer. We switch places at the blackboard. "First things first. What's the worst thing that could happen to a lax bro like Troy Richards?"

Naomi raises her hand a second time.

"Uh . . . Naomi?"

"He could get hit by a car."

"We're not actually trying to hurt the guy," I say, grimacing. "Just his reputation."

"Premature balding?" Tatum offers.

I run a hand through my hair before I can stop myself.

"Does he have an embarrassing childhood stuffed animal or a baby blanket we could steal?"

"What's wrong with having a baby blanket?" Naomi sulks.

"What about any embarrassing fears?"

"Spiders." I think on it. "And the penguin from Wallace and Gromit."

"I mean . . . same?"

"We could turn off the hot water to the locker room while he's in the showers? Steal his clothes?"

"What is this, summer camp?"

"*Oh!* Easy. We screw with his car." Tatum snaps her fingers.

"My uncle works at an auto body shop in the next town over. He once dealt with a guy whose ex-wife poured bleach in the engine—"

"The Chimaera is off-limits," I interrupt, crossing my arms. "It belongs to Mr. Richards."

"And we care . . . why?"

"I'm with Andrew, let's not break the law—"

"Guys. Guys. You're thinking about this the wrong way," I interrupt again. "It's a hell of a lot simpler. The worst thing in the world? . . . *Troy. Could. Lose*"—I point to the photos one by one—"his girl . . ." I look at Tatum. "His friends . . . ," At Naomi. "And his college lacrosse scholarship." Finally, my attention lands on Sassi.

Sassi cracks her gum in her mouth, chews, and blows a bubble until it pops.

"He's cheating on Jennifer."

We all turn to stare at Naomi, everyone surprised to hear her speak in such a clear voice. When the reality of her words hits me, my feet and heart and everything in between suddenly feel like they're made of cement.

There's no way . . . unless . . .

"How do you know that?" I ask, afraid to hear the answer. "I mean . . . are you sure?"

"I overheard Chloe and Zoey talking about it a few weeks ago. He's sleeping with Zoey."

"If he's sleeping with one of them, he's sleeping with both," Tatum mutters, one eye on me.

"Gross."

"And . . . accurate?"

"*Guys—*"

"That's what you get for dating a lax bro! No offense, Sassi."

"None. Freakin'. Taken."

I grimace and stare out the window, looking toward the empty parking lot and remembering just how sad Jennifer seemed on our first day back. Then, I turn to the blackboard and rearrange Sassi's photos, writing above them with a piece of chalk:

OPERATION: KILL THE LAX BRO

"You mean that . . . metaphorically," Naomi peeps. "Right?"

I nod.

"Too bad," Tatum mutters. She shrugs when we look at her. "What? Like you've never thought about . . . ?" She draws a line across her neck with her finger, beheading style. "Look, I'm just saying. If I could? I'd do something super bloody. Macabre. To send a message, y'know? The dude and his entourage owe me so much money, maybe it would knock some sense into all of them."

Naomi mumbles something in response.

"Jesus, Naomi. The amount of time we'd save if you *enunciated*—"

"I'd poison him."

The three of us blink at her in a shocked, stony silence. Tatum finds her voice first.

"With what?"

"Mushrooms. Rat poison. Or maybe just . . . arsenic? Mr. Levitan keeps it in the lab for the AP class." Naomi blushes, and even though her voice is quiet, it's also steady, matter-of-fact. "Arsenic is tasteless, and hard to trace. It would be less bloody, too."

"I dig it."

Sassi shifts uneasily, and I pivot to look at her.

"Sassi, I promise we're taking this seriously—"

"Yeah . . . me too." She tugs the sleeves of her sweatshirt over her hands. "And *I'd* stab Troy Richards in the heart with his lacrosse stick. That freakin' sport is the only thing he's ever cared about, after all."

Tatum mimes applause.

"All right . . . well . . . any more questions?" I ask. As an afterthought, I put quotation marks around the word *KILL* on the board.

The girls share a look. And although it takes a moment, I realize that for once, they are all smiling. Not only that, but I am too.

"What do we do first?" Naomi asks.

11

this kiss

SASSI DeLUCA

When the weekend arrives, it's impossible to ignore the way the daylight slithers across my carpet before disappearing entirely at 4:57 p.m. Sharp. After the sun, the next to drop are the dads. The honorably underpaid and deep-fried. Followed by their kids with undiagnosed seasonal affective disorder, sunlamps not included. But for those of us lucky enough to have our own car, or those with a friend of a friend who can borrow their old man's for the weekend, it's time to make the holy pilgrimage to our most sacred house of worship.

The one. The only.

The Hancock Mall.

If you're someone who has never been here before, the first thing to know is that the name is a lie. Technically, there are two malls. Each one a four-story glass building that is connected to the other by a narrow sky bridge, like two kids with their fingers stuck in a rope trap. The New Mall and the Old Mall. Both have fluorescent lights and black-and-white tile straight out of the '80s, and I wouldn't be surprised if the slop in the food court is even older. Yet, with the free air-conditioning, and the movie theater, and the not totally insignificant detail that there's literally nowhere else to go, it's paradise.

Beggars and teenagers can't be choosers.

I park outside of Macy's and head directly for the Old Mall food court. Where, even though they don't serve it, it always smells like broccoli. A handful of restaurants line the room, including obvious crown jewels like McDonalds, Johnny Rockets, and Papa Gino's, and at the center, surrounded by a spattering of neon-orange tables, is a decently operational merry-go-round. When I was younger, my parents and I would come to the mall every weekend for brunch at the Cheesecake Factory, and we'd stay late to ride my favorite wooden horse. Who I named Man o' War, for obvious reasons. My mom called him Manny.

Dragging my attention away from the merry-go-round, I claim a seat in the outermost ring of tables. I'm careful to put my back to the windows so I can see everything and everyone. The chairs are bolted to the floor, making it impossible to get comfortable. I'm sure it was an intentional choice, to make sure shoppers spend more time on their feet.

Speaking of.

I clock Tatum in line at Panda Express, and my eyebrows soar high under my bangs when I see the Limited Too bags dangling off her elbow. Can't say I pegged her for the type. Tatum sees me and waves, and a moment later she drops into the seat across from me.

She slaps a bulging Styrofoam to-go box on the table between us.

"'Sup, Sassafras."

Tatum opens the lid and an explosion of hot Chinese American food floods my nose: Soy. Salt. Plastic.

My stomach grumbles.

"You want a bite?" Tatum asks, mouth full. She ignores the chopsticks and twirls a fork into a snowball of noodles. Toying with her food and my patience.

"Skooch." I nod to the table next to us.

"What? Don't want to be seen with me?"

"No. I do not."

Tatum rolls her eyes. But she obligingly moves one table over, placing herself so we can both watch the merry-go-round, and so anyone looking at us would think we were here separately. Present circumstance aside, I don't need anyone knowing I'm on speaking terms with Tatum Stein.

It's something I'm trying to forget myself.

My gaze goes to a clueless-looking freshman couple who clamber onto the merry-go-round. At the last second, they sit face to face in one saddle. Whoever he is, he kisses her. And whoever she is, she laughs.

Ew.

"Troy and I came here on our first date," I mutter. When my brain realizes what my mouth has said, my cheeks flush hot. "We saw a movie with our friends."

"Cute."

I scowl and cross my legs tight at the ankles. I should just leave it there, but suddenly I have to say so much more. I want to. The memories started as soon as I passed through the revolving doors, and now, it's like the only way to prove to myself that it was all real is to talk about it out loud.

"One time we—"

"No offense, but I didn't join Andrew's little group project for talk therapy," Tatum interrupts. "If you expect me to play therapist, I'm going to need a copay."

"You're such a jerk."

"Yep. And I take cash or Visa." Tatum cracks her neck like a glowstick and pushes the rest of her food aside. I swear the smell is only getting stronger. "What now, James Bond?"

I do a scan of the food court, my eyes glossing over the pink-and-red decor that popped up weeks ago for everyone's third-favorite Hallmark holiday. Valentine's Day is days away, and it seems like everyone and their brother is out shopping for their respective other halves. Insignificant or otherwise.

However, with Andrew still under house arrest and Naomi working her part-time job at Blockbuster, tonight it's just Tatum and me reporting for duty.

Lucky me.

"Can I ask you something, DeLuca?"

"I mean. You just did?"

Tatum snorts and slouches low in her chair, kicking my legs out of the way to make room for her surprisingly humongous feet. "What do you think really happened at the Maxwell party? Andrew doesn't have the stones to punch anyone, especially Troy Richards. But then where did his bruise come from?"

"It wasn't Troy, if that's what you're asking."

"How can you be sure?"

"One, I was there. Two, Andrew would have told us. Three, Harper Lee." I sigh when Tatum gapes at me, at a complete and utter loss. "Sorry. I take it you didn't pay attention in eighth-grade English?"

"Uh—"

"Harper Lee? *To Kill a Mockingbird*?"

Tatum burps.

"Gross. All right, well, my point is, Andrew was hit on the right side of his face. Which means that whoever hit him was left-handed, and Troy is a righty." I hesitate, thinking hard. "Have you seen him, by the way?"

"*Shah.* The eagle and the eaglet are at the seven-fifteen viewing of *Varsity Blues*. I caught them arguing over what to watch. She wanted *She's All That.*"

"You do know that *eaglet* means 'baby eagle,' right? Not 'girl eagle'?"

"I look like I care?"

"What about the Stern twins?"

"The ravens are nested outside the Old Mall. Last I saw, they were flying north by northwest."

I frown, and now it's Tatum's turn to sigh, disappointed.

"They're buying push-up bras."

I nod and stand, when suddenly, Tatum yanks me back down. My tailbone hits the seat.

"Tatum!"

"Check it. See that rent-a-cop?" Tatum points across the food court. There is a man doing rounds in a banana-yellow polo and high-waisted joggers. He has a walkie on his hip and keeps a hand over it like he's packing an actual weapon. "That there's Reggie. He could be a problem."

"How, exactly?"

"Easy. Ever since he accused me of shoplifting—"

"Accused? Were you actually?"

"Well, yeah. But that's not the point—"

I snort. And I'm not looking at her directly, so I can't be sure, but I think I feel Tatum smile. Meanwhile, on the opposite side of the merry-go-round, Reggie pauses to chat with two old ladies on scooters.

"What's so funny? I'd like to see you try."

"That's the difference between you and me, Tatum. *I* never got caught."

Tatum looks at me, mildly impressed, and I feel something warm blossom in my stomach. At first I think it's embarrassment. Then I realize it's pride.

Like any self-respecting preteen with too much time on her hands and some unspeakable something to prove, I had a shoplifting phase. But it was nothing too fancy, and no mom-and-pop stores. Ever. After my parents divorced, my dad tried to recreate our family afternoons at the mall to cheer me up, and I would ask him to buy me a purse or a bag. Anything with pockets worked, the lumpier the better, and when he wasn't looking I'd fill it with jewelry. Then, when the teller scanned the bag out, they would unknowingly deactivate the security tags on whatever was inside.

I never set off an alarm.

I never got caught.

So I stopped.

"You're crazier than I thought," Tatum says, squinting at me like she's seeing me for the first time. "Oh, another thing. Do you think we should come up with a safe word?"

"Please, no."

"Have a little fun." She juts out her bottom lip. "Besides, if I see Troy coming, how am I supposed to stop him from seeing you?"

"Break his knees?"

Tatum huffs and I take one last look around the food court. This time my gaze falls on the blazingly colorful storefront across from us. Candy Palace. I don't remember when, or why, or how he convinced me, but Troy and I once spent an entire evening sampling fudge and sharing Bubble Tape like Lady and the Tramp. Somehow, even though I never told him, he figured out that sharks are my favorite animal, and the date ended with him buying me a gummy hammerhead the size of my face.

And when we kissed, he tasted like Pixy Stix.

"Baby Bottle Pop," I blurt out, surprising myself. "That's our safe word."

"And here I didn't think you had a sweet tooth—"

"Can you leave already?"

"But I sat down last!"

I cross my arms, and Tatum groans. Reggie heads for us, and she reluctantly takes off speed-walking in the opposite direction. Exhaling, I take Tatum's chopsticks, finish her lo mein, and exit the food court. But I make sure to recycle the Styrofoam before I go.

And now it's my turn.

I find Zoey and Chloe exactly where Tatum said they'd be, taking advantage of the 5-for-$25 sale at Victoria's Secret and arguing about the value of cheeky versus boyfriend panties. They are each gripping one side of a pair of underwear that has *UR WELCOME* spelled on the crotch in sequins, and it's anyone's guess who the winner will be.

"—it's not like anyone is going to see them!"

"Just because I wore your Monday pair on Tuesday *one* time—"

"Chloe!"

Chloe relents. She drops her end and Zoey slingshots the offensive pair out of sight. To kill time, I lap the room like it's an ice-skating rink, swooping up an armful of clothes without looking too closely at what I'm grabbing. Eventually, Chloe disappears into the dressing rooms, and I seize the moment to corner Zoey. As nonthreateningly as possible.

"Hiya, Zoey."

"Hi, Sassi."

We blink at each other, and I tilt my head to the side to mirror her stance. Neither of us says anything else, and the aisle fills with the crackle of a new J.Lo song. I haven't spoken to the Stern twins in ages, but the fact of the matter only smacks me in the face right now: We used to be friends before I was dating Troy. Even after the breakup, Chloe held me when I cried. Zoey told me it was his fault. Chloe painted my toenails and fingernails and paid for me to get my first Brazilian wax. Zoey answered every late-night phone call. And they both said all the right things.

It's not you.

It's him.

He's a boy.

He's too young.

He's too old.

He's gay.

You deserve better.

He panicked.

You lucked out.

He'll come back.

You'll move on.

Eventually, and apparently sometime after the universal chunk of time in which it's okay to grieve a breakup had passed, the Stern twins stopped talking to me. As did all the guys on the lacrosse team, even the ones I thought were just as much my friends as Troy's. And after every painful second that Troy put me through, that might be the worst part. Realizing that it wasn't just Troy who didn't love me.

None of my "friends" did.

"Who are you here with?" Zoey asks, lazily looking over my shoulder. I hesitate just long enough for her to propose an answer to her own question. "Is it Kyle?"

I smile in a demure no-comment-I'm-so-in-love-tee-hee kind of way.

"Do you know where the beauty section is?" I ask. Zoey looks at my arms, and I grit my teeth when I realize that I, of course, managed to grab an ambitious G-string off the rack. Zoey jabs her thumb over her shoulder toward the section I was just in, and I pretend it takes me longer than it does to find what I need.

NEON NECTAR. MARVELOUS MELON. ELECTRIC GRAPE. KOOL KANDY.

"What do you usually use?" I ask without turning around. "Lip gloss? Lip stain? Lip oil?"

"ChapStick."

I shudder. Forcing a smile, I walk back to Zoey, stopping close but not too close, with two tubes of watermelon-flavored gloss in hand. I station myself in front of the nearest mirror and apply a coat to my lips. Then I pucker. Swipe. Smooch.

"Y'know, Zoey . . . this would look great on you."

"Hm?"

"Check it. I just can't pull off this color like you can."

Zoey, always a blood sucker for a compliment, turns around.

It's not entirely a lie. The color would suit her fine. The only thing I'm not being honest about is that Troy is allergic to the synthetic watermelon flavoring in this particular gloss. Which I only know because I wore the same kind on a date to Canobie Lake Park, and we had to leave early after making out at the top of the Yankee Cannonball. It's not a fatal allergy or anything, but it's just enough that if Troy were to, hypothetically, make out with someone who isn't his girlfriend, his lips would swell to the size of a cantaloupe.

For days.

"Seriously," I press. "Try it on."

But Zoey doesn't take the gloss. Or the bait.

"I insist," I literally insist.

Finally, insatiably, Zoey grabs the gloss and plants herself in front of the mirror. Puckers. Swipes. Smooches. "Tastes like spring break," she says, pleased with herself. Then she checks the price.

"What's wrong? You don't like it?"

"Hmm? Oh yeah, I guess. But my babysitting money hasn't come through yet."

"I can buy it for you."

Zoey narrows her eyes at me. "Why?"

Now I'm the one who hesitates. Good freakin' question, Zoey. Because like I told Andrew and the others, for this plan to work, we need Zoey to think the gloss is her idea.

Chloe returns from the dressing room before I can think of a good or bad response.

"Hi, Sassi!"

"Hiya, Chloe."

"Oh snap. Do you guys, like, remember coming here with

your mom in middle school?" Chloe smiles in a way that makes me know to be wary of whatever she says next. "We got fitted and everything by that lady with the unibrow, and when they didn't have your size we started calling you—"

"*Duracell.*" Zoey finishes the thought, giving me an obvious up-down.

My cheeks flush redder than my hair, and I'm suddenly aware that every surface in this stupid store is a mirror: the walls, the ceiling, the floor, the tables, even some of the sequins on the more ambitious-looking DDs. Growing up, I didn't wear a bra for the longest time because my mom said I didn't need one. But when our little girl gang wanted to go bra shopping, she agreed to drive us. Then, when it was my turn, the woman in the dressing room happily announced my bra size. To everyone. Which was, and is, a horrifying AAA.

Hence the name. Duracell.

Mean girls can be brutal.

And sometimes pretty clever.

"Are you ready to go, Zoey?"

Zoey nods. Chloe dumps her returns onto the pile in my arms, and the two of them breeze on by. The twins exchange less-than-discreet whispers, and I watch their reflections like a fun-house mirror, only getting bigger and bigger as they get farther and farther away. For a moment, I hope the security alarm will go off and stop them in their tracks. Not that I have any idea what I would do then. Either way, it doesn't, and they continue into the Old Mall.

Until someone in a neon windbreaker smashes into them from the opposite direction.

12

there she goes

TATUM STEIN

"*Jesus Christ—*"

"Tatum!"

I don't stop to apologize. Instead, I pull myself up to standing, pushing off Zoey, or Chloe, like a springboard, and keep running toward the New Mall. Over their bickering, I can hear Reggie huffing and puffing and sloughing behind me, and I don't waste time looking back to see Sassi's reaction. No matter how badly I'm dying to.

"Hey! Stop! *Please!*"

My Docs punch the ground as I fly to the sky bridge. Shoppers step out of the way when they hear me coming, but there's no need. I ran on the track team for the first half of my first freshman year, and Coach Mike said that if I got out of my own way I might be able to swing a college scholarship.

What a turd.

I burst through the next door on my right and take the stairs to the roof three at a time. Then I hurl all my weight at the emergency exit, opening the door as far as it will go. Once the alarm starts to sing, I double back the way I came, crouching against the banister with my Limited Too bags tight to my chest. Reggie appears a minute later, a new record for him, and heads for the roof without looking twice. Once the door closes I count to five and head for the parking lot at a leisurely pace.

No one looks twice. Or once.

It's not hard to figure out which car belongs to Sassi. Even without the lavender butterfly seat covers, the overlapping *MY KID IS AN HONOR STUDENT* stickers would kind of give it away. I jump up to sit on the hood, and I fish my pipe out of my pocket. I started smoking the fall after my mom died in order to trick myself into thinking I had some kind of control over my life. Now, when I light up, the air tastes like October.

"What. The. Fuck."

I glance up to see Sassi coming toward me.

"Are you sure that's what you want to say?"

"Sorry. Let me try again." She steamrolls up to me, and there might as well be smoke coming from her nostrils, not mine. "Feet. Off."

I snort and stand to greet her, politely tapping the ash over the side of the car. "Aren't you going to thank me?"

"For what, exactly?"

I sigh and make a show of checking my watch. Cinderella smiles back at me, bashful, which reminds me that I need to be home soon to throw dinner in the microwave. I slide my pipe back into its place.

"Because by this time tomorrow, Chloe will discover a new tube of lip gloss in her purse. Courtesy of yours truly."

"You planted it on her?"

I take a crinkled receipt out of my pocket.

"And before you ask, *yes*. I bought it fair and square. Just in case."

"But that wasn't the plan, Tatum. We need to make sure *Zoey* uses it!"

"Chillax. Chloe is as dumb as a stump and won't question where it came from. And as soon as Zoey sees her sister has something she doesn't, you know she'll snag it for herself. Signed, sealed, delivered . . . I'm your *savior*."

Sassi hesitates, chewing aggressively on the inside of her cheek. She looks from me to the Old Mall and back again but doesn't smile. I blow smoke in her direction and she flaps it away with both hands.

"Go on. Say it."

"How will I ever repay you," she deadpans.

"For starters, you can give me a ride home. I'm late, and I still need to figure out dinner for my sisters."

"You don't have a car?" she asks. I shake my head. "How did you get here in the first place?"

"The bus."

"Crazy thing about busses, they run both ways."

I press my hands in front of my heart, prayer position, when she makes no sign of caving. Sassi pushes the heels of her hands into her eye sockets.

"Fine!"

Beaming, I toss my bags into the back seat and scramble in at shotgun. To no surprise, the inside of Sassi's car is outrageously clean, almost sterile. Sassi slides in with significantly more grace and her hands automatically go to a permit-perfect 9:00 and 3:00 on the steering wheel.

"Are your parents out of town?" Sassi asks, eyes on her

mirrors. I realize she's looking at my Limited Too bags and connecting the dots. We pull out of the parking spot, and I'll admit that I'm impressed she drives stick.

"Kind of." I shrug. "My mom died. Their mom's a deadbeat."

"And your dad—"

"Is still in prison."

"Jesus, Tatum. I'm sorry. I didn't know."

"No need, I've got it handled. During the week, Sarah and Eliana are busy with school, and I swap weekends with their mom. Tomorrow we're doing tie-dye."

Sassi drums her French manicure on the steering wheel. But whatever she's thinking, she never gives it airtime. Eventually she sighs and steps on the gas.

"I'm an only child," Sassi admits.

"I can tell."

"What does *that* mean?"

I snort and rest my feet on the dash. Sassi grips the wheel until her knuckles show, but she doesn't tell me to put them down.

"Why are you *really* going along with Andrew's plan?" she asks, sharply changing the subject. "What's in it for you?"

"I'll show you mine if you show me yours."

"I'm serious, Tatum!"

"And I am too," I say, shrugging. "Troy owes me money. And has been blackmailing me for drugs. But if this scheme actually works, I might be able to recoup my investment."

"This is just phase one," Sassi reminds me. She slows at the crosswalk outside the New Mall and I strain forward against my seat belt to point.

"Look."

The Stern twins cross the street mere feet away from us, but neither of them can see beyond the glow of Sassi's headlights. Their shopping bags look a little rumpled but otherwise no worse for wear.

"God, I hope Andrew's stupid plan works," Sassi mutters, watching the girls walk to their car. Someone behind us honks and she eases forward to the exit. "What are we supposed to do now?"

"Now . . . we wait," I say, watching the twins for as long as I can. Once they disappear, I look back at Sassi, puppy-dog eyes at the ready. "Or . . . we could get burgers?"

Sassi rolls her eyes and exits left toward McDonald's.

13

truly madly deeply

NAOMI KING

Valentine's Day has always been my favorite holiday. But don't worry, it's not like I'm expecting a sudden uptick in my social status. I'm an outcast and a hopeful romantic, not clinically insane.

Late last night, the PTA moms went all out decorating the high school. There are streamers and balloons in all the major hallways, plus bowls of candy and individually wrapped condoms in the bathrooms. Like most of the Hancock girls, I'm dressed in pink and red from headband to toe, with a necklace of plastic candy hearts that my mom gave me before I left home. Ever since we were little, our parents have always given my sister and me matching baskets of goodies to kick-start Valentine's Day. Usually with a Mad Libs or two and a new outfit. One year my dad gave me a Beatles CD, and "Love Me Do" became our unofficial anthem.

As Mel and I grew up, we got in the habit of handing out valentines and homemade cookies to everyone in our respective homerooms. In kindergarten, Sebastian Fitzgerald yanked one of the bows off my new dress, and after I stopped crying, my mom told me that *that* meant he liked me. The next year, in first grade, my teacher Mrs. Feynman helped all of us decorate shoeboxes to collect our valentines, and I could barely wait to count my haul on the living room floor. Because if there was one more or less than the total number of kids in class, it was a big deal.

Who loved you? Who *hated* you?

The first and only time an anonymous valentine was slipped into my locker was in sixth grade. I never figured out who it was from, but to be honest, I didn't really try that hard to find out. Nothing could top a secret admirer.

Not even the truth.

"Tatum!"

I catch sight of Tatum hunched over one of the water fountains with her shoulders up to her ears. She doesn't turn around when I say her name, but she does when I get too close to ignore. Unlike me, she's dressed in a dark miniskirt and fishnets. I try not to let my disappointment show. She, however, doesn't bother.

"Um . . . hi?"

"Hi." I take a steadying breath before I can talk myself out of it. "I made these for you." I swing my school bag off my shoulder and riffle through the front pocket with both hands. A moment later I hand Tatum a plastic Tupperware and a thick envelope. "Happy Valentine's Day!"

Tatum grimaces, pinching the envelope between her thumb and pointer finger like it's a dirty sock. Her nails are freshly and sloppily painted with twinkling lime-green polish, and it reminds me of the time my dad let Mel and me paint his nails. Tatum sniffs the corner of the envelope before tearing it open. Inside is a homemade card, but instead of anything pink, I made sure to go all black with hers. Next she holds the Tupperware up to the light.

"I . . . um . . . made snickerdoodles?"

"I didn't get you anything," Tatum says, flat.

"Oh, no worries." I loop both thumbs through my bag and begin to rock forward and back on my feet. "You didn't have to, or anything. I just really love Valentine's Day."

"No kidding," Tatum muses, taking in my outfit. "Did you bake something for Andrew, too?"

"Um . . . no?"

"Uh-huh, sure." She smirks. "You have any updates on you-know-whomst?"

I stop sharply with my weight in my heels.

It's almost been a full week since Sassi and Tatum planted the watermelon lip gloss on Zoey. Ever since that night, the four of us have been watching Troy like a kettle of hawks, waiting for an incriminating rash and the demise of his newest high school romance. But so far, nothing. No swollen lips, not even a pimple. Troy's skin and relationship look as clean and healthy as ever, meaning that either I was wrong or Sassi was.

And she never is.

"No, but—"

"I knew I should have done something to his car. Maybe there's still time."

"Andrew said not to—"

Tatum interrupts me by pointing over my shoulder, a sudden and unmistakable horror in her eyes. But I don't have to look behind me to guess what's coming our way, because there is one thing about Valentine's Day at Hancock High that even I don't like.

The glee club.

"Well, your love is a potion, stir with a spoon—"

Every year, the Hancock boys and girls a cappella clubs take over the high school, dividing the hallways into respective territories like the Sharks and the Jets from *West Side Story*. The boys are dressed in red pants, white shirts, and clip-on bow ties, and the girls are in white pants, red shirts, and water bras. The two clubs compete to raise the most money by selling singing valentines, and Mel told me that they've mastered the art of popping up when you least expect them. But for a bargain price of $3.99, anyone can send a rose and a swarm of Off-Broadway hopefuls to traumatize their crush in the middle of third period. Or, if you're like most people, embarrass the crap out of your friends.

This time it's the boys, and they descend on someone's locker like a cloud of cicadas. Poor Mary Edwards tries to make a break for it, but they corner her with a horrible Barenaked Ladies cover.

"It's been one week since you winked at me! Now I'm floating high like a bumblebee!"

"Jesus. They get worse every year." Tatum shakes her head, her wild curls tumbling over her shoulders. "I didn't think that was possible."

"I think the idea is sweet," I admit, struggling to keep a smile.

Tatum shrugs and walks away without saying goodbye. I hurry to catch her.

"Wait. Tatum? Did you hear what I said before? Don't do anything until we talk to Andrew about . . ."

Tatum whips around, and the ice in her gaze makes me trail

off. She takes another look at the cookies I gave her, sighs, and disappears around the corner.

Adjusting my bag, I exhale through my mouth and begin the climb to the second floor.

The science labs always seem to smell like rotten flesh, thanks to the anatomy students who boil down a full-size pig every semester and then string up the bones in the windows to study. I take a deep breath before entering the chemistry room, and I exhale only slightly when I see that the chair next to mine is empty.

"All right, everyone. Settle, settle." Our teacher, Mr. Sam Levitan, stands tall as he scarfs down the remaining half of his daily tuna sandwich. Although I can't imagine him drinking, he has a beer gut that is always in competition with the funny ties he likes to wear. Today's is a banana with a mustache.

"Hi, Mr. Levitan," I squeak out.

Mr. Levitan nods hello, his head bobbing an awful lot like the Taco Bell bobblehead on the dashboard of my dad's car. He watches me slide into my assigned seat at the very back of the room. There is an eye wash station directly behind me and a row of empty test tubes waiting patiently on a cart to the side.

"Ms. King, make sure you're paying close attention today. When your lab partner arrives, you'll need to catch him up."

"Okay."

"Thank you. Now, today we are going to finish the ammonia fountain exercise that we started earlier in the week. If I can get everyone to grab a clean flask and—"

"Ehem?"

I, like everyone else, look to the door, dismayed to see the girls glee club poking in from the hallway. There are six of them in total, and they are all twittering in a way that reminds me of birds sitting on a wire.

"Greetings, ladies." Mr. Levitan's voice is tight. "Who are you here to terrorize?"

The girls settle themselves and step inside, assuming a loose half-moon formation in front of his desk. Each of them holds a single red rose. Mr. Levitan sighs and moves to give them more room. It might be his first Valentine's at Hancock, but he knows his place.

"Where is Troy Richards?"

The door opens a second time, and Troy himself saunters in, either not knowing or not caring that he's a full five minutes late. I know the odds are against us, but I still do a quick scan. Just to be sure. His blue jersey is untucked from his jeans at the front, and his hair is dashingly rumpled at the back, almost as if he just woke up from a nap.

Still no adulterous lesions to speak of.

"Perfect timing, Mr. Richards. These girls are here for you."

"Me, really?" Troy stops where he is, swagger dialed up to the max. The rest of the class laughs, more than ready to be entertained. "Ready when you are, ladies."

The glee girls tighten their ranks. One of them hands Troy a rose, and another produces a stainless-steel tuning fork. She taps it against the nearest tabletop.

DIIIIIIING.

"Everybodyyyy, yeaaah . . . wants Troy's body, yeaaah . . ."

While Mr. Levitan seethes next to them, the girls sing a remixed Backstreet Boys single. After one of them breaks free for an inspired solo, Troy leads a standing ovation. Once they are finished, Troy turns in a full circle with his arms outstretched, basking in the attention from all sides of the classroom, like the conductor of a grand orchestra. He leads us in a whooping round of applause, and the glee girls bow.

"Thank you, ladies." Mr. Levitan pushes his horn-rimmed glasses up on the bridge of his nose, and he frowns when they don't immediately leave. "Is there . . . anything else?"

To all our surprise, the ringleader of the merry troop smiles, and another girl steps forward to hand Troy a second rose.

DIIIIIIING.

"Anticlimactic, unsanitary, unsanitary, anticlimactic—"

Laughing, Troy makes his way to our station while the club launches into their version of a Beastie Boys tribute. He drops his things next to me, without looking at me. But it's safer that way. As Troy sits down, he tosses the roses aside and picks at a wedgie with both hands, and I force myself to look away before he or anyone else catches me staring.

"Well. Now. Don't hate me, it's Kyle—"

At the front of the room, Kyle Hennessy turns around in his chair, and he and Troy exchange an air high five.

"—throw your stick around, let's get hostile—"

"How many more of these do we have?" Mr. Levitan asks through his teeth.

All four remaining girls hold up their roses, and Mr. Levitan collapses behind his desk, properly defeated. The singers continue with their performances one by one, and my attention drifts from the growing rose pile in front of Troy out the window to my left.

Outside, I spot Tatum pacing on the lawn beside the school marquee. It has had the same message on it since before the holidays, but the janitor must have changed it earlier today.

CONGRATS CLASS OF '99
GO BIG OR GO HOME!

Tatum stares at the building, desperate, and when she sees me looking back at her, she waves both arms above her head. But I have no idea what she's trying to say.

"Anticlimactic, unsanitary, unsanitary, anticlimactic—"

"Mr. Richards?"

Because I'm looking the other way, I barely hear Mr. Levitan's voice over the girls.

"—MR. RICHARDS?!"

Troy lurches away from our table, his chair making a harsh SCREEEECHing sound across the floor. I whirl around, and I see he is scratching at himself with both hands.

"AAAARRRGHH—!"

Troy lets out a bellow of pure agony, and when he tries to unzip his pants, I scream. People around us start to whisper, confused, but not all too worried.

Mr. Levitan makes a beeline for us.

"Calm down, son. Did you spill something on yourself? What—"

But Troy doesn't wait to explain. If he even could. Roses, singing valentines, and everything else forgotten, he bolts down the aisle, shoving Mr. Levitan and the glee club out of the way before he disappears into the hall.

And it's only now that I realize.

It was no wedgie.

14

u can't touch this

ANDREW GARCIA

"—I don't want another milkshake, I don't want another french to fry, so—"

I swallow a groan and drop my head on my textbook. Typically, the library is one of the few spots where you can find peace and quiet, and today it's the only place people can seek refuge from the glee club. So it's packed. Luckily, I found a table between the sections for World War I and World War II, but the wall on my right is made entirely of warped glass, and it's the only thing standing between me and the Faith Hill massacre happening next door.

"—this Hershey's kiss, this kiss—"

Giving up on studying, I close my book and stand to crack my back. Heads still turn to follow me as I leave, but perhaps with less frequency than when the news of my lacrosse suspension first broke. That said, even the librarians whisper as I go.

Omnipotent hypocrites.

I step into the hallway just in time to catch the end of the performance, and I try not to react too much when I see that the glee boys are singing to Jennifer and Chloe. Jennifer is wearing a pink sweater vest and matching skirt, and when she turns, I spot a tiny heart brooch pinned to her collar. She applauds at the end of the song, so I do too, and we are both shocked when the boys hand a rose to Chloe instead of her.

"Chloe, did you send yourself a valentine?" Jennifer teases. "Again?"

But Chloe just squeals. She kisses one of the boys on the cheek and the glee-ers skip off, leaving behind an awkward silence that's even more silent and awkward than awkward silences usually are. Jennifer sees me, and she gives a shy little wave.

"Hi, Andrew." She nudges her sidekick into mumbling hello. Clearly, it's her attempt at a public truce. "Chloe, you can get going. I'll catch up with you and Zoey later."

"Are you sure?" Chloe pouts, casting her dewy eyes on me. I maintain what I hope is an innocent expression as she does a full-body audit, from my Nikes to my backward baseball cap. When Jennifer nods, she begrudgingly leaves us.

"Happy Valentine's Day," Jennifer says, testing the waters when I don't say anything right away.

"Thanks . . . you too."

"Did you get any valentines?"

I make a show of emptying my pockets, and she smiles.

"Remember when your mom sent you to school with her cupcakes?"

"I wish I didn't." I make a face. "They were awful."

"Yeah . . . I think *memorable* covers it."

I laugh and follow Jennifer into the stairwell, but neither of us is in a rush to go anywhere. The traffic in the school eases to a gentle ebb of bodies, with most people headed off to class above and below us.

"And how many singing valentines have you been victim to today?"

"Oh . . . zero," Jennifer admits. She absent-mindedly twirls the end of her ponytail, and I notice a new charm bracelet on her wrist. I catch a glimpse of a tiny lacrosse stick and a telltale *#1* made of sterling silver. "Troy's not exactly into public displays of affection, y'know?" she says.

I resist the urge to scowl, not wanting to disagree too harshly and scare her away. But this is Troy we're talking about, the same guy who sprinted shirtless down the hallway after he passed his scoliosis test. Not like it's something you study for.

But . . . whatever.

"Jennifer . . ."

"Yeah?"

Jennifer looks at me patiently and cocks her head to one side like a puppy. I'm ashamed to admit there is a part of me that is dying to reach over and snap the bracelet off her arm, one tacky charm at a time. But another, sadder part of me is realizing she might not want me to. So instead of whatever supersuave thing a normal guy might go with, I say the first thing on my mind.

"You have spinach in your teeth."

Jennifer gasps, then laughs. She covers her mouth and the offensive fleck of spinach with her hands.

"What! Where? Tell me!"

I'm not quick enough, and she bares her teeth at me. Shamelessly. Not caring how it looks, and not knowing how effortlessly beautiful she is. That's what I've always liked about Jennifer: She doesn't know how pretty she is, and she's not afraid of looking like a fool. She's also a bit of a slob.

"Little to the left."

"Did I get it?"

"No. Left. Left."

Jennifer runs her tongue over her front teeth, both of us laughing like idiots. I never thought it would be a piece of spinach that did it, but I suddenly realize that Sassi was right.

Whatever I've been feeling all these years . . . it is love. Probably.

"Can you just get it for me?"

"I—"

"Please, Andrew?"

I nod and move closer. I cup Jennifer's chin in my hand, and tenderly, I slide my thumb over her gums. It's not gross, and it's not intimate or anything, until Jennifer puts her hand on mine. I've never been one for Valentine's Day, or the Hallmark movies that my mom watches year-round, but this sure does feel like one of those moments that people like to talk and write and rap about.

I hate that I'm about to ruin it.

"Jennifer . . . we need to talk about what happened on New Year's."

She pulls back so fast that I'm left holding the air.

"I'm sorry to keep bringing it up," I continue, lowering my hand. "I didn't mean to corner you or anything. But you're not exactly giving me a lot of options. I need your help, and you're not answering my calls."

"I can't talk on the phone when my folks are home. We only have the landline, and they're always listening in."

"You need to tell them, and everyone, what really happened at Hilary's. I want us to tell the truth. Together."

"I don't see how that will help you get your spot back on the team—"

"Don't be delusional, Jennifer. This isn't about lacrosse," I interrupt. "You can't be with a guy who . . . who . . ."

"Who *what*, Andrew?"

I don't trust myself to say something nice, so I don't so anything at all.

"I'm *happy* dating Troy, okay?" Jennifer says, voice low. She nudges the toe of my sneaker with her own. "You don't have to worry about me. I'm a tough cookie."

"But I do worry about you."

"Why?"

"Because I—"

"ARRRRRRRGH!!!!"

There is a bloodcurdling howl from the floor below us, and Jennifer and I instinctively leap apart. I crane my neck over the stairs just in time to glimpse Troy sprinting to the ground floor. It happens so fast I think I must have imagined it, except—

"Was that *Troy*?"

The next thing I know, Jennifer is zooming after him, and I'm running after her. The emergency alarm goes off a second later, an indicator that Troy must have bulldozed through the nearest exit. By the time I make it to the first floor, Troy is halfway across the parking lot, moving even faster than he did at last year's playoffs. He's holding his belt with one hand, and because of that, he fumbles and drops his keys. The top is down on his dad's convertible, and he settles for hurling himself directly over the door and into the driver's seat. Once right-side up, he braces one foot on either side of the steering wheel, and he claws at his boxers like there are fire ants in his pants.

And then it dawns on me . . . Sassi's absurd plan actually worked.

But Zoey didn't waste time kissing him on the lips.

"No fucking way," I mutter.

A swarm of onlookers gathers at the convertible, and I join them. I catch sight of a neon windbreaker in the crowd, but it disappears a moment later. Jennifer pushes through the otherwise captive audience, and I'm a little surprised by how forceful she is. She pulls on the driver's-side door, but the car is still locked.

"Troy! Are you okay—"

"HOSPITAL!"

Jennifer scoops up Troy's keys and lets herself into the car, shoving him to the passenger seat. But when she tries to start the engine, a death rattle comes from somewhere deep inside. It sounds awful . . . and it smells worse. And for a second, Troy goes still. His face is red, eyes dark. Livid. Before he can do or say anything, more students come running out from the school, led by the panting Mr. Levitan. He and Kyle Hennessy, a senior who's already committed to playing lacrosse at Middlebury next fall, are the first ones to reach us. Naomi trails at the very back of the mob.

"What's going on?" Mr. Levitan demands.

"The car won't start!" Jennifer says. "I think he's having an allergic reaction or—"

"Does he have an EpiPen?"

Jennifer goes blank-faced. She doesn't know.

"He doesn't," I call out.

Not that anyone thanks me.

"Come with me, son. I'll drive you."

Jennifer nods and helps Troy out of his car. Meanwhile, Mr. Levitan jogs to the teachers' lot, returning in a mustard-yellow Buick. He and Jennifer ease Troy into the back seat, and a moment later they peel out. One of the younger lax bros is dumb enough to stand and silently wave goodbye, and Kyle smacks him on the back of the head. As soon as the Buick is out of sight, Kyle pops the hood on Troy's car. From where I'm standing, I can't tell what he's looking for, but a moment later he holds a hand above his head for everyone to see.

There something . . . dripping . . . off his fingers. Like blood.

Except it's inexplicably and confusingly . . . neon blue?

"Glitter."

Tatum materializes next to me like a phantasm. Thankfully, people are too distracted to pay us any attention.

"Don't tell the drama department." She winks at me.

"Tatum . . ." I mutter, keeping my voice low. Suddenly, I feel sick to my stomach. "I told you the car is off-limits. It's not even Troy's. It's his dad's."

"Right. And like I told you . . ." Tatum smirks and slides her sunglasses firmly into place. "We're at war."

15

one headlight
TATUM STEIN

The auto shop that my uncle Isaac owns, Al & Sons, is smack on the border between the towns of Hancock and West Valley. After Grandpops passed, the business was left to Isaac and my dad, the titular sons, before going to Isaac in full after my dad's third and final arrest. When they were kids, my grandparents started out in Southie, but as soon as my dad and Isaac got old enough to find trouble, of which there was plenty for two unsupervised boys in South Boston in the '60s, my bubbie moved everyone to the suburbs. Like my dad, Isaac never graduated from high school, and as recently as a few years ago, there were rumors he and his old crew were involved in the Gardner Museum heist. Rumors Isaac is more than happy to stoke after his second Sam Adams.

Al's consists of a garage bay just big enough to fit two cars side by side, plus the inner office, if you are feeling generous enough to call it that. There's room for a tiny standing desk, a computer, and a water cooler, but no air conditioner, no guest chairs, no magazines. Nothing to encourage spending any more time on the premises than necessary. As for decoration, there is a single wall of photos across, crooked but framed, all of them snapshots of Isaac's time at Hancock High, including a black-and-white photo of his lacrosse team winning state in 1975. When I was little, I loved visiting the shop with my dad on the weekends. There's always been something about the smell of fresh rubber, be it new tires or new shoes, that makes me want to lick things. Even now, it's not all bad. The office shares a wall with Dirty Water Pizza next door, and most days I can count on the Greek ladies working the counter to slip me an extra slice and a hunk of baklava. Today I had planned on saving the snickerdoodles that Naomi gave me earlier for my sisters, but after eating one on my way over, I physically couldn't force myself to stop.

Naomi might be a certified space cadet, but she's got a gift.

The front door swings open, triggering the beastly bell that Isaac installed last summer.

"Yello?" I say on instinct, not looking up or away from the office computer. Against my better judgment, I agreed to help Isaac design new graphics for the shop, and I've since been trying to teach myself how to use Microsoft Paint.

The man who enters doesn't respond. But something about his silence, or the sheer amount of oxygen being sucked out of the room by a stranger, causes me to look up. When I see a police officer glaring down at me, I nearly do a double take.

"Picking up?"

"Oh. I don't actually work for—"

"You're sitting here, aren't you?" the officer interrupts, brittle. He loops both thumbs behind his belt buckle, as if his holster needs any more spotlighting. His white-blond pornstache is combed to perfection, and the officer doesn't bother taking off his sunglasses. I make eye contact with my reflection.

"Fine. How can I help? *Sir?*"

"Isaac called me."

"He did?" I frown. My uncle isn't exactly known for going above and beyond with his customers, let alone talking on the phone. I grab the clipboard under the desk. "What's your name?"

"Michael Richards."

My pen halts in the middle of writing today's date. "What kind of car is it?" I ask, my voice sounding far away.

Not that I don't already know.

"1992 TVR Chimaera." Troy's dad tips his head, evaluating me without seeing me.

As I write down his details, I rack my brain for any and all information that I have about Mr. Michael Richards. But unlike his prodigal pain-in-my-ass son, it's not much. At a glance, Mr. Richards looks like the kind of guy who will call you "bud" or "buddy," but only because he forgot your name. Or he couldn't be bothered to learn it in the first place.

He's also just as terrifying as Troy.

"And did Isaac tell you why he—"

"Michael!"

I see myself flinch in the sunglasses. Isaac comes as far into the office as he can, but Mr. Richards's presence takes up so much space that there's not enough room for the three of us. There is a thumbprint of grease on Isaac's face from picking his nose, and he spits a wad of chewing tobacco toward the trash can at my feet. Which he misses.

"Don't worry, Tate. Michael and I go way back." Isaac indicates the photo wall with his chin, specifically the snapshot of his team. "We both played lacrosse in the glory days."

"Of course you did," I say. Through my teeth.

"He was a beast on the field. And if he hadn't torn his ACL—"

"Where's the car, Isaac?"

My uncle jerks to attention and leads Mr. Richards toward the auto bay, and I wait for them to step out before I follow. I'm careful to catch the door before it closes, and as I hustle in the opposite direction, around the back of the shop, I spot Mr. Richards's cruiser at the curb. For what it's worth, he's taking up two parking spots.

"Asshat," I mutter to myself.

Troy's Chimaera is sitting half in, half out of the farther bay, exactly where the tow truck dropped it after school today. Isaac and Mr. Richards keep their backs to me as they talk, and I hide behind the dumpsters to better listen in.

". . . the fuck, Isaac?"

"I'm betting it was those Trapelo kids. You remember the rivalry. You know how it is."

"I do . . ."

Their voices drop to murmurs, and I shuffle closer. I don't know what is causing it, but I can't shake the gut feeling that I know Mr. Richards from somewhere. Somewhere besides the obvious, that is. I thought I knew all the cops in town—then again, I do avoid them, for obvious reasons. But the smug look. The sunglasses. The pornstache. Finally, he turns to the street, and his shadow snaps it all into focus. There's a reason I'm able to recognize him better from afar. Because in truth, I've only ever seen him at a distance.

On the second-worst night of my life.

". . . drained about a gallon of glitter from the engine. Whoever it was, they knew something about cars."

Ruh-roh.

I step farther behind the dumpster, just in case.

". . . fix it?"

"Absolutely. This is nothing. Not like the Chevy . . ."

At that Mr. Richards claps a hand on the spot between Isaac's neck and shoulder, and oddly enough, the gesture reminds me of how Troy had his hand in Jennifer's back pocket. Casual, territorial. As the two of them head back the way they came, I go in the opposite direction, fishing my cigarettes out of my pocket, and I time it so that by the time they get back to the door, I'm leaning casually against the side of the building.

"Smoke break," I say, lighting up without looking at them. I keep my voice sour, indifferent. "How's the car?"

"She'll be okay," Isaac says. "Michael's boy is the lacrosse captain at Hancock, just like his old man. My money says a rival team is behind the damage. Hancock and Trapelo have been pranking each other like this for decades."

"If they're not careful, someone's going to get hurt," Mr. Richards mutters.

"Go sports," I offer.

I exhale and Mr. Richards physically turns his nose up at the smoke. Without saying goodbye, he heads for his cruiser, and once Isaac disappears into the office, I let my mask drop. I exhale again, harder this time, as if that will make me feel any better. Because for all their scheming and kumbaya-ing, both Andrew and Sassi failed to mention that Troy's dad is a cop, and not just any cop.

He's the cop who arrested my dad.

16

let me clear my throat

NAOMI KING

"Naomi..." Andrew trails off, his concern instantly quadrupling my own. "No offense... but are you *sure* you can do this?"

I don't trust myself to respond, so I don't. But I at least manage a shrug with one shoulder. For as long as I can remember, my palms have always gotten sweatier when I'm nervous, and it's something that Mel and my parents still love to tease me about. When I was six and she was ten, Mel and I were the ring bearers in our aunt's wedding in upstate New York. But I got so nervous walking down the aisle that when I tried to give my aunt's ring to the pastor, it right slid out of my fingers and under a pew.

Currently, I'm sitting in the back seat of Sassi's car, behind Sassi and Andrew in the front, with a Tupperware of my leftover snickerdoodles on the console between them. Splayed across my lap is the cheerful-looking Lisa Frank folder I've been using for AP chemistry, and inside is today's homework from Mr. Levitan. Which, on Sassi's orders, I offered to bring Troy after school.

Seeing as how he missed class for obvious reasons.

Thanks to us, Troy spent the better part of his Valentine's Day squeezing Jennifer's hand in the ER. Most people seem to think that the bizarre reaction around his nether regions was set off by a spill in Mr. Levitan's classroom, and I even overhead Principal Clancy give Mr. Levitan a verbal warning. However, despite any initial victory we might have felt, no one has managed to connect the dots from Troy back to Zoey.

As the silence in the car stretches from awkward to certifiably insane, Andrew begins to crease and uncrease one of Sassi's butterfly seat covers between his thumb and pointer finger. A nervous tic.

"Maybe Naomi could just leave it at the door," he suggests. He's speaking to Sassi, not me.

"No. We need eyes on Troy." Sassi squints through her windshield with a dainty pair of opera glasses. "I want to know exactly what he thinks happened today. After what Tatum did to the car . . . he has to know it's not a coincidence. And we need to know if he suspects anyone."

"But what if he does?" I whine. "What if he thinks it was me?"

To that, Sassi doesn't have an answer. But the look on Andrew's face tells me we're thinking the same thing.

When Sassi and Andrew picked me up after dinner, I was surprised to see that Sassi had changed out of her school clothes into an all-black ensemble. Reconnaissance chic. Then again, she does seem to take everything as seriously as possible, so I should just be grateful she's not making Andrew and me wear ski masks. Sassi has accessorized with a black beanie and black fingerless gloves, but she still has her Harvard sweatshirt tied around her waist.

"This is why I told Tatum not to touch the car," Andrew mutters. "I didn't want to get Mr. Richards involved. But even if she hadn't, your plan didn't exactly—"

"My plan worked like a freakin' charm." Sassi tosses her hair over her shoulder. "It's not my fault Zoey slid straight into third base."

Andrew and I grimace.

"What's so bad about Troy's dad?" I ask.

"He's . . . a character."

"Monster," Sassi corrects him.

"And . . . what do I do if *he* opens the door, not Troy?"

Andrew exhales all his air through his nose.

Troy's house is located at the very end of a dead end street. It's not particularly big or small; the walls are shingled navy blue, and the front door is painted red, like a clown's tongue. There is a Christmas wreath hanging above the door knocker, and something tells me it hasn't been taken down in years. Sassi was careful to park out of sight of the wide living room windows, seemingly with the expertise of someone who has done it many times before.

"Naomi—"

"Enough, Andrew," Sassi interrupts. "Naomi's a big girl. She doesn't need you trying to scare her." She reaches for another cookie without taking her eyes off the house. "You can do this, Naomi. In and out. Got it?"

"Got it."

"Good. Now get out."

I risk one last look at Andrew, and he's frowning hard enough that the scar in his eyebrow furrows into a lightning bolt. I slide out of the back seat before my brain can catch up to what my body is doing, and I keep my eyes on my Skechers as I trot to the front door. Like most things in my closet, my sneakers were hand-me-downs from Mel, and because they are a half size too big, I'm wearing my biggest pair of fuzzy socks to help them fit. They used to light up, but they haven't in ages. When I ring the bell, I can feel Andrew and Sassi watching me from the car. I wonder if it's too late. Maybe I should just leave the homework on the stoop.

Before I can decide, the door opens.

"Oh! Hi, Naomi." Jennifer Lee is standing in the doorway to the Richards home. And even if she wasn't backlit by the hallway, I don't think I'd be able to tell which of us is more surprised to see the other. She looks tired, but she puts on a brave, polite, not-tired face. Like Sassi, she's changed out of the clothes she wore to school today, but I try not to think too hard about who she got her oversized Green Day shirt from.

"I have Troy's homework," I say quickly, and I hold out the folder in the air between us. It's less a shield than a flag of surrender. "Mr. Levitan asked me to—"

Suddenly, a mass of muscle and blond hair tackles me off the landing.

"No! Bad dog!"

It takes me a moment to realize what happened. The next thing I know, there is wet grass under my back and a massive, wriggling dog on my front. Jennifer hustles to drag the golden retriever off me, and I can feel the dog's heart thumping wildly against my own.

"Sorry! She's really friendly, but she'll go feral if she smells food," Jennifer says, lovingly hip-checking the dog away from my face. "My parents are out, and I didn't want her to be alone. So I brought her over while I'm taking care of Troy."

"Thanks," I manage, rising shakily to my feet. This time, I do wipe my hands on my legs, not that it helps with the drool. "What's her name?"

"Belle." Jennifer blushes. "I loved *Beauty and the Beast*. We went to see it three times in theaters."

I nod and pet Belle, who loses interest in me the split second I show interest in her. She trundles off in the direction of the street.

"Is Troy expecting you? I can wake him up if you want." Jennifer tucks a strand of glossy hair behind her ear. "He's been napping since we got back from the hospital."

"No, that's all right," I say, trying not to sound too eager. "Is he okay?"

"Yeah, the nurses said he'll be fine. Thank god."

"Does anyone know what happened?" I ask, my voice sliding up an octave. At least.

Thankfully, only Belle seems to notice that I've gone ultrasonic, and she huffs at me.

"I'm not sure." Jennifer frowns. "I mean, talk about bad timing, right? Troy says he sat in something, and then the whole thing with his car . . ." She shrugs. "The lax bros think it was a rival team messing with them."

"And what do you think?"

"Does it matter?" Jennifer asks, tilting her head to one side. My stomach tightens into a lump. I hate the idea that she's the only one who doesn't know about Troy and Zoey.

"No, I just . . ." I take a breath. I can't outright tell her the truth, but maybe I can lead her closer to it. "Does Troy have any allergies? Sometimes I bring in food from home, and I don't want to risk making something that might hurt him. Unless . . . maybe it's not a food allergy?"

"That's sweet of you to think of him," Jennifer says, missing the hint entirely. "But I don't think so."

"You should ask him. Sometimes I can get rashy when my mom uses this one kind of detergent. It's so bad, and it can even happen if I hug someone who used the same kind. Maybe it was something like that?"

"Rashy . . . right."

I'm saved from responding by the sound of Belle barking at something in the distance. Or someone.

"Did you walk here?" Jennifer asks, scanning the block.

"Erm, no. My mom is actually, kinda, *definitely* waiting for me in the car," I shrill. "Bye!"

"Bye . . . ?"

I avoid Jennifer's bemused brown eyes and force myself to walk at a normal speed to the street. I nearly break into a run when I see Sassi's car, and I quite literally throw myself onto my stomach in the back seat.

"Are you okay?" Andrew asks, eyes going wide at the grass stains on my overalls.

Sassi snorts, licking the last bit of sugar off her finger.

"We're in the clear," I manage, surprised by the jolt of pride I feel when they both smile at me. "Troy doesn't know it was us."

"Good," Sassi says, shifting her car into gear. "Now for the fun part . . ."

now

17

my own worst enemy

JENNIFER LEE

Troy's body continues to spiral—slowly—where it hangs off the ceiling fan. Sassi has finally stopped pacing the perimeter of the yearbook office, and Tatum tries and fails to make herself comfortable on one of the chairs closest to me. She's begrudgingly agreed to keep the overhead lights off, but even if they weren't, there's too much blood on Troy's face to tell if his eyes are open or closed. Not that I know which would be better.

Naomi follows my gaze.

"How'd they even get him up there like that?"

Tatum punches Naomi on the arm. Twice.

"*That's* what you're wondering?"

"Why'd you ask us to come here, Andrew?" Sassi demands, rounding on him. She crosses her arms tightly over her sweatshirt. "You said you needed help? Great. Fine. But what do you want us to do? The guy's freakin' *dead.*"

Naomi covers her mouth with both hands, about to blow chunks. I instinctively step closer to rub circles on her back.

"I can go get Clancy and—"

"No. No one leaves this room," Andrew says, his voice hoarse. "Remember? The killer is out there . . . or in here . . . or, whatever."

"You just left your girlfriend alone to come find us!"

"I'm not his girlfriend," I mumble, guilt rising with the bile in my throat. But everyone ignores me, even Andrew.

"Andrew's right," Naomi says through her fingers. "We can't trust anyone outside this room."

"Oh, but we can trust everyone *in* it?" Tatum hisses.

"What does that mean?"

"You know what it freakin' means—"

"If there *is* a killer in the school, isn't that even more of a reason to get help? People could be in danger!"

Tatum huffs and pokes Troy's calf with her finger, causing him to rock ever so slightly from side to side. All of us track the motion in horror. The only dead body I've seen before now was at my grandfather's open-casket funeral—and the thing I remember most is how the funeral parlor got his lips all wrong. They were glued too tightly, like he was humming, or keeping a secret. Which everyone knew he wasn't capable of.

"He's . . . stiff."

"If rigor mortis has set in, he's been dead for at least two hours," Naomi whispers, more to herself than any of us. No one bothers asking what vampire novel she learned that from.

"Weren't you supposed to meet Troy at some point?" I ask, my attention going back to Tatum. "Wasn't that why you were waiting in the stairwell?"

"Yeah. Troy said to meet him at eleven-thirty." Tatum shudders. "I guess this means he didn't stand me up . . . for once . . ."

"What about you guys?" I say, turning to Andrew and the others. "When was the last time anyone saw Troy?"

"I've been working the bake sale with Andrew's mom since my dad dropped me off," Naomi explains. "I sold Troy a cookie when the lock-in first started. Chocolate chip, I think. Does that help?"

"Can anyone else confirm that?"

"Jesus, Tatum. Are you suggesting *Naomi* did this?"

Naomi recoils at the suggestion.

"Well . . ."

"I also saw Troy at the beginning of the night," Sassi chimes in, coming to Naomi's defense. "Moose brought booze, and all the seniors had a drink in Principal Clancy's honor. Kyle can vouch for me."

"Except Andrew and I saw you on the third floor, moments before we got here and found Troy," I say, holding Sassi's gaze as best I can. Something crackles in her eye.

"Like I said, Kyle can vouch for me."

Tatum snorts. "Of course he can."

"And what is *that* supposed to mean?"

"Oh, nothing . . . nothing . . ."

"I didn't see Troy at all tonight," Andrew admits, shifting anxiously from one foot to the other. "We've been avoiding each other since the Trapelo game."

"So . . . who *do* we think it was?" Naomi asks.

"Is now really the time to—"

"My money's on Ms. Jeffers. I always thought she had the hots for him."

"Seriously, Tatum?"

Naomi gags again, echoing my sentiments. But Sassi slips Tatum a five-dollar bill from her bra when she thinks I'm not looking.

"Naomi was right. We should call the cops—"

"And what do you think will happen when people hear that Jennifer and I found his body?" Andrew says. His voice sounds near to breaking, and he gestures wildly with both arms. "Everyone at this school knows how much I hated Troy. Don't you know what they'll think?"

"They'll think you killed him," Naomi murmurs. My hand goes still on her back.

"Yeah, that . . ."

"Well. Did you?" Sassi asks, matter-of-fact.

"*No*," Andrew whisper-shouts. "That's why I need your help. Because together, maybe we can—"

Tatum makes a farting sound with her lips.

"Hold up. There is no *we*, Andrew. You made that very, very clear when everything went to shit last month. When *you* threatened to kill Troy . . . in front of everyone."

Andrew runs both hands through his hair, desperate to regain some semblance of control.

"And I said I'm sorry. Okay? All I'm asking is that we use the rest of the lock-in to track down who really did this. Thanks to Principal Clancy, no one is going anywhere for the next few hours. Which means we have an advantage. Once the night is over, we lose our chance. I'm not asking you to lie to anyone, just to wait . . . and to help me find Troy's killer in the meantime."

"Holy freakin' moly . . ."

"I'm with Sassi on this one," Tatum mutters. "You're deranged,

Andrew. Give me one reason we shouldn't walk out of this room screaming. Right now."

"Because I didn't do it, and the best way of proving that is by finding whoever did," Andrew insists. "And because . . . we're . . . friends?"

I'm expecting the girls to keep arguing—or at the very least, for Tatum to laugh in Andrew's face. But again they surprise me, and again the room goes quiet.

I manage to look away from Troy's body long enough that I can look—really look—at the others. Sassi's skort is askew, her lips swollen, and despite her bravado, she is nervously twisting and untwisting her ponytail through her fingers. Next to me, Naomi is biting her lips so hard that the bottom one has started bleeding—but she seems to be thinking about Andrew's words. Meanwhile, even if Tatum is sitting down, her arms are crossed so tightly that it looks like she's trying to hug herself. She might be acting tough, but she's just as scared as the rest of us. Andrew is the last person I look at, as discreetly as I can manage, and my stomach drops when I see his face.

Because he's wearing the same exact expression I saw on New Year's Eve—moments before everything with Troy went to shit.

"I'm in," I whisper. "I trust you, Andrew."

"Tatum?"

"Yeah, whatever."

"Naomi?"

"Okay."

"Sassi?" Andrew presses. He senses her resistance, as do we all.

"If it makes you feel better"—Tatum shrugs—"it's not like anything we do is going to bring your ex back to life."

"Thanks, Tatum..."

Sassi groans and flips over to redo her ponytail—apparently a nervous habit. When she stands, her face is eerily calm. "Fine," she says, brisk. "But if we're really doing this Scooby-Doo bullshit, we do it my way. Capisce?"

"Sure. Quick thing, though." Tatum shoves her hand under Sassi's nose. It takes me a moment to realize she's wearing a watch, and Sassi nearly goes cross-eyed trying to read the face. "Need I remind everyone there's an attendance check at midnight? If we're not in the gym in five minutes, everyone is going to come looking for us."

"What about Troy?" I ask. "Don't you think people will notice *he's* missing?"

"Not much we can do about that..."

"I say we show our faces. Give ourselves an alibi and buy time to figure out next steps."

"Why do we need an alibi if we didn't actually kill him?"

"Jesus, Naomi. It's a figure of speech—"

"Are we just supposed to leave him . . . here?" I press.

Everyone goes silent at my question, each of us trying and failing not to stare at the bloody jersey swaying in front of us.

"Yes?"

There's no use in protesting further—we don't have the time, and it's obvious that neither Sassi or Tatum has the patience. Andrew loops an arm around my waist and steers me toward the hallway, but at the very last second I hesitate. Something tugs at the back of my mind.

"What is it, Jennifer?"

"My charm bracelet. Earlier, I gave it back to Troy," I whisper. "The one he gave me for Valentine's Day. If anyone finds it . . . it could connect me to the crime scene."

Andrew stiffens and follows my gaze, his eyes raking over Troy.

"We'll find it. I promise," he says.

Again, I believe him. And I follow him and the others into the hallway.

march

18

all i have to give

SASSI DeLUCA

There's a running joke told by, for, and about our school that Hancock High was designed by the same dude who built the state prison. Where the rumor came from is anyone's worst guess, but as I wait in the windowless room outside my advisor's office, I can't say I'm not considering its truth. In a desperate effort to spruce up the joint, there are a handful of plants spaced across the bookcase of self-help tomes. Most of them look plastic, but one is definitely dead. Meanwhile, I keep my gaze riveted to the clock, tapping out the seconds with my heels on the elephant-gray carpet. And in case you were wondering, yes.

The clock *is* a full two minutes slow.

"Hi, hon!"

My college advisor, Ms. Jeffers, blows in from the hallway. Only twenty or twenty-two minutes behind schedule, depending on which clock you're using. Today she is dressed in skin-tight cheetah-print pants, clogs, and an ugly oversized sweater, all of which make it hard to tell how old she is. But I've always assumed she's just a few years older than I am.

She hasn't had the optimism squished out of her.

"Sorry I'm late! Traffic was a beast." Ms. Jeffers beckons me with her acrylics. "Come in, come in . . ."

I paint on a smile, shifting the drinks carrier and matching pastry bag out of my lap as she fumbles with the key to her inner office. When my mom used to drive me to school, stopping at Dunkin' was part of our morning routine. I don't go as often since she left, but on really bad days, or really good ones, I like to make an exception. Even my stepmom knows about my sweet tooth, and she'll unabashedly use Dunkin' to soften me up.

Their Boston Kreme is to die for.

"What do you have there?"

"One chocolate frosted doughnut and one hazelnut iced coffee with extra ice and extra cream," I say, shaking the bag in front of me. "It's nothing, really. Just a teeny tiny thank-you for agreeing to meet me before homeroom."

"Oh my! In that case, you are very, very welcome." Ms. Jeffers casts me a conspiratorial look over her shoulder. "Don't be shy, lady. Make yourself at home!"

I nod and follow her in, placing the doughnut and both of our drinks on the edge of the desk. Earlier today, I opted for my usual Harvard sweatshirt and jeans, and now I'm careful not to move my arms any more than I have to. The sun came out fast, and in my defense, it was still winter when I woke up. I had no idea the pit stains would be this bad. It actually seems a little rude of the weather to be so nice, if I'm being honest.

Like the waiting room, Ms. Jeffers's office is sparsely but colorfully furnished. There is a wailing couch with one end permanently dented into a butt shape, plus a set of beanbags. As has become our custom, Ms. Jeffers crashes into a beanbag at full force, and I take the chair at her desk. If you were to walk in unknowingly, you might suspect that the roles of advisor and advisee were reversed.

If you knew us better, you'd know for certain that happened a long time ago.

"All right, hon. Talk to me."

"I just wanted to check in," I begin, legs crossed, hands in my lap. "I haven't received my acceptance letter just yet, and I wanted to know, if you know, if there is anyone else who has heard back."

"From Harvard?" Ms. Jeffers clarifies.

I nod and she smiles at me. Sympathetic.

And it's the gosh darn *sympathy* that makes me want to absolutely freakin' *rage*.

"Like most schools, Harvard mails out regular decisions in the beginning of March," Ms. Jeffers says. She points to the tear-off calendar on her desk. Each day is stylized with different movie quotes, and I obligingly tear to a new day. Today, March 1. Valentine's Day was already full two weeks ago. And despite the best efforts of our merry band of misfit toys, by now the memory of Troy's public humiliation has become just as stale as the discount candy I bought at CVS the next day.

Troy's still the man.

He's still dating Jennifer.

He's still going to Harvard.

He's still . . . *Troy Richards.*

Even if the same can't be said for his car.

"If we can count on the reliability of the postal service, you should expect to hear back from schools before the end of the month. Or . . . early April."

"April?"

Ms. Jeffers winces at my tone. She shuffles to the cabinet behind her desk and begins riffling through the bottom drawer, pausing only to rip off a hunk of doughnut.

"Remind me, hon. What other schools are you waiting on?"

"You don't understand. I have to go to Harvard. It's where my parents went. And met. And . . ."

"And?"

I am suddenly aware of the wetness in my underarms.

"Harvard is . . . the only place I applied to."

Ms. Jeffers sits on the corner of the desk farthest from me, no longer meeting my eyes. I recognize the top sheet of paper on the stack in front of her, a copy of the contact information for various staff members at Harvard, including the admissions office.

"As I'm sure you are aware, Sassi, it's an open secret that Harvard takes one student from Hancock every year. And Troy Richards committed last November."

"I know, but—"

"I realize this may surprise you, but this was a very competitive senior class." Ms. Jeffers motions for me to pass her the rest of her doughnut, and I miraculously resist the urge to chuck the bag at her head. "No two candidates are the same. Applications are thoroughly vetted by each admissions office, and every school looks at the full profile of a given student. Not just their grades."

"And Troy plays lacrosse."

"Yes . . . that too."

I grab my coffee and chug, ignoring the scorching sensation as hot liquid hits the roof of my mouth.

"Unless Harvard revokes Troy's acceptance, it's unlikely anyone else from Hancock will be admitted for the fall semester. Even you." Ms. Jeffers absent-mindedly flips through her papers. It's only now that I see she's holding a brochure with a group of brazenly smiling teenagers and, of all things, the Eiffel Tower on the cover.

She slides it toward me with one of her acrylics.

"Have you considered a gap year, Ms. DeLuca?"

I choke on my next sip.

"If not," Ms. Jeffers backpedals, revealing a brochure for Framingham University, less than an hour away, "there are smaller schools with rolling admissions that you could still apply to—"

When her phone rings, Ms. Jeffers holds a single finger in my direction to keep me in my seat. She takes a bite of chocolate glazed before answering. "Hello?" she asks.

Whatever she hears on the other end causes Ms. Jeffers to frown, and she puts the phone down in the cradle.

"Wrong number?" I guess.

Ms. Jeffers shakes her head. "It's the strangest thing, but this has been happening all week. I could swear I heard someone breathing . . . but they hung up." She shrugs it off. "Where were we . . . ?"

"You want me to apply to Framingham University," I say, a half guess. Ms. Jeffers nods, delighted that I'm willing to be my own bearer of bad news.

"Bingo."

"But it's a safety school!"

"Better to be safe than sorry."

I'm on my feet before I can even pretend to consider the tacky brochures. My heart is in my ears, loud enough that I can't hear what Ms. Jeffers says next, and when I storm out of her office I almost don't recognize—

"Tatum?"

Tatum stands at the bookcase across the room, curls knotted under a beanie. When she turns, I realize she's fist-deep in the jar of lollipops that Ms. Jeffers uses to lure in freshmen. She's also wearing a heinous DIY-looking tie-dyed crop top.

"Morning, Sassafras."

"What are *you* doing here?"

Tatum selects a mystery-flavored Dum-Dum before putting the rest back on the shelf. "I could ask you the same thing. But . . . I don't care?"

I cross my arms and immediately uncross them when I remember the pit stains. Tatum clocks the brochures in my hand, but if she knows what it is, she doesn't say anything. Ms. Jeffers's voice comes from close behind me.

"Tatum! This is a surprise. You two girls know one another?"

"Nope."

"Yup."

"Barely," I say, forcing a toothless smile.

Tatum ignores my vitriol and points at the same dying plant I noticed earlier. "For what it's worth, Ms. J, that li'l guy needs sunlight, pronto."

"Silly me. Thanks, Tatum." Ms. Jeffers laughs. "I never suspected you'd be a plant lady!"

"You didn't?" I mutter.

Neither of them acknowledges me.

"Eh, I'm not really. I'm just used to taking care of things," Tatum says, shrugging.

Something in her voice makes me stiffen. But before I can

overthink it, I yank open the door and stand with one foot in the hallway, one foot in the office, waiting for Tatum to follow. Once she does, I try to keep an inconspicuous but consistent gap between us. We're already halfway down the hallway when I realize I accidentally scooped up Ms. Jeffers's list of Harvard contacts in addition to the brochures.

"Looks like we're headed the same way," Tatum teases. She chomps into her fresh lollipop with her front teeth, and the sound makes me wince. The building has already begun to fill with eager-beaver types headed for their respective homerooms, and I swerve to avoid a gaggle of freshmen coming the opposite way. I sigh through my nose.

"Lucky me..."

19

smells like teen spirit

TATUM STEIN

Sassi tucks her hair behind her ears with both hands, and for some reason she makes it a point not to raise her elbows any higher than her rib cage. She's so focused on what she's doing that she doesn't notice I've already swiped one of the brochures she was carrying in her armpit, and it's only when I emphatically flip the pages open in front of us that she does.

"Hey! Give that—"

"Well, well, well. What's some prim Harvard legacy like you doing with a flyer for Framingham University? Unless . . . ?"

Sassi answers the question by ripping the paper out of my hands.

"Mind your own beeswax, Tatum. I am going to Harvard. Framingham is just a safety school."

"Buzz-buzz, babes . . ."

Sassi creases the brochure once, twice, three times, apparently determined to fold it into nonexistence. Once she's done, the flattened square reminds me of the origami cootie catchers my little sisters are always bringing home from elementary school. But Sassi doesn't seem like the type to leave things to chance. Instead, she shoves the evidence of her visit to the advising office deep into her messenger bag and marches down the stairs to the first floor. I follow at a safe distance.

"Hey, unclench your booty hole, Sassi. You don't have anything to be ashamed of," I say, surprised to realize I mean it. "As much as I hate to burst your bedazzled little bubble, no one gives two hot shits about where you go to college. I certainly don't."

"Thanks..."

"Just saying! But look, if you do want to talk about it, everyone tells me that I'm a really great listener—"

"Literally no one says that, Tatum." Sassi stops in front of Principal Clancy's office, both of our images reflected on the trophy case along the opposite wall. "Besides. Have you ever even tried applying to college? I mean, aren't you repeating senior year for . . . what . . . the second time?"

I hold up three fingers, then lower two, flipping her the bird.

"I'm a super-super-*super*senior, actually. State law allows you to stay in high school until you're twenty-two."

"Wait a sec . . . how old *are* you?"

"Never ask a woman her age. Or her body count."

"Ew. Don't make me vom." Sassi makes a face at the thought. "Are your grades really that bad?"

"Appreciate the concern, but my grades are fine. The thing working against me is my attendance record."

"And criminal history."

"Sure. That too."

"It still doesn't make any sense." Sassi gives me a shrewd look. "Don't you *want* to leave?"

I hesitate, surprised at how deep her words cut. I can't remember the last time someone asked me what I wanted.

The first bell rings bright, a ten-minute warning shot before the start of classes. Sassi cringes at the sound but doesn't move. Instead of answering right away, I stare at the trophy case. I'm always amazed by how easy it is to recognize the people in the black-and-white photographs if you try. Not that I actually know them; I'm not that old. But from here, they look like all the students roaming the hallowed halls of Hancock High. Blur your eyes just right, and it could be anyone smiling back at you.

Winning. Hopeful. Happy.

"I'm serious, Tatum. You're smart enough to know there are other options. If not college, you could get a real job. Probably. So what on earth is keeping you here?"

"My sisters," I admit.

That's all I say, but Sassi nods like she can read my thoughts. Honestly, maybe she can.

"They're lucky to have you looking after them."

"Easy for you to say. You're not in charge of family movie night." I smirk. "Roll your eyes at me all you want, but I have more important things to worry about than studying for the SAT. And as much as this school sucks, I got a great thing going here. I have clients. I have a business. And I make *bank*."

"Even so, you can't stay here forever." Sassi gestures to the half-empty hallway. "For what it's worth, it's okay to be selfish from time to time. And thinking about your future is certainly one of those times."

"Thanks for the advice, Sassi. But you can bet your bottom dollar I'm going to ride the Hancock train as long as I can."

Sassi fiddles with the zipper on her bag. I'm fully expecting her to continue lecturing me about the benefits of higher education and following my dreams.

Instead, she surprises me once again, and she does it by staying silent.

The second bell rings at five minutes to go, and Sassi jumps to attention. She takes the crumpled brochure out of her bag and, startling both of us, holds it out to me. She doesn't say anything more, and I don't either. But something tells me we might be thinking the same thing. Because the flyer and what it represents mean something different for both of us, and yet it might also mean the exact same thing: safety.

I pocket the brochure before Sassi can start gloating.

Suddenly, the cafeteria doors at the far end of the hallway fly open with a rush of incoming students, followed by a roar from within. Like a foghorn.

HoOOOOOoot!

A roided-up, raged-out foghorn.

HOOOOOOOOT—HOOOOOOOT!

Inside, the cafeteria is a complete and utter bloodbath of school spirit. There are crowds of kids cheering and screaming and yodeling while the boys lacrosse team finishes a vicious push-up competition. One guy on top of each table. I've never managed or cared to tell the difference between the members of Troy's meathead entourage, but it doesn't matter. They're all cut from the same cloth, and that cloth is a reversible mesh pinnie. Plus calf socks and cabbage hair. Also, for some ungodly reason, most of them like to lug around a gallon jug of water throughout the day, and anyone who cares that much about hydration has some serious damage. It's a real choose-your-own-adventure of eating disorders.

I catch a glimpse of balloons and face paint before the doors swing shut. From where we're standing, it looks like the entire cafeteria is riveted in place by the revelries. Even the lunch ladies.

"There's a pep rally after school," Sassi says. "I totally forgot about it. Next week is the beginning of the lacrosse season."

At that moment, Hootie, a guy dressed in a full head-to-talon owl costume, jogs by us. The door blows open with his entrance, just long enough for us to hear the mob issue another welcoming howl.

HOOOOOOOOT!

This time, seconds before the doors close, I see him.

At the back of the cafeteria, Hancock's unprecedented, untouchable, and, in my personal opinion, unbleached asshole, Troy Dickhead, holds court with his loyal subjects. Jennifer stands next to him, with his arm and a letter jacket around her shoulders.

Troy is the only one of his crew not doing push-ups. Unlike the rest of us, he has nothing to prove.

"'Sup, guys!"

A tiny crocheted bucket hat appears between Sassi and me, and underneath the hat is Naomi. Her bag is made of the same vomit-colored yarn. I wouldn't be at all surprised if she made them both herself.

"Jesus, Naomi! Do you always sneak up on people like that?"

"Sorry," she squeaks, inexplicably out of breath. "I wanted to find you before homeroom. I didn't realize the pep rally is tonight, and Andrew wants to talk about—"

"Hang on. I *really* have to pee."

Naomi and I stare at Sassi, equally confused by the interruption, and she groans out loud. Sassi checks over her shoulder to make sure that no one from the cafeteria is watching us. Once she has the all clear, she drags us both into the closest bathroom.

"Hey! Careful—"

"That hurts—"

"Tatum, check the stalls."

Sassi releases us and I throw her an exaggerated salute. Then I kick open the stall doors one by one with the chunky heel of my boot.

"You don't have to do it like—"

"Like what?" I ask. I slo-mo ninja kick the last door and Sassi massages her temples with both hands. Thankfully, there's nothing in here except the two-ply.

"Look, we all need to be more careful. Andrew, too," she explains, and I realize she sounds like I do when I'm trying to explain to my sisters why they can't stay up late to watch reruns of *CatDog*. "If someone hears us talking about Troy, we could get—"

"What?" I snort. "Detention?"

"Exactly."

Naomi looks just as horrified as Sassi by the prospect, but I shrug and chuck what's left of my Dum-Dum at the trash can—perfect shot. Not that they care. Without really thinking about what I'm doing, I reach into my bag for my favorite Simpsons lighter and my lucky pipe. It's only when I see Sassi glaring at me that I remember my manners.

"Oh . . . you want a hit?"

"*No!*"

"Smoking will kill you," Naomi chirps.

"If I'm lucky."

"My point, Tatum, is that if we want to take down Troy, we need to be discreet." Sassi looks directly at me. "The stunt with the car was anything but."

I frown and blow smoke in Naomi's direction, and she hacks like a geriatric cat with a hairball.

"I told you—"

"And Andrew told *you*. You shouldn't have touched the car! Mr. Richards loves that thing more than his own son."

"And that's my problem . . . *how*?"

"We're lucky Troy thinks it was a rival school that poured the crap in. Otherwise—"

"Andrew wants to do something. *Today*. At the pep rally," Naomi interrupts, bouncing up and down on the balls of her feet. "That's what I was coming to talk to you about. I think we should vote on it. Y'know . . . to be fair?"

Sassi and I exchange a glance.

"It's a perfect opportunity," I admit. "Everyone will be in the gym tonight. All eyes on Troy. Maybe . . . we could pull the fire alarm? Or load pudding cups in the T-shirt cannon? Or—"

"Slow down. I *don't* think it's a good idea," Sassi says. "Messing with the pep rally isn't messing with Troy. It's messing with everyone."

"So?"

"So? Do we really want to . . . I dunno . . . burn that big of a bridge?"

"The only reason not to burn a bridge is because you still want to use it." I shrug. "Do you?"

Sassi sighs and turns to check herself out in the bathroom mirror. But after a moment, her eyes slide to me and my tie-dyed shirt.

"Grab the freakin' kerosene."

20

spice up your life

NAOMI KING

I was seven years old when I confirmed that my entire existence was a huge mistake.

My dad was downstairs, in the kitchen, talking to one of my aunts or uncles or second cousins, and the adults were too busy swapping war stories about the bare-bottom method to see me tiptoe in. My parents had a strict no-dessert policy if we didn't clear our plates, but Mel and I were newly addicted to the Flintstones sherbet Push-Ups our mom had brought home. Desperate bellies, desperate measures. What I remember most is hiding on the stairs while my dad laughed at someone's inside joke. He doesn't laugh as much these days; he's older than most dads and spends every evening sleep-watching MTV. But when he does, he laughs with his full heart and stomach. I've always loved hearing him like that, and I still do.

Naomi is our happiest accident!

And it didn't really bother me. At first.

But when seven-year-old Naomi told eleven-year-old Mel

what the adults had said, Mel was aghast. For weeks after she never left my side, as if to show our parents, and anyone else who might dare to ask, that we were a package deal. Sisters. A team.

I know it might not seem like a lot, but four years is a long, long time. In school, and in all the other real-life ways. And sure, it can be fun to have an older sister—but those four years become *light-years* when one of you is in middle school and the other is acing her permit test. After Mel got her license, she spent the weekends with her friends, and our parents would seize the opportunity to hit up Costco, their shared house of worship. To this day, my mom and dad are at their happiest sampling the newest and most improved items in the store.

Meanwhile, I've always preferred to stay in the car.

Upside-down in the back seat, feet on the headrest, I plowed through every copy of the Boxcar Kids and the Baby-Sitters Club that our library had on the shelves. Not to mention the contraband editions of *Teen Beat* magazine that Mel squirreled away from our mom. After reading *The Borrowers* for the first of many times, I began imagining tiny fairy-sized people running around me, telling me about their adventures as they slid down the seat belts like a waterslide. On rainy days, I'd stare out the back window and pick raindrops to race down the glass. I got good at keeping myself company, and as I got older, it seemed like my parents were always tired, run ragged by Mel and her cosmopolitan teenager demands. They were grateful that I was quiet in comparison. Easy. Although for the record, it's not that I ever liked being alone.

I just wanted to make things easier for them.

BeeeEP-BEEP . . . BEEeeep . . .

The screen on my Game Boy blinks off for the final time, and I half-heartedly tap the bottom against the countertop. Nothing. My game has been on the fritz ever since Troy got to it, and even though I replaced the batteries, nothing I do can fix the mouth-shaped crack in the screen. I sigh and look out the windows of the chemistry lab. From here, I have a bird's-eye view of the Hancock parking lot, and I watch from on high as people zoom off with their friends for second lunch. There is an aging oak tree tucked alongside the building, and the uppermost branches barely scratch the glass. The flag on the pole withers at half-mast, and from inside, there's something about the sunny suburban bliss that seems almost fake.

"Naomi?"

I swivel around fast and immediately jam my knee on the side of the table. Andrew and Tatum watch me from the hallway, and Andrew sheepishly knocks on the inside of the open door before they come in.

"You okay?" Andrew asks.

"Fine . . . I'm fine . . ." I say, clearly not. "Is Sassi coming?"

"Yeah. She's going to snag her camera from the yearbook office and meet us in a few minutes." Andrew gestures to the stool next to me, Troy's seat. "Can I sit?"

I nod, and he plops down. Meanwhile, Tatum takes a lap around the chemistry lab, pausing to examine the cabinet of chemicals behind Mr. Levitan's desk. He always keeps it locked, especially after Valentine's Day.

"Did you have lunch in here?" Tatum asks, without turning around.

"Oh . . . no. I usually eat in the bathroom."

"Right . . ."

The three of us plunge into an excruciating silence, and I absent-mindedly twist back and forth on my stool, dragging my Skechers on the ground.

"Y'know, I've never told anyone this . . ." Andrew hesitates, his words an olive branch. "Sometimes I like to eat my lunch on the roof. The entrance from the south-side stairwell has been broken for years, and Troy and I used to go up there all the time when I was a freshman. It can be nice to be alone. Serene."

"Really? You don't think it's . . . like . . . super weird?"

"Nah. Just normal weird," Tatum calls over her shoulder.

Andrew smiles at me, rolling his eyes in Tatum's direction. Today he's wearing a striped collared shirt and jeans, and when he bends to open his backpack, I try not to stare at the inch of skin above his boxers, but Tatum makes no such effort.

She smirks when she catches me looking.

"Here you are," Andrew says, handing me a brand-new shampoo bottle. According to the packaging it smells like Blaze of Glory—and according to Andrew, it's Troy's favorite. I discreetly sniff the top and turn it over to read the ingredients.

"*Four* in one? What's the fourth?"

Andrew just laughs.

"Are you sure you know what you're doing?"

I nod, heat rising in my cheeks.

"And . . . what exactly *are* you going to do?"

I gesture for Andrew and Tatum to follow me to the emergency eye wash station, which they do. I'm more than aware that they are watching my every move, and I squirt out just enough shampoo to make room inside the bottle. Once that's done, I open the cabinets at eye level and begin collecting everything else we might need.

Scale . . . goggles . . . stirring rod . . . gloves . . . funnel . . . Scoopula . . . dropper . . . beakers . . .

Andrew's eyes go extra wide.

"There are two ingredients we're going to be working with. Calcium hydroxide and potassium thioglycolate," I explain, returning to my station. "Calcium hydroxide is harmless on its own. You can use it in cooking, pickling vegetables, home brewing, and even making tortillas."

"Yum? I guess . . ." Tatum sighs.

"The second ingredient, potassium thioglycolate, breaks down keratin bonds. And lucky for us, the school keeps plenty of it in stock for the AP anatomy kids." I shimmy a pair of goggles over my glasses as I talk. "Put them together, and we're making—"

"Nair!"

Andrew laughs and drums his hands on the table and I smile wide enough to show my teeth. I got my braces later than everyone else in my grade, and I still remember the first time I smiled without them. Because that was when Mel said I was "actually pretty." The worst part was that she thought she was being nice.

In the way that only a big sister can.

"Tatum, could you please . . . ?"

Tatum nods. She returns to the chemicals cabinet, and with one quick swipe of her student ID in the doorjamb, she's in.

Andrew whistles.

"Where'd you learn how to do that?"

"Hebrew school," she says, shrugging. "How do you spell *thioglycolate*?"

I join Tatum behind Mr. Levitan's desk and grab two containers before closing the cabinet, careful to leave things exactly as we found them.

"The thioglycolate will weaken the follicles. Mixed with the calcium hydroxide and a little Blaze of Glory, it should remove Troy's head of hair in one wash . . . or less."

I hand Andrew his own set of goggles.

"What's this for?" he asks, frowning.

"Chemical burns."

"I don't want to blind the guy—"

"We won't," I promise, shaking my head. "I'm going to dilute the formula to cover the smell. Don't worry. It will work. And it won't be permanent, either. His hair will grow back after a few weeks."

"Jesus," Tatum mutters, twirling one of her own curls around her pinkie.

"This is amazing, Naomi," Andrew cheers, almost vibrating with excitement. He holds out his fist in the air between us, and I stare at it for a moment, not quite sure what to do.

Then I bump it.

"Booyah," I whisper.

"Sorry . . . am I interrupting something?"

The three of us turn to face the hallway, but Sassi's gaze is locked on Andrew and me.

"No," I say hastily.

"Now, that's a dang shame."

Andrew laughs and slides his hands into his pockets, careful to put a safe distance between the two of us. It's impossible to misunderstand her meaning, or his reaction. I avoid the sympathetic look that Tatum shoots in my direction.

"How's it going in here?" Sassi asks, perching on the stool next to Tatum. "We ready to go?"

"Almost."

"You should see this girl in action, Sassi," Andrew says. "She's going full mad scientist on us."

"It's not that hard," I say. "You just have to use the right ingredients."

"I don't think anything in a kitchen could be this dangerous—"

"Have you ever heard of ergot poisoning?" I ask. All three of them shake their heads. "Ergot is a fungus that grows on grains. Like rye or wheat. If you wanted to, you could grow the stuff on a piece of bread for months, and that fungus will contain hemotoxin. Symptoms of ergot poisoning include dizziness, convulsions, and psychosis."

"So you're saying if we actually wanted to kill Troy, we just need to make him a sandwich?" Tatum suggests.

Sassi kicks her in the shin.

"You could also extract cyanide from apple seeds," I add, chewing thoughtfully on the inside of my lip. "Or plums. Peaches, apricots . . . but it's supposed to take a while."

"And you learned all this where, exactly?"

"A book."

Sassi and Tatum laugh, and Andrew gestures for me to continue. I move slowly as I scoop the ingredients from their containers into beakers, and even though I know it's safe, I hold my breath as I stir them together. Tatum does too, her cheeks inflated like she's a puffer fish. To top it off, I use the funnel to pour the new chalk-white mixture into the bottle of Blaze. Andrew stays by my side until I remove my goggles.

"Okey-dokie. That should do it."

"Do what, Ms. King?"

The four of us sit up fast.

Mr. Levitan is standing at the front of the room, staring at us, with his brown bag lunch in one hand and a gigantic stack of papers in the other. Today, his tie features a hippo in a lab coat.

Mr. Levitan's eyes flash to the supplies splayed across on the countertop, and Tatum casually shifts to block the borrowed chemicals from his view.

"Shouldn't you kids be at lunch?"

"Sorry for the mess, Mr. Levitan. It was my idea." Andrew is the first one to collect himself from the surprise. "Sassi and I are in Mr. Dyson's class, and we both missed out on lecture this week. Naomi was just helping us catch up." He pauses to throw me a megawatt smile. "She's great at this stuff."

I gulp and resist the urge to peek at him from the corner of my eye. I know he's just being nice, but it scares me how easily he lies.

"And you?" Mr. Levitan asks Tatum.

"Adult supervision?"

Mr. Levitan sighs, but instead of questioning us any further, he just chomps into a baby carrot with a hair-raising *crunch*. Eager for a distraction, I look at the papers in his arms.

"What are those for?" Sassi asks, reading my thoughts.

Mr. Levitan peers over the edge of his glasses as if seeing the printouts for the first time. Groaning, he lowers himself into his chair.

"Clancy roped me into the planning committee for lock-in," he admits. "I'm responsible for marketing and ticket sales."

Mr. Levitan turns over the top page for us to see. Besides the actual details for the infamous end-of-year celebration, there is a surprising number of palm trees around the border of the flyer.

"The theme was Principal Clancy's idea. Thoughts?"

"Tropical," Tatum offers.

Mr. Levitan sighs again. "It doesn't feel entirely appropriate, does it? Especially considering that the night is supposed to commemorate the students we lost."

"My sister told me that . . ."

I trail off when Andrew puts his hand on my knee, everything in my body buzzing at hyper speed before going very, very still. It takes me a moment to realize that, based on Mr. Levitan's expression, his thoughts are also suddenly not here. An unmistakable shadow passes over his face. A brisk knock causes all of us to turn and see Principal Clancy in the doorway. She's dressed in a concrete-colored pantsuit and matching glasses, and her cheeks flush when she sees the crowd. It reminds me of all the times my mom caught my dad feeding our childhood cat scraps from the table. One part embarrassed, two parts guilty.

"Good afternoon, all. Sam, could I see you for a second?"

Mr. Levitan pushes back from his desk with both hands and follows her into the hallway.

The rest of us remain silent until their voices fade to a pleasant mumble. Tatum speaks first.

"Sam?"

"Do you think Clancy and Mr. Levitan . . . ?"

"God, I hope not."

"Why? He's not wearing a ring."

"Really?" I say, surprised when Andrew nods vehemently. "I can't believe you noticed something like that."

"I notice lots of things," Andrew says, smiling. He follows Tatum out of the lab and into the hallway, and Sassi drags her stool as close to mine as she can once they're gone.

"Hi."

"Hi?"

"Don't fall for it."

"Fall for what?"

"It. *Him.*" Sassi gestures vaguely in the direction Andrew disappeared. "I see that love-struck look on your face. But I'm telling you right now, if you can't keep your heart out of this, I'm pulling the plug on all of it. Got it?"

"Got it."

"Um . . . Naomi?"

Sassi and I look up, both of us surprised to see Andrew watching us. He hovers in the doorway, clearly intent on saying something, and I have no idea if he overheard us.

"What is it?" I hear myself ask.

"Just . . . thanks for all your help today," Andrew manages, fiddling with the straps on his bag. Neither of us can look the other in the eye for longer than a nanosecond. "I think it's really cool that you know all this freaky stuff."

I nod, not trusting myself to speak, and he leaves, saluting us with a peace sign as he goes.

"Freakin' lax bros," Sassi mutters.

21

killing me softly with his song

ANDREW GARCIA

As much as Sassi may deny it, there is one person at Hancock High who has just as much power as Troy Richards. But it's not Principal Clancy or any of the geriatrics on tenure, nor is it the guidance counselors and their Myers-Briggs tests, or the moms who rule the PTA. No, the person Tatum and I are meeting is even more obvious and less obvious at the same time. An enigma, unseen and unspoken to, everywhere and nowhere at once. Like Batman, but with more chest hair.

I'm talking about Sean Collins . . . our janitor.

"This is awesome, Sean," I say, picking up the pace to follow his retreating form down the underground hallway. "We really appreciate this."

Sean swings his head to look at us without stopping, like a bloodhound on the hunt. He always wears the same work boots and coveralls, which he uses to display an eccentric collection of decorative iron-on patches. Sean walks with a limp, and between that and his thick Irish accent, there's a rumor that he was a paramilitary fighter who fled Ireland for the States. But if anyone actually took the time to ask, Sean would be the first to tell you he doesn't have enemies. Not anymore.

"You two caught me at a good time." He sniffs. "Besides, I owe her for . . . you know . . ."

I don't actually know, but when I try to catch Tatum's eye, she just smirks and ducks to avoid a spiderweb.

"Are either of you kids going to tell me what you're up to?"

"Please," Tatum snorts, "where would be the fun in that?"

Sean turns right down the next hallway.

"By the way . . . where . . . are we?" I ask, trying to keep my voice steady. Whatever I was picturing when Sean agreed to help us, it wasn't this. I click on the miniflashlight attached to my keys, but it seems like neither Sean nor Tatum needs it to know where we're going. In fact, when we reach an intersecting corridor, they stop at the same exact time, and I almost face-plant into the flaming dice patch on Sean's shoulder.

"Hear that?"

I shake my head and Sean holds a finger to his lips. As the quiet presses in on us, I realize I can hear something—a telltale rhythm that I mistook for my own heartbeat.

"The gym," I say, realizing.

The basketball team must be running drills above us.

Sean nods and continues onward, not checking to see if we're following. "There are two tunnels under the school"—he gestures with one gnarled finger, and I crouch to avoid bonking my head on a pipe—"one north to south, the other east to west. They connect to the external generators on the outside and meet up . . . here."

Sean stops short once again, and I nearly double over at the stench of cat hair and garlic wafting off him. If memory serves, he has three cats: Fluffy, Spot, and Dame Judi Dench. Breathing heavily, Sean points at a set of double doors ahead of us, a harsh white light glowing at the edges.

"Be quick, yeah?"

Tatum checks her watch and frowns. "Dammit. We're behind schedule."

"Whose schedule?" I ask.

"Mine."

Tatum leads the way through the double doors, and on the other side we find the basement. The room is twice the size of the average classroom, with obnoxious fluorescents to keep the otherwise windowless space in an eternal state of daylight. There is a matching set of doors across the room, and from what Sean told us, the hallway on the other side leads directly to the boys' and girls' locker rooms. In the center of the room are two rolling bins full of dirty towels, and beyond them we spy two industrial-sized washing machines. Tatum shoves the towels out of our way, and she wheezes when she catches a whiff. The washing machine is in the middle of a cycle, and I can feel it vibrating through the linoleum. Because as is tradition, the boys are washing their white game-day jerseys for tonight's pep rally.

I join Tatum in front of the machine and stare at our reflections on the porthole window. We're both distorted and sudsy, and I grimace when I see a pair of tighty-whities go pinwheeling by with the rest of the jerseys.

"Is it true you guys don't wash your jerseys between seasons?" Tatum asks me suddenly.

"Yeah. For good luck."

"Yucky."

From her bag, Tatum produces a brightly colored box that is completely squashed in one corner. On the front is a picture-perfect image of four girls with identical smiles and brightly patterned tank tops, one of whom is holding a single finger to her lips as if she's keeping a secret. Because tie-dye is so scandalous.

"My sisters are going to be pissed when they realize this is missing," Tatum mutters. She opens the box from the non-crushed end and curses when one of the plastic toppers rolls under the dryer. "This better be worth it."

"It will be."

She tries to open the door of the washing machine, but it resists and buzzes angrily.

"Need any help?" I offer.

Tatum ignores me. She grabs the door with both hands, and although she manages to yank it open on the second try, she also lands smack on her butt, water gushing onto the floor. Undeterred, Tatum pops back to standing and yanks on a pair of kid-sized gloves from her kit. She passes me one of the empty bottles and I obediently fill it with tap water from the sink.

"Do you think we need to worry about Sean ratting on us?" I ask.

"Nah. That guy doesn't know Fritos from Doritos."

I blink at Tatum, mystified.

"He's a few crayons short of a full set," she tries again.

Ah. I nod and give the bottle back to her, and Tatum produces a mason jar next. I recognize the smell immediately.

"Vinegar?"

"Any girl worth her salt knows you need vinegar to make the colors stay." She shakes the bottle with both hands. "And if you get the dye on your normal clothes, you can combine the leftover vinegar with baking soda to lift stains. The mix also works great for removing blood."

"And you know that . . . why . . . ?"

Tatum rolls her eyes and mixes the vinegar with the dye powder.

"I don't have as many colors left as I thought . . . but this should still do the trick. You might want to close your eyes for this part."

Gracelessly, Tatum squats at the front of the machine and squirts the entire bottle of dye inside. It splatters across the damp fabric like something out of a horror movie. I inhale sharply. Whether you are on the team for four minutes or four years, one of our many unspoken rules is that every athlete is responsible for leaving their jersey better than they found it. Literally. Metaphorically. Spiritually. Your victories are the team's victories, and when you are wearing the uniform, you represent everyone who has come before you, or will ever come after. Before we got to high school, I remember when Troy and I were assigned our first jerseys at lacrosse camp. The numbers were given out at random, and I somehow ended up with number one. Until Troy asked if he could have it, so I gave it to him. I don't remember what his reasoning was, but I didn't care about it, and he did.

At least . . . I think that's what happened.

"Holy moly. If you could see your face right now." Tatum sits back on her heels to gawk at me. "Earth to Andrew."

"What? For a lot of the guys, the jersey is the most important thing we have."

Tatum rolls her eyes.

"Why on earth do you care about this stupid sport so much?"

"What do you mean?"

"Dude. Am I supposed to believe you all get off on running around and hitting other guys with your sticks?"

I scowl and cross my arms.

"I've always played sports. But lacrosse was the first one I was really good at. Being a part of the Hancock team gave me purpose, and a legacy, and a path to the next stage in my life, whatever that may be. Besides, and I see you rolling your eyes, whenever the team is together, it feels like we can do anything. You know what I mean?"

"No," Tatum admits. She gives me an evaluating stare. "But . . ."

"But?"

"It does sound kinda lovely."

She kicks the door shut and the machine automatically restarts.

"Your turn, Garcia."

I nod, but my feet don't move right away, my entire body paralyzed as I watch the soap take the color and spread it around . . . and around . . . and around. I reach one arm behind me to make sure the shampoo is still in my backpack, and when I feel its shape, I duck out to the locker room side of the basement. Tatum stays where she is, keeping the doors just slightly propped open with her toe.

"Good luck," she whispers, and I can't tell if she's being serious or not. "You're gonna need it."

I don't respond.

Somehow, the varsity locker room looks both completely different from and exactly the same as the last time I was here, to clean out my locker. Maybe it's because I always entered from the opposite side, so from here everything is inverted. Backward. The room also has a distinct, dreadful smell, one I never noticed before.

And, as I knew he would be, Troy is in the showers.

Singing.

"No, I don't want no scrub—"

Every step down the aisle brings back a memory, and I fight to stay focused as I get closer and closer to his painfully pitchy voice.

"—a scrub is a guy that can't get no love from me—"

Freshman year. Tryouts. I couldn't get my locker open because I was so nervous, and Troy let me share his.

"—hangin' out the passenger side—"

Sophomore year. Crying on the bench when my dad didn't make it home for my birthday, and Troy staying late to comfort me. He didn't say anything, and I didn't either. But it meant the world.

"—trying to holla at me—"

I turn the corner and stumble over a pile of Troy's shit—clothes, pads, lacrosse stick, sneakers, backpack. His stuff is spread out everywhere, and it's all I can do not to fall flat on my face.

"Kyle, that you?"

The shower curtain closest to me peels open and I dive into one of the aisles. I imagine Troy looking around the corner in confusion. But a moment later, he goes back to singing. Quickly, quietly, and holding my breath until I might burst, I creep up to the very edge of the showers and swap out Troy's shampoo for Naomi's doctored bottle. I don't linger to see if he uses it. Instead, I flee, and when Tatum sees my flustered expression she narrows her eyes. But she doesn't ask, and we let ourselves out the way we came in.

Where I immediately come face to wart with the colossal growth on Sean's nose.

Talk about a jump scare.

"Sean!"

But Sean just blinks at me, bored and confused. I don't think he's moved an inch. Literally. Maybe Tatum was right about the Frito thing.

"All set, kiddos?"

"Yeah, we're good. Th-thanks, Sean," I stammer.

"Appreciate you keeping this between us, big guy," Tatum adds. She tosses Sean a plastic baggy, and he catches it with surprisingly catlike reflexes.

"Next time, bring the fruity stuff."

Tatum nods as Sean limps back the way we came, and once his back is turned, she and I share a glance.

"Did you do it?" she asks.

"Yes." I nod. "And if we did this right, there won't be a next time."

22

quit playing games (with my heart)
SASSI DeLUCA

"Alessandra!"

There are only two women on all of planet Earth who still use my full name, and even though I know, I know it's not *her*, I stop short outside the gymnasium.

There are a dozen PTA moms selling baked goods by the doors, which means it takes more than a moment to spot Mrs. Garcia behind a festive cupcake tower. Like the others, Andrew's mom is wearing a blue-and-white *I* ♥ *LAX MOMS* T-shirt. But unlike her gal pals, she beams at me with a real, sincere smile.

In fact, her enthusiasm is almost enough to make up for the fact that it's her and not my own mom hawking overpriced pastries.

"Hi, hon! I haven't seen you in ages!"

"Hiya, Mrs. Garcia. How are you?"

She wiggles out from behind the table to hug me. Mrs. Garcia was the de facto Fun Mom of our neighborhood growing up, bankrolling our lemonade stands with whatever was left in her pantry or buying us out if no one else showed up. That said, everyone within a two-mile radius knew never to eat her cooking. Let alone her baking. Mrs. Garcia pulls away to examine me, running both hands up and down my upper arms.

The sudden dose of affection gives me goose bumps.

"I'm good, I'm good. But what's this I'm hearing about *you* these days?" She gives me a happy little shake. "Congratulations on Harvard!"

"Thank you. That means a lot."

"You're the one who earned it, missy! And you deserve it too. Your parents must be so, so proud of you. I know I am!"

I shrug, hoping it's not totally obvious how much her words mean to me.

Or that I haven't talked to my mom in almost a year.

"You're too sweet, Mrs. Garcia," I say. I shift my hulking camera bag to the opposite shoulder, and her eyes widen when she notices it for the first time. On Andrew's orders, I stopped by the yearbook office to sign out the kit, and I've been too excited to put it down. There's a deep purple mark from where the bag hangs off my shoulder, but it looks worse than it feels. "I didn't realize you'd be here today. Not since Andrew . . . um . . ."

Mrs. Garcia's smile withers.

"Yes . . . well. I've been coming to these types of things since I was a Howler, and I couldn't leave these ladies understaffed." She gestures to the moms behind her, and because her back is turned, Mrs. Garcia doesn't notice the dirty looks they give her in return. "So I'm here. For the team. With cupcakes!"

"Of course," I agree, listless. "Cupcakes. For the team."

Mrs. Garcia and I stand awkwardly in the bustling swarm of jocks, nerds, and drama rats, and I fight the impulse to give her a second hug.

Andrew has never been one to talk about his parents. Even when we were younger, and it was still cool to love your family. Now I doubt he's stopped long enough at any point this semester to consider how his lacrosse suspension has changed his mom's life too. Because if there's nothing to do in Hancock at our age, it must be even worse for the adults. There were plenty of times after my parents' divorce that I caught myself staring across the driveway and wondering what it must be like in the Garcias' little nuclear family. Mr. and Mrs. Garcia met when they were students at Hancock High, and from what I can tell, they've never lived more than ten miles away from their hometown American Dream. But as I got older, I realized that Mr. Garcia is never really around. He's always traveling for work, and Andrew's life *is* his mom's life. I wish I could tell her that I understand. Or that I think I do.

I wish I could promise her that it will all be okay.

I'll make sure of it.

"Mom?"

We turn to see Andrew watching us from the stairs with a mixture of unease and embarrassment. I don't know why, but suddenly I feel caught in the act.

"Hi, sweet pea. Look who I found!"

"Hi," Andrew says, not sharing her enthusiasm. "Mom, I'm sure Sassi needs to get ready for—"

"I know, I know, but I haven't had the chance to ask her about your new club!"

"Our . . . our *club*?" I echo.

Mrs. Garcia squeezes my arm one last time before releasing me, and I hold Andrew's look of panic over her shoulder.

"Yes! When I told Andrew he needed to find a replacement for lacrosse, it didn't even occur to me that you'd be looking for new members." Mrs. Garcia laughs to herself. "But now he won't give me any details! Tell me, Sassi. What is this mysterious club you guys are in?"

"Women and gender studies," I deadpan.

Andrew snorts and quickly tries to pass it off as a cough.

"It was nice seeing you, Mrs. Garcia, but Andrew's right. I should grab a seat," I say, lifting my camera by way of explanation.

"Of course, hon. But promise me you'll come over for dinner soon, okay? I know Andrew loves spending time with you."

"Mom!"

I bite back a smile. "Promise. I'll see you inside, Andrew."

"Yeah, I'll catch up in a minute."

Before I go, Mrs. Garcia snatches one of the cupcakes from the top of her tower, tossing me a conspiratorial wink as she presses it into my hand. I swallow my guilt and walk away, cradling the dessert like a baby bird in my palm.

Our school auditorium is barely large enough to fit the senior class, meaning that for the all-school events like this, everyone files into the gymnasium. At the center is the lacquered court for the basketball and volleyball teams, freshly buffed to perfection according to Principal Clancy's high standards, and there are bright red fold-out bleachers along the walls. Everyone is in high spirits. But between the nonstop chatter and the heavy footfalls as people find their seats, it feels like the gym is smaller than normal.

Or like the walls are closing in on us. Fast.

"Sassi!"

I pause when I see Kyle hiding in the corner under the bleachers. Instead of his lacrosse uniform, he's gone incognito in sweats with a dingy white towel over his head. But I'd recognize him anywhere.

Not that *that* means anything.

"Hiya, Kyle."

"Do you have a sec to—"

"No, sorry." I wave my camera in his direction without looking too closely at him. "I'm on the clock."

Kyle pouts but doesn't try to stop me as I walk away and find a place to sit.

At that moment, two underclass girls dressed in the team's blue practice jerseys rush by me, bumping my bag. I almost mistake them for middle schoolers—I swear the freshmen just get smaller every year. Without apologizing, the girls scamper to claim a spot in the first row with the rest of their flock.

The oh-so-cleverly nicknamed *laxtitutes.*

Before every lacrosse game, each player on the boys team picks a girl to wear his practice jersey, and the laxtitutes take it upon themselves to dress up with hair ribbons and temporary tattoos and glitter. Lots of glitter. Their job is to keep spirits high for the home games, and they specialize in creating the most obnoxious chants.

But you don't have to take my word for it.

"Kyle, Kyle, he's got style—"

"Moose, Moose, on the loose—"

"Troy, Troy, he's our boy—"

"At least they're consistent."

I don't hear Naomi as she approaches, but she takes the seat next to me in the bleachers, careful to leave a larger-than-necessary distance between us. Soon the cheerleaders take center court, and the crowd applauds nervously. The last time I was sardined in the bleachers like this was on Halloween. The seniors are the only ones allowed to come to school in costume, and it's a tradition for them to put on skits and dance routines for the underclassmen in the gym. Last fall, Troy and his lax bros were the center of attention. They all dressed up as postal workers, which might not seem particularly inspired, but the crowd lost their marbles when Troy popped out at the last second wearing a carboard box.

Only a cardboard box.

I offer Naomi my untouched cupcake, and she takes a surprisingly massive bite. I try not to stare at the frosting in her teeth, but when she grimaces it's impossible not to.

"What's wrong?" I ask.

"It needs more baking powder."

"You can tell that just from one bite?" I say. I whistle when she nods. "Maybe you should take over. The PTA needs all the help they can get."

"Maybe." Naomi sighs, unconvinced. She looks around the room, eyes going wide behind her glasses. "This is my first pep rally. I didn't go to any last fall."

"You're not missing anything," I assure her.

But we both know that I'm lying.

As the cheerleaders dance their little hearts out to a zappy Madonna mash-up, I fish out my camera and turn my viewfinder to the crowd. Mr. Levitan is talking to Principal Clancy under the basketball hoop, and she is batting her eyes in a way that I'd truly like to unsee. Next I spot Jennifer and the Stern twins sitting on the side of the bleachers closest to the exit. Today they are dressed in matching spandex shorts and jerseys for their respective lax bro counterparts. The only thing different about their outfits is that Jennifer is wearing her usual letter jacket around her shoulders.

"Troy never let me wear his jacket," I mutter, more to myself than to Naomi.

"It's not his."

I lower my camera an inch to stare at Naomi. Stunned.

"Whose is it, then?"

"What do you mean?"

"What do *you* mean, what do I mean?"

"It—it's Jennifer's jacket," Naomi stammers, surprised by my surprise. "She's on the *girls* lacrosse team. You didn't know?"

"Wait. We have a girls team?"

A giggle slips out of Naomi before she can stop it, and she slaps a hand over her mouth. "Yeah. They're actually ranked higher than the boys," she says through her fingers. "Jennifer made MVP last year as a freshman."

"How do *you* know all this stuff?"

"My sister is at BU on a lacrosse scholarship."

I shake my head. But in my defense, it's Hancock High. None of the girls' sports teams have funding from the school. Let alone fans.

Although that does explain how Jennifer and Troy met in the first place.

Almost as if she can hear us, Jennifer turns to look in our direction. When she shifts, I can see that she is the only person sitting on a blue-and-white seat cushion—most likely a gift from Troy. A vinyl throne for the Hancock queen.

"Why do you think she's dating him?" Naomi murmurs, following my gaze. "I mean, *you* dated him. What's so special about Troy?"

"Oh. I mean . . . I always thought the most special thing about him was that . . . he's *not* special," I admit. "He's normal. He's *fun*."

Naomi considers this, pressing her hands between her knees. Her voice is even lower when she speaks again, and I lean in to hear her over the crowd.

"Do you think Andrew is in love with her?"

"Who? Jennifer?"

Naomi nods. She's smarter than I give her credit for.

"I do. What's not to love, right?"

Naomi hesitates, then nods in agreement. The jealousy on her face is obvious. At least, it is to me. But what she says next stops me from commenting on it.

"What happened between you and Kyle Hennessy?"

"What do you—"

"I saw you dodge him just now."

Naomi's words strike me as funny, and it begins to dawn on me that this is the longest one-on-one conversation we've ever had. Bechdel Test be damned. But Andrew was right: No one pays enough attention to her, and she notices way more than I give her credit for.

"Nothing that will ever happen again," I say.

I freakin' *vow*.

Naomi and I sit in silence for the rest of the cheerleaders' routine, each of us floating somewhere in our own mind as one of the flyers crash-lands on her spotter. I raise my camera a second time, and when Naomi turns away, my attention lands on her profile. There's an obvious yearning in her face when she talks about Andrew and Jennifer. As much as she might think she hides it, her heart is out on her sleeve, and it's *so* obvious that it will be crushed. But she knows it too. Naomi puts her chin in her hand and sighs, and I realize she'd be pretty if she stopped picking at her zits.

Quickly, without thinking, I snap her photo.

"Greetings, earthlings."

Tatum is the next one to appear. But instead of sitting by either of us, she sits in the row directly in front, her back to Naomi's shins.

"Nice outfit, Tatum," I say, taking in her floor-length leather coat. The collar is trimmed with some kind of faux dead animal.

"I'm in mourning."

Ahead of us, the cheerleaders finish in a pyramid—and the flyer falls a second time. Typical. The crowd cheers and Tatum taps on the shoulder of the guy in front of her.

"Pay up, Frankie."

Frank Reynolds frowns and hands her a wrinkled dollar bill. I can almost feel my eyes bug out of my head.

"Do you bet on everything?"

"Eh. I don't like horses," Tatum says, shrugging. "But I got five bucks that says Clancy tries to get us to do the wave before the night is over."

I shake my head in disbelief as Frank hands her another bill.

"Tatum, did you know there's a girls lacrosse team?"

"Where? At Hancock?"

Andrew plops down in our row before Naomi can explain, and she slides all the way into me to avoid accidentally touching him. Out of respect for her and her broken heart, I don't complain.

"Did you see who's here?" Andrew asks us, his voice subdued. I follow his gaze to the far side of the room.

"Holy freakin'..."

Mr. Richards stands alone in the corner, hands in his pockets. He must have come straight from work, because he's still wearing his uniform. I didn't know Mr. Richards at all before I was dating Troy, and once I met him, I really wished I hadn't. He allegedly lost the hearing in his right ear during his last tour in the army, and he still refuses to see a doctor. As a result, he always speaks way louder than necessary, and one way or another, all conversations end with someone yelling. As I watch, I catch him checking out the cheerleaders' butts.

Until *he* catches *me* staring.

"Good evening, everyone..."

Principal Clancy steps forward, microphone in hand. There is a sudden burst of static, and the crowd shrieks. She moves the mic away from her mouth.

"We're going to get started lickety-split, but please remember to check out the bake sale happening right outside. All the money raised tonight goes directly to support your Howlers, which is integral for their upcoming spring season. Speaking of..."

The overhead lights flash once, and Principal Clancy hoofs it out of the way. The cheerleaders line up at the door, holding their pom-poms in the air to make a tunnel. Seizing their moment, the Stern twins jump up and unravel their newest artistic masterpiece, a banner that unironically says *GO HOOTERS!*, for the boys to burst through.

I rise to my feet with Naomi, and Andrew, and Tatum, and everyone else.

HoooOOOOT!

HOOOOOOOT . . . !

In addition to the cheering, people start stomping their feet double time. It feels like thunder. But I'm ready. I raise my camera, everything narrowed to a point.

And . . . nothing.

No running.

No screaming.

No lax bros.

No Troy.

The applause dips and soars back even louder. But to everyone's surprise, a full minute passes, and another, and still the team doesn't show.

"I bet he's too embarrassed to show his face," I whisper to Naomi, failing to keep the glee out of my voice.

Before she can answer, the lights shut off. All of them. The gymnasium is plunged into total and unwavering darkness, and the laxtitutes scream-squeal with glee.

"What happened?" Naomi whispers.

Before I can answer, the lights come back on.

Instead of running through the banner like they usually do, the team must have slipped out from hiding somewhere underneath the bleachers. Because suddenly, all the lax bros are standing in a perfect X in the center of the room. Stoic. Silent. Each player has his arms crossed behind his back and a towel over his head. Just like Kyle did, I realize. Something about seeing them all perfectly frozen feels off. Ominous. Like we're about to watch a séance. Because of the shift in energy, it takes me a moment to realize that their white jerseys are a different color.

But instead of the tie-dye that we had planned on, they are all a bright, bright pink.

"Tatum . . ."

"I only had red!"

Troy stands tall at the center of his squad, and once the roar from the crowd dies down to a manageable hum, he is first to remove his towel.

"Holy—"

"No way!"

"Troy!"

Troy's head is as bald as a baby's. Aside from his eyebrows, there isn't a whisper of blond hair left on his skull, and with my camera I can even see the tan lines around his ears. At first people whisper. Then they giggle.

And I snap pictures like freakin' crazy.

Despite the reaction from the crowd, Troy continues standing with his hands behind his back. He waves at someone along the side of the court, and Principal Clancy jogs out to hand him the microphone. She, like everyone else, doesn't hide the fact that she's staring.

"Hi, everyone," Troy purrs into the mic. He looks into the crowd, ignoring the hubbub and making intentional eye contact one person at a time. "Thank you for coming out tonight."

Andrew and I share a glance over Naomi's head.

"As most of you guys know," Troy continues, his voice turning heavy, "I lost my mom to breast cancer when I was in elementary school."

No.

Freakin'.

Way.

I think I almost black out with rage, because Naomi grabs my elbow to keep me upright.

"No. Fucking. Way," Tatum mutters in front of us.

My thoughts exactly.

"This spring is my senior year," Troy continues, even-keeled as ever. "Which means this is my last season playing lacrosse for Hancock."

Someone behind us wails, and Troy holds up a gracious hand in their direction.

"I've grown so much from my time here at this wonderful school. And I realized I wanted to do something special before I graduate. So, at the risk of sounding cheesy, I talked with the boys, and I'd like to dedicate this season to my mom. Also, in her honor . . . *all* the money we raise this year will go to cutting-edge research at the Dana-Farber Cancer Institute."

The crowd bursts into another wave of whispers, and I look for Mr. Richards to see his reaction. But he's vanished.

As for the rest of the gym, you can practically *hear* the panties drop.

Troy lowers the microphone, and at his signal the player on his left steps forward to stand shoulder to shoulder. He takes his towel off.

"Andrew . . ." I say through my teeth.

One by one the boys remove their towels, revealing that they've all shaved their heads in honor of Troy's mom. Without his locs, Kyle looks older than he did before, and although I try to catch his gaze, this time he ignores me. Unusually somber. Seeing his frown makes me break, just a little.

And the crowd is freakin' loving it.

"What did you guys *do*?" I hiss.

"My formula couldn't have been strong enough for the entire team," Naomi whispers, hugging herself. "He must have made the others do it, after . . ."

I don't hear what she says next. Because at that moment, Troy points at Principal Clancy, and she pulls a rope to release the volleyball net that is tied to the ceiling above us. I didn't realize it before, but the net is filled with colorful red and white balloons, and once released, they cover the ground like we're witnessing a winning presidential election. The music comes back on, breaking the spell, and the lax bros hoot and holler as they start stomping on balloons. The crowd screams with renewed vigor, but to me, each pop sounds like a gunshot. In the middle of the chaos, Troy laughs, jubilant and more powerful than ever, and he places his hands on his hips. I realize he is looking for someone in the crowd, and when he points, for a heart-stopping moment I think he's pointing at *me*. But he's not.

It's Andrew.

"I promise you this, everyone: We have a spectacular season ahead of us," Troy says. He presses the microphone tight to his mouth, practically kissing the static. "You know what they say. If you can't play nice . . . play lacrosse."

now

23

hypnotize

JENNIFER LEE

Things are normal inside the gym—so normal that I could cry.

Kids snicker and jostle and yawn as they take their seats in the bleachers. Most people are riding out the final stages of a ubiquitous sugar-high, but we step around the legs of one girl who is already fast asleep and drooling on the shoulder of a friend. A glance at the clock above the basketball hoop confirms that it's only a few minutes after midnight, meaning we're just in time for the attendance check. It also means we have a full five hours left between now and the end of the lock-in.

Five hours to find Troy's killer.

Tatum leads the way, without meaning to, to the bleachers on the far side of the court—the rest of us are too numb to do anything but follow. Suddenly, the lights are too bright. The floors too squeaky. The air too stale. I can't believe that no one is looking at us. Pointing. Screaming. But even with the sleep-deprived zombies, it seems like the crowd is too distracted to pay any real attention. There's a uniquely familiar tinge to the air that something big, something important, something major, is about to happen.

Does anyone even notice that Troy is gone?

Does anyone care?

"Good evening, everyone!"

Principal Clancy takes the center of the gym, a microphone in one hand and the power cord roped around the other. Like a noose. Tatum shoots Andrew and me a warning look before she breaks away to sit at the very back of the bleachers. Meanwhile, I rub my throat absent-mindedly, the image of Troy's bloated neck popping in front of my eyes like the Whac-a-Mole game at Chuck E. Cheese.

There's a painful burst of static from the mic, and Principal Clancy adjusts her grip. Like me, she checks the clock, but the gesture is purely for theatrics.

"Or should I say . . . *gooooood morning!*"

The room groans in response.

Andrew finds a seat as the last remaining stragglers are shepherded into the gym by the school's college advisor, Ms. Jeffers. From up here in the bleachers, we can see everything. More importantly, everyone else can see us. Still standing, I hesitate for only a moment in the aisle, and I look from Andrew to the Stern twins on the opposite wall. Weighing my best options—if there are any. Sassi and Naomi have both conveniently disappeared, assuming their respective positions among the crowd.

"Can I sit with you?" I ask.

Andrew also hesitates. Because like me, he's acutely aware of the fact that the Stern twins are gloating at us. But he nods. I sit next to him without smiling, and without realizing it, he mirrors my posture. Shoulders hunched. Hands pinched between his knees. Eyes on the exits.

"You look like you're about to puke," I whisper.

"Yeah, you too."

I do a quick scan of the gym while Principal Clancy vamps for attention.

"Just a few housekeeping things before we get started," Principal Clancy says. "First up! If you've lost something, please tell a chaperone and we will escort you to the lost and found in the front office. Second! If you've found something, kindly do the same. And third—"

Suddenly, the lights flicker on and off.

On and off.

Andrew reaches for my hand, but when he intertwines our fingers, it only makes my heart go heavy. As soon as the lights come back on and stay on, Principal Clancy picks up where she left off.

"Please put your hands together for our very special, *special* guest, Jonathan the Not-So-Great . . . hypnotist extraordinaire!"

The crowd cheers with varying degrees of enthusiasm, and Andrew claps without releasing my hand. When nothing else happens, the applause begins to fade—all except for the lax bros, who automatically compete to see who can be the very last person to clap. Eventually, The Notorious B.I.G. starts blasting over the speaker system, and the PTA moms squawk in disdain.

But the rest of the gym eats it up. No—devours it.

Finally, the hallway doors fly open, and Jonathan the Not-So-Great jogs in like a pro wrestler, striking various poses along the way. I'm not sure what a hypnotist extraordinaire is supposed to look like, but in his cheap suit and suspenders, he seems more like a used car salesman—or even one of the wacky inflatable tube dudes plopped outside the Maxwell dealership.

He also has no idea that—for some of us—his performance is merely tonight's intermission.

"Hey-hey, kiddos!" Jonathan the Not-So-Great skids to a halt next to Principal Clancy, and even though he certainly doesn't need it, she hands over the microphone. "Thank ya for having me! I hear that tonight is a celebration of all the hard work you've put in this year . . . Well, maybe not you seniors. But the rest of you, good job!"

Now, that gets a real laugh.

I spot the AP chemistry teacher, Mr. Levitan, setting up several folding chairs down the middle of the court. Meanwhile, Jonathan the Not-So-Great holds up a hand to block the overhead lights, scanning the oily faces in front of him as if he were looking out to sea.

"Can I start by getting a few volunteers? Let's say . . . two from each grade?"

Immediately, hands go up, everyone eager to volunteer themselves—or the unlucky person sitting next to them. In fact, Andrew and I are some of the only people who don't offer to participate, and I shoot him an unsteady glance.

"Andrew . . . do you think they're in the room with us right now?" I whisper. Neither of us needs to be a hypnotist to know who I'm thinking about. Andrew rubs the back of my hand with his thumb. "Maybe Tatum was right," I say. "Maybe it was Ms. Jeffers."

"No way. Ms. Jeffers is just as likely to have done it as my mom is."

"I mean . . . maybe . . . ?"

Andrew laughs in a wooden kind of way.

"Don't tell me you're serious, Jennifer. What exactly would my mom's motive be?"

"You," I say, no longer joking. "It's like you said, everyone in town knows that you and Troy were at each other's throats. Don't you think a mom would do anything to help her kid?"

Andrew and I share a glance.

"—*you. You. You. You.* And . . . *you!*"

Out of the corner of my eye, I see Jonathan the Not-So-Great high-five his next victim—volunteer—while they clamber out of the second row. He points at someone buried deep in the bleachers, and I do a double take when the crowd shoves her forward and onto the court.

"Okay, kiddos." Jonathan the Not-So-Great clicks his heels with glee. "What's everyone's name?"

"Kyle."

"Moose."

"Zoey."

"Chloe."

"Wow! Anyone ever tell you girls that you look just alike?"

The audience snickers.

"I'm Emily."

"Mary Anne."

"Simon."

"And I'm . . . um . . . Naomi?"

Andrew and I share a nervous glance. Although why I'm suddenly so nervous, I can't be certain. Maybe it's just the fact that Naomi looks smaller than she usually does, her braids pulled forward in a half-hearted attempt to hide her face.

Or maybe it's because the girl most people at Hancock call a snitch is sitting in front of the entire school, and what she knows could ruin all of us.

"People in my line of work love events like this." Jonathan the Not-So-Great begins talking even faster, like a carnie. "Because you teenagers are *open-minded*. Your brains are still developing. Which means that unlike the adults, you tend to make *veeeeeery* good subjects." He stops in front of Chloe, taking as much time as possible to roll up his sleeves. "Young lady, have you ever been hypnotized before?"

"Me? *Psh.* Nope."

"And are you hypnotized right now?"

Chloe giggles.

"No. I mean . . . duh?"

Jonathan the Not-So-Great nods, his expression giving nothing away. Then he snaps his fingers in front of her eyes once—only once—and her chin drops onto her chest.

Everyone gasps.

"*I mean . . . I mean . . .* I don't know if I'd agree with you," Jonathan the Not-So-Great echoes, exuberant. He raises her arm above her head and lets it drop for emphasis. Like a puppet whose strings have been cut. Like a forgotten Slinky on a bottom step. Or like any other overused metaphor that ends with something dropping—dead.

"Can I get the rest of you to switch seats? Please?"

The remaining participants hesitate, then do just that—and it's a bizarre game of musical chairs as everyone tries to avoid Chloe's motionless body. Once they are settled, Jonathan the Not-So-Great begins to prowl up and down the row, hands locked behind his back.

"You. What's your name again?"

"Kyle."

"Kyle? Good name. Great name. A strong name ... And you, dear?"

"Naomi."

"Nice to meet you, Naomi. Kyle, do *you* know Naomi?"

"Erm ... kinda?"

"Well, I hope so. Otherwise this might be ... awkward."

Jonathan the Not-So-Great flicks Kyle on the forehead—and he collapses, face-planting into Naomi's crotch. She's not going anywhere anytime soon.

"I'm going to count backward from ten to zero," Jonathan the Not-So-Great explains. I can't tell if he's talking to the crowd or his guinea pigs. Maybe to him it's all the same. "With each number, I want you to ease and fall, ease and fall, *ease and fall* into sleep. Every muscle from your nose to your toes, *nose to your toes,* is deeply relaxed by the time I reach the number one. Breathe in deeply ... and ..."

The hypnotist's voice slides into a new rhythm. Slower. Peaceful. Sage. He walks down the line, left to right, and each person he taps slumps, defenseless, at his touch. Naomi's legs shoot out in front of her at an angle, and Kyle rolls all the way out of his chair and face-first onto the floor. Jonathan the Not-So-Great chuckles, nudging Kyle's side with his dress shoe.

"There's a special term for this boy ..." He smirks. "A flopper!"

Suddenly, someone shrieks on the far side of the gym, and everyone turns to see the source of the sound.

Underneath the basketball hoop, near where the teachers have gathered to watch, there is a second person splayed out on the floor—a woman with blond hair covering her face and a tray of overcooked cupcakes spilled around her. Andrew gasps next to me, but the sound is lost to a roar of laughter.

"Mom . . . ?"

"Ah, not to worry! Not to worry . . . This happens every now and then," Jonathan the Not-So-Great calls out, but the way he jogs across the room, I don't entirely believe him. "Some minds are easier to hypnotize than others. Even from a distance. Watch."

He snaps his fingers, and Andrew's mom startles awake. I don't know who I'm more embarrassed for—her or Andrew. Jonathan the Not-So-Great and Mrs. Garcia speak in whispers, and after a moment of consideration, she nods. Jonathan the Not-So-Great gestures for the crowd to start clapping, which they do, and Mr. Levitan brings forward an extra folding chair. They make a spot for her on the end closest to Naomi, and Andrew's mom smiles sheepishly as she sits down.

"She's okay, Andrew," I say, tugging on his hand. His entire body has gone stiff, arched toward the folding chairs, and his mom, like a magnet. "Look, she's okay."

Several heads turn to stare at us, and the skin on the back of my neck grows hot. But my hands remain clammy. The feeling reminds me of playing outside in the snow during the winter, past curfew, and coming into a shockingly warm house. Too hot and too cold all at once.

"Just when I thought this night couldn't get any worse . . ." Andrew mutters, bringing me back to the present.

"Now," the hypnotist sings. "You kiddos want to see something *really* fun?"

It's a rhetorical question, and the crowd goes silent. Amused.

Afraid. In fact, I don't know who's more captivated—the audience or his literal captives. Jonathan the Not-So-Great goes down the line again, but this time in reverse order. Right to left. Chloe, or Zoey, is still passed out cold, and he positions her limp wrist directly above her head.

"*Hard and strong, and hard and strong, and hard and—*"

This time, when he releases her arm, it stays exactly where it is. Like she's a scarecrow. But before anyone can applaud, there is a fresh burst of screams—Moose has a boner. The lax bros hoot and haw in delight as Principal Clancy flutters a hand over her heart.

"Next up. The *instant* I touch your shoulder, the *instant* you feel me touching your shoulder, *laugh. Laugh and laugh, and laugh and laugh—*"

In an instant, every single volunteer does just that. Giggling. Chuckling. Belly-laughing. Snorting. Or, in Mrs. Garcia's case, braying like a donkey. Kyle wraps his arms around his belly and rolls across the floor, kicking into high speed with the heels of his sneakers. Meanwhile, Naomi is laughing so hard I can almost see the tears behind her glasses.

There's nothing remotely funny about it.

"*—and sleep!*"

They drop again. Naomi nuzzles into Mrs. Garcia's shoulder, and the gesture would be sweet if they weren't on display for the whole school to gawk at. Something about the scene makes my heart twinge—I haven't cuddled either of my parents like that since they stopped reading me bedtime stories.

"Are there any questions, suggestions, or bad jokes from the audience . . . ?"

Nearby, a boy in the grade below me stands up.

"How did you learn to control people's minds?"

"Hypnosis is not mind control," Jonathan the Not-So-Great fusses. "In fact, I bet that most of you have spent your day in a trance at least once or twice. Right? Y'all a bunch of daydreamers? Big thinkers? You see, everyone drifts in and out of flow throughout the day . . . and the people I have selected tonight were almost certainly hypnotized *before* they walked in the door."

"Andrew . . ." I begin, then trail off. Too stunned to say it, but too afraid not to consider it. "Could someone have been hypnotized to kill . . . ?"

Andrew shushes me, but there's no need. Jonathan the Not-So-Great is busy making his volunteers jump around like wild kangaroos, and no one is paying us any attention.

"That's *crazy*, Jenn."

"I'm not crazy—"

"I didn't say *you* are," Andrew counters. Based on the set of his jaw, now is not the time to split hairs. "I mean . . . maybe? I guess it's possible. But what's the motive?"

Before Andrew can stop me, I pop to my feet.

"Hi, I have a question," I call out, my voice brittle. "Can someone be hypnotized to do something they really, really don't *want* to do? Something they would never do normally?"

"Well, it depends on—"

"I thought you said you could make them do *anything*?"

Jonathan the Not-So-Great grins wickedly in answer.

"Let's go to the beach."

This time, he doesn't touch them. He doesn't need to. Everyone crashes in their chairs at the exact same time, and Andrew's mom fans her face, desperate, with both hands. Meanwhile, Naomi starts building invisible sandcastles and Kyle rips off his shirt—and the girls in the audience lose their minds at the sight of his four-pack. At which point Zoey also tries to take off her shirt—until Principal Clancy sprints over to pin down her arms.

The lax bros groan in disappointment.

"Better apply some sunscreen," Jonathan the Not-So-Great sings, handing an invisible bottle of sunscreen to Mrs. Garcia. She passes it down the line and drops to her knees behind Naomi, rubbing the lotion over her shoulders just like my parents did when I was a little kid. Ears to fingers. Much to my dismay, my dad always brought the same sunscreen to the beach. It came out of the tube bright purple but turned white the more you rubbed it in, and he'd rub until it was completely gone or I cried—whichever came first. Now Mrs. Garcia rubs vigorously at Naomi's arms, so much that I'm surprised it doesn't hurt. Then again, it's not like either of them would know.

"Will they remember anything?" I ask.

Jonathan the Not-So-Great frowns up at us, and for a moment, I wonder if he can also read minds. Because just as I feared it would, his attention lands on Naomi. Instead of answering me, Jonathan the Not-So-Great helps Naomi and Mrs. Garcia to their feet, positioning them across from one another.

"Do either of you girls speak Latin?"

Still under his control, they shake their heads like rag dolls.

"Great, great ... *You do now.*"

He snaps.

Naomi and Mrs. Garcia stand up as straight as possible,

each one the perfect mirror of the other. I have no idea how it's possible, but they both start speaking a mile a minute, their words tangled and coming straight from the back of the throat.

"See, the greatest thing about Latin . . . it's a *dead* language," Jonathan the Not-So-Great teases. "So these ladies can share their *deepest, darkest secrets* without any of us knowing. *Deepest* and darkest . . . *deepest* and darkest . . ."

Naomi magically moves faster and more frantic with every passing word. Unlike Andrew's mom, she starts gesturing wildly with her hands, and it becomes obvious to even the sleepiest viewer that something is wrong. She's hysterical. Naomi grabs Mrs. Garcia by the arm, pointing at the door to the hallway. When she grabs her throat and pretends to choke herself, I bite hard on my tongue to keep from making a sound.

Then Naomi points into the audience—at us.

"She wouldn't . . ."

"Wouldn't she?" Andrew mutters through his teeth. "Troy told me she's a snitch."

His tone makes me frown.

"I thought Naomi was your friend?"

"She is, but . . ."

"Is everything okay, young lady?" Jonathan the Not-So-Great asks, clocking her distress. Naomi shakes her head, her braids smacking her right in the face. "Okay, then. *Tell us.*"

Within the very same sentence, without stopping to draw breath, Naomi switches back to speaking normally, and the force of the change causes her to stumble.

"I'm . . . I'm . . ."

Andrew squeezes my hand. Like me, he's waiting on the knife edge of his seat for Naomi to answer. To confess. Because suddenly we are seconds away from her telling everyone that my boyfriend's corpse is waiting for us in the yearbook office—and if Andrew thought people were going to be suspicious of him before, there's no way they'll believe any of us now. Whatever happens next, it all hangs on Naomi's words.

Which she delivers at the top of her lungs.

"I'm in love with Jennifer Lee!"

april

24

always be my baby

NAOMI KING

I started my job at Blockbuster the same weekend Mel left for BU. My parents wanted me to skip my first day to make the drive, and the memories, with all of them. But I surprised everyone and said no. Merely out of a newfound sense of obligation.

And, fine, a little bit of pride.

It was the first time I was doing something that Mel hadn't done before. So while the three of them packed up the Subaru, I watched from the front stoop. My parents must not have realized that that Friday night was my first alone. Otherwise, they would have tried to say something profound before hitting the road. We've always spent Friday nights together as a family, with ice cream from Cold Stone Creamery for dinner and maybe a rom-com or two from Blockbuster.

The local Blockbuster is a stand-alone building with a bright blue awning splashed at the center of town. Across the street are a bank and a pet shop, and around the corner are the TJ Maxx and a funeral parlor. Suburban bliss. Whenever we went to the grocery store, my dad would stop at Blockbuster on the way home so that Mel and I could each pick out a movie to watch after dinner, even though we all knew Mel would get the final say. I've always loved how the place smells, like microwave popcorn and wet paper. And I quickly memorized every aisle, down to the eggplant-colored carpet. Which is the reason my manager, Beatrice, offered me the job. That and her sciatica, which makes it hard for her to chase away the little boys that like to linger in the Adults Only section. My uniform consists of your basic khakis and a royal blue polo, and my favorite part: the name tag that looks like a mini clapboard. Most of the time I'm busy sorting returns from the drop box or alphabetizing shelves or helping customers find a movie they don't remember the name of. We also do video game rentals, which most people don't know. Beatrice spent thirty minutes training me on my first day, and everything else I've learned from watching movies on my shift.

Don't split up in haunted houses, do follow your heart, life is like a box of chocolates, and, of course, Han shot first.

At the moment, I sit cross-legged as I paw through a box of Cracker Jack. My teeth are coated with nuts and sugar, and I have one eye on the *Sailor Moon* rerun on the overhead TVs, the other on Sassi as she prowls the aisle of period movies.

"Which do you prefer?" Sassi asks. "1949 or 1994?"

"1949 has Elizabeth Taylor."

Sassi sighs, skeptical, but puts back the VHS in her left hand and brings her final selection to the checkout station. *Little Women*, 1949. Today she has paired her usual Harvard sweatshirt with bike shorts, Princess Diana style, and despite showing up twenty minutes early with bagels from Dunkin', she looks more like the disgruntled celebrities on our news rack than she usually does.

"Do you have a Blockbuster card?"

"Nope."

"Oh. Um . . . how do you usually rent movies?"

"The library."

Sassi rolls her eyes when she sees mine nearly bulge out of my skull.

CLANG!

We flinch when someone drops a return in the slot facing the parking lot. Taking my cue, I push out of my seat and grab the tape from the metal collection bin. When people use the drop box, I can't see who is making the return, but I like to guess based on the movie they chose. *The Land Before Time:* a young family who moved to town for the public school system. *War and Peace:* the grumpy man at the post office who feeds pigeons on his lunch break. *I Know What You Did Last Summer:* a new divorcee. This time it's *Dead Poets Society,* and I pop the tape into the player on my desk, not at all surprised to see the telltale black-and-white twinkle on my screen. Snow.

Because regardless of who rented what, they always forget to rewind.

"Do you have to do that every time?" Sassi asks, leaning over my station to watch.

"More or less."

"I hate that saying. Of course it's more *or* less." She leans in closer, mesmerized by the flashing colors as I rewind double time.

"I mean, we have a tape rewinder, but I like to do it this way."

"Doesn't it spoil the movie if you've never seen it before?"

I shrug. By now, I must have watched hundreds of movies backward, and I've never really stopped to think about it.

"Sometimes they're happier this way."

Sassi ponders my words, and I offer her my Cracker Jack. Which she takes. Then we watch in silence as a bright young boy ignores his father's criticism and triumphs in his high school play. All is well. Unroll credits.

DING!

The bell above the door chimes, but neither of us needs to look over to know that it's Tatum, thirty minutes late—we can smell her musk before we see her. When she rounds the corner, she is wearing an oversized black-and-white flannel as a dress, and she's carrying her skateboard under one arm. Before I can reclaim my spot, Tatum makes herself at home in my chair, her Doc Martens kicked up on my keyboard. She examines the prize from my Cracker Jack.

"Did I beat Andrew here?" Tatum asks, munching away. "It's been weeks since the pep rally. I thought he'd be raging to go."

"Do *you* see him hiding anywhere?" Sassi gestures to the empty store. The weekend rush won't start for a few more hours.

"Just thought I'd ask. I can't stay long. I have to pick up my sisters from Hebrew school." Tatum sighs and digs her purple pipe from her pocket. "So, were you able to talk to your boy toy? Do we know what happened last month?"

"Kyle's not my boy. Toy *or* otherwise," Sassi mutters. "But . . . yeah. And according to him, it was all Troy's idea."

"Shocker . . ."

"Apparently, the team showed up to the locker room and Troy was waiting with a bald head and clippers. He told them that he buzzed it himself and then convinced them to do the same. I guess there's strength . . . and stupidity . . . in numbers."

"Was the thing about his mom a lie?" I ask. Sassi shakes her head. "Gosh . . . I didn't know she died . . ."

"Don't feel bad." Tatum shrugs. "My mom's dead. And I *still* think he's a dick."

"If Kyle is telling the truth, that means Troy probably hasn't told anyone about the shampoo. No one knows we did anything."

"*He* might not know what happened."

"Please. We're talking about Troy Richards. He's evil . . . not dumb." Tatum lights her pipe with a Simpsons lighter. "We got lucky with people thinking the lip gloss was a chemical spill, and the car was a rival team. But after this, he has to know that someone is actively fucking with him."

"There's nothing that could point back to us," Sassi insists. "Right, Naomi?"

"Right. I was careful."

"Right. She was careful," Sassi quips, head bobbing on her neck. "Besides, by now the lacrosse season is in full swing. The lax bros have enough to worry about. Last year, Trapelo High stole Hootie and mounted him on the roof. To which Troy and his goons responded by taking a *literal* shit on the Trapelo lacrosse field."

"Allegedly."

"Sure. They took an alleged *literal* shit on the Trapelo lacrosse field."

Tatum frowns, thinking. She takes a second drag from her pipe, and I cough on her exhale.

"Can you not do that in here?" I ask weakly.

Tatum stares at me. She doesn't say anything, but she walks to the video drop box and bends over, breathing through the slot toward the parking lot. "Noob," she mutters.

"Thanks."

DING!

The front door opens again, and all three of us turn to look at more or less the same time.

"Hi... Jennifer?"

"Hi, Naomi," Jennifer says, smiling at me before casting a wary look at the others. Although she's wearing her usual letter jacket, underneath she's dressed down, in fluffy pajama pants that make me wonder if she just got out of bed. "Hi... everyone. Didn't expect anyone else to be up so early."

No one responds. I offer a little wave of hello.

Jennifer lingers, waiting to see if either Sassi or Tatum will invite her into our team huddle. Which they don't. She disappears down the rom-com aisle, and I watch her ponytail flounce away.

Tatum leans across the magazines to pinch me on the arm.

"Ow!"

"Aren't you going to do something?"

"Like what?"

"I dunno! The whole point of meeting here was to avoid being seen together, right?" Tatum jerks her head to the exit. "So kick her out or something before Andrew shows up."

"Me?"

"You," Sassi adds. She nudges me forward, and when that doesn't work, she gives me a solid shove in Jennifer's direction.

Jennifer is standing all the way at the end of the aisle. I resist the urge to wipe my hands on my khakis as I get closer. She doesn't seem at all surprised when I stop next to her, and she points at the overhead TVs.

"I love *Sailor Moon*."

"Really?" I say, unable to hide my surprise. But by some small miracle, I manage to resist telling her that I've been playing the same five episodes on a loop all week. "Me too."

"Tuxedo Mask was, like, *totally* my sexual awakening," Jennifer laughs, and I relax a bit when I realize that she's laughing at herself. "God, don't tell Chloe or Zoey I said that. They'd never let me hear the end of it. As far as they know, it was the guy from *Sixteen Candles*."

"Michael Schoeffling?"

"No, I think it's Jake something . . ."

"Michael Schoeffling plays Jake Ryan," I explain, adjusting my glasses.

Jennifer merely "ahs" in response, and I hastily look around the aisle for something else to talk about. She also senses the awkwardness, and she fiddles with the silver charm bracelet she's wearing.

"Are you sure I can't help you find something? It's pretty slow right now; I have the time. And I mean, I'd like to help, if I can."

"Well . . . maybe. My mom just sent me over while she's at the bank." Jennifer sighs, apparently less than impressed by the selection in front of us. "If I don't find something good, we're going to be stuck watching *The Graduate*. Again."

We both laugh at her bitterness.

"You should try *Pretty in Pink*," I say, reaching around her to take the VHS off the shelf. "Trust me. Moms love *Pretty in Pink*."

"Thanks, Naomi. You're my hero." Jennifer grins at me, but

her expression fades slightly when her eyes go over my shoulder. "Hey... can I ask you something kind of random?"

"Of course."

"Are you friends with those older girls?"

I almost forgot we have an audience, and an attentive one, at that. When I turn around, Sassi becomes intently focused on the ceiling tiles, and Tatum buries her face in what's left of my Cracker Jack.

"Um... maybe?" I admit. Because the truth is, I don't know the answer to Jennifer's question. But she doesn't seem to find my response weird.

"Be careful, okay? I don't trust them. Especially Sassi."

"Sassi?" I whisper. "What did she do?"

Jennifer sighs and steps around me, casually but intentionally planting herself between me and the others. At first I wonder why she bothers, but then I realize it's so they can't see her mouth moving.

"Look, I don't like talking poorly about people behind their back or anything, and I'm not the kind of girl who wants to shit-talk her boyfriend's ex. But based on the stories Troy has told me... Sassi *really* hurt his feelings."

"I mean, I think Sassi would say the same thing about Troy."

"That's rich. She's the one who broke up with him."

"What?"

Jennifer nods, and even though I know I shouldn't, I look back at Sassi, now innocently flipping through a copy of *Teen Beat*. Because according to her, Troy ended things with her on the night of their junior prom. That's the reason Andrew reached out to her in the first place. That's why she cares so much about taking Troy down.

If Sassi's lying about prom, what *else* could she be lying about?

"Just be careful, okay?" Jennifer sighs, tucking a flyaway piece of hair behind her ear. "You can't trust girls like that."

I nod and stare hard at the carpet. Jennifer takes the VHS from my hand and I follow her to the checkout. Both Sassi and Tatum have made themselves scarce. I don't risk looking at Jennifer again until she breezes out the way she came. Once she's gone, I restart the *Sailor Moon* episode from the beginning, and the other girls pop out from behind a door very clearly labeled EMPLOYEES ONLY. Although I don't know why I'd think that would stop them.

"What did she say to you? Was she suspicious of us or anything?"

"No. We just . . . talked."

"About what?"

"Um . . . movies?"

BRING-BRIIIIING!

The phone rings, causing all of us to jump, and Sassi and Tatum raise their eyebrows at me when I ignore it.

"We've been getting robocalls the last few weeks," I say, shrugging. "You pick up, but there's no one there. If it's important, they'll call back."

BRING-BRIIIIING!

I buckle under their judging stares, and I answer the call on the last ring.

"Good morning, Blockbuster, this is Naomi. How can I help you?"

"Hey, Naomi."

I'm startled to hear a real human on the line.

"Andrew?"

Something in Andrew's voice immediately puts me on high alert. Sassi and Tatum watch me, confused, and I put the call on speaker. The three of us crowd around my station to listen.

"Where are you? Sassi and Tatum and I are all here waiting," I say. Tatum silently jabs a finger toward her Cinderella watch. "You're late."

"I have a video on hold, but I'm not going to be able to make it to the store today."

"Um . . . okay?"

Tatum booty-bumps me out of the way. "What are you talking about, stud? Is everything okay?"

"Thanks. Bye."

The line goes dead a second later, and we all share a glance of confusion.

"What movie was he talking about?" I mutter, more to myself than to them.

Sassi face-palms in reply.

25

i want you back

ANDREW GARCIA

My mom's laughter zigs and zags its way upstairs and through my open bedroom door. Typically, she likes to spend Sundays working in the yard on her never-ending gardening projects, and I planned on making a mad dash to the car before she could stop me. Instead, I freeze at the sound of voices in our kitchen, even though Sassi will be furious that I'm late. My dad isn't home for another week, but I haven't heard my mom laugh this way in ages.

Not like . . . this.

I shove my feet the rest of the way into my Nikes without lacing them, and I jump the bottom step. But because I'm in a rush, it isn't until I'm in the kitchen that I realize who the other voice belongs to.

"Going somewhere, sweet pea?"

For the second time in five minutes, I freeze.

Troy and my mom are sitting side by side at the circular table in our breakfast nook. She must have just made a fresh pot of coffee, and I can smell the Folgers from here. Troy smirks at me over the edge of my favorite Teenage Mutant Ninja Turtles mug. He doesn't even blink.

"Morning, Andrew."

"Morning, Troy."

"Look who stopped by!" my mom squeals. She's too distracted by the return of her prodigal son to sense the tension in the air. "When I saw Mr. Richards at the pep rally last month, I asked if I could borrow his power tools for a weekend. Troy came over just now to deliver them."

"It's my pleasure, Mrs. Garcia."

"Please, *Katie.* You know that!"

"Right, right, sorry . . . Katie."

They laugh and clink their mugs like a pair of daytime talk-show hosts. I force my feet across the kitchen one tile at a time and lean on the refrigerator with my arms folded. Hoping to convey some sense of control while trying to avoid the rainbow of kitschy magnets and holiday cards. Not that either of them bothers looking in my direction.

"Where have you been hiding all semester, young man? I've been working on that meat loaf recipe you liked so much!"

"The team is keeping me extra busy this year. We're four and oh for the season so far, but with the Trapelo game coming up, the guys need all my attention"—Troy shoots me a pointed glance—"now more than ever."

I clear my throat loudly.

"Mom, I'm gonna head out—"

"C'mon! Stay for a sec, Andrew." Troy relaxes into his seat, both arms along the top of the nook. I hear the threat in his voice, even if my mom doesn't. "Katie, would it be all right if I talk to our boy here for a moment? Alone?"

"Of course." My mom smiles, taking Troy's empty mug as she stands. "I'm sure you two have a lot to catch up on. I'll be out back. Holler if you need me."

I try to catch her gaze on her way out of the room, but she simply puts their mugs in the sink and disappears through the screen door.

"Where you off to so early on a weekend?" Troy asks, innocently tilting his head to one side. "I'd think you'd still be sleeping. Especially since you don't have practice to worry about."

"I have errands to run. Nothing crazy."

"I'm sure it can wait."

I hesitate, Troy's stare boring into my own. With his new hair, or lack thereof, his eyes stick out brighter than they did before. Their icy blue color is a perfect match to the vinyl seating behind him, and it gives the overall impression that he is exactly where he's supposed to be. Adding insult to injury, my mom's cat, Stanley, seizes the moment to dart into the kitchen, and instead of me, he makes a beeline for Troy's lap.

"Hey, little man . . ."

Troy coos and scratches Stanley under the chin, not at all concerned about what my decision is going be. He already knows. Scowling, I swipe the phone off the counter and use the call history to dial, careful not to turn my back on him in the process.

"Good morning, Blockbuster, this is Naomi. How can I help you?"

"Hey, Naomi."

"Naomi King?" Troy crows. "What a fucking creep."

My grip tightens around the receiver.

"Andrew? Where are you? Sassi and Tatum and I are all here waiting. You're late."

I press the phone as tightly to my skull as I can, hoping against hope that Troy can't hear the other side of the call. "I have a video on hold, but I'm not going to be able to make it to the store today."

"Um . . . okay?"

"What are you talking about, stud?" Tatum's annoyance crackles over the line. "Is everything okay?"

"Thanks. Bye."

I hang up with a quick, silent apology and a mental plea that they will understand something is wrong. Troy is still watching me, and I consider sitting across from him but don't. He plops Stanley onto the table, the cat purring incessantly as Troy runs both hands down his spine, one immediately after the other, just the way he likes.

"What are you doing here, Troy?"

"I wanted to see how you're doing. Your mom was right. We haven't talked in—"

"And whose fault is that?" I snap. "You're the one that got me kicked off the team. I'm exactly where I am *because* of you." I lean both hands on the table, unable to keep the fury out of my voice a second longer. "Jesus Christ! You were my *best friend*, Troy. How could you? How could you do *any* of this?"

Stanley mews pitifully when Troy stops petting him. I'm not sure who looks more disappointed.

"We've *all* been thinking about you, you know." Troy sighs, slowly shaking his head from side to side with exaggerated pity.

He even has the audacity to sound upset. "The team is different without you around. Moose is letting in goals left and right, and our offense is slower than ever. We're just . . . we're not *clicking* the way we used to. Or the way we need to, in order to make it to state. I'm not sure if you heard, but we almost lost to Sudbury last—"

"I heard," I interrupt. "Don't tell me you came here for advice."

"I didn't."

"Then what—"

"I want you to come back."

Every muscle in my shoulders goes slack, and if my hands weren't already flexed on the table, there's a chance I might slump straight to the floor. But *relief* isn't the right word for what I'm feeling. It's complete and total . . . resignation. Because after everything that's happened, everything the two of us have done to one another, I realize that the girls were right all along. Troy will always think he's in control. If only because he's . . . *him.* He truly believes that he can snap his fingers and I'll come running, that he can change his mind and fix both of our problems. That it's easy. That it's his choice. That it's possible to forgive and forget, as long as he's the one doing the forgiving.

To him . . . everything is just one big game.

"What are you talking about, Troy?"

He grins and runs a hand over his bald head.

"I'm trying to tell you that the team needs you. We need your spirit. Your muscle. And, admittedly, that anger—"

"If this is your version of an apology, it fucking blows . . ."

Troy throws back his head to laugh.

"It's not. But there is one condition."

"Of course there is..."

Troy smiles and throws a tiny piece of plastic on the table between us. It takes me a moment to realize what it is, and when I do, I try not to react.

The nozzle from Tatum's tie-dye kit.

"What's this?"

"Save it, Garcia. You've always been a shitty liar." Troy turns his focus back to Stanley, wrapping the cat's tail around his fist as he speaks. "At first I didn't want to believe that something was up. I mean, I knew you might try and get back at me. I would have. But the shit with my car?" He frowns, a muscle twitching in the side of his neck. "*You* know how my dad is. Which made me realize, there's no way you're *that* stupid. So you must be working with someone else. Right?"

Troy tugs a bit too hard on Stanley's tail, and the cat yelps.

"You're hurting him."

Troy ignores me.

"It wasn't until the jerseys, and my hair, that I realized it wasn't a coincidence. And there's no way you could be in so many places at once." Troy narrows his eyes at me. "Seriously, Andrew? My fucking *hair*?"

Stanley cries out in pain.

"Stop it, Troy."

Troy releases Stanley. The miserable cat makes a break for it, and he streaks out of the kitchen without looking back.

"Here's how this works, Garcia. You tell me who was helping you with your little revenge scheme, and I'll put in a good word with Clancy. Best-case scenario, we can get you back on the field before the Trapelo game. Thoughts?"

"Just one: Get out of my house."

Troy blinks at me, genuinely surprised, and when I make no other attempt to respond, he holds both hands in the air, palms to me, and rises to leave. I immediately back up, putting extra space between us. Just in case.

It only makes him smile.

"You're sure about—"

"*Out.*"

Troy shrugs and crosses the room, but he lingers at the counter before he goes. Next to the box of Mr. Richards's power tools is the picture of us that used to hang in the front hallway. Troy stares at the broken glass for a long, long time, and then he shoves the picture into my arms, forcing us into a brief tug-of-war. Face to face. Inches apart.

"You were right about one thing, Andrew," Troy growls. "You were my best friend."

"So?"

Troy releases the frame, and what he says next makes my blood run cold.

"So just imagine what I'd do to someone who wants to be enemies."

26

wide open spaces

TATUM STEIN

The house is quiet when I get home with dinner. Too quiet to mean anything good.

"Sarah? Eliana?"

I drop my grocery bags from Stop & Shop on the floor. Unlike the colonial McMansions splashed throughout Hancock, the house where my sisters and I live is the same flat two-bedroom ranch house that my parents bought in the '80s. Sarah and Eliana share what used to be my parents' bedroom at the back of the house; once they were old enough, I helped them paint the slanted ceiling with their hand- and footprints so that they'd feel some sense of ownership. I sleep in the room off the kitchen, one I've never bothered decorating more than hanging up a Talking Heads poster on the outside of my closet. I kick off my Docs next to the groceries, and it's a quick walk to the living room, where I find—

"Isaac?"

I stop as I turn the corner. Because Sarah and Eliana are

sitting on the couch like porcelain dolls, and Isaac is sandwiched between them. He's still wearing his coveralls from the shop, and I grimace at the thought of an oily snow-angel butt print he's guaranteed to leave behind.

"You're home late," Isaac says.

"No, I'm not." I flash him my Cinderella watch. "How we doing, girls?"

My sisters blink at me. Sarah is the younger and smarter member of their dynamic duo, smart enough to know that someone in the room is in trouble but not quite old enough to understand who or why. She taught herself to read with a weathered copy of *My Father's Dragon*, and to this day she's still a bit dragon crazy. In contrast, Eliana is already boy crazy, and I blame one too many Disney Princess movies. Last year, I made the mistake of letting her choose her own outfit for picture day, and we now have a photo of Eliana in a turquoise skirt and a plastic crown on our wall.

"They're good," Isaac answers for them. "We've just been watching TV, waiting for you."

"And here I am."

"Here you are."

"Eliana, Sarah, can you put the groceries away?" I ask, every single one of us aware that I am not asking. "I got frozen latkes."

The girls at least cheer at that, scampering away without a backward glance.

"To what do I owe the pleasure, Isaac?" I ask, perching on the armrest of the couch farthest from him. All the furniture in our house is mismatched and well-loved. If not by us, than by whoever left it on the curb.

"You're short on rent. Again," Isaac says, his voice clipped. "Need I remind you, with your father indisposed, *I'm* footing the bills—"

"That's a laugh—"

"—and I expect to see a return on my investment." Isaac reclines into the couch cushions, crossing his legs with one ankle over his knee. "In case you've forgotten, kiddo, you work for me. I give you the merchandise, and you turn a profit. Just like your father."

This time I don't have a comeback. Witty, snappy, or otherwise. Because he's right. The past few weeks I've been distracted by Troy, and because of that, I haven't been making my usual numbers, which, more importantly, means Isaac isn't making his numbers. And even if he's my uncle, he can always make my life more miserable than it already is.

Suddenly my attention falls on the coffee table at Isaac's knees. In the center is a large copper-colored envelope. I didn't notice it until now.

"What's that?"

"You tell me. It arrived for you."

"Oh yeah? What is it?"

Isaac flips the envelope over and reads out the return address, one syllable at a time. There's no way of misunderstanding the bitterness in his voice.

"Framingham University, Office of Admissions."

Sassi's face flashes in my mind's eye.

"Since when are you going to college?"

"I'm not, I just—"

Isaac snorts. "Let me stop you right there, Tate. College isn't for people like us."

"What do you mean?"

"We don't need it. In fact, we're better off without it. Why would you want to pay some old schlub to tell you how to think? That shit ain't the real world. You got everything you need, here." Isaac taps the side of his head with a blackened finger.

"Just because you didn't do anything with your life doesn't mean I can't."

Isaac crows with laughter. "Fine. Let's play this out for a sec. How are you going to afford tuition payments? And who will look after the girls if you're off frolicking down frat row?"

"I'd never leave them—"

"Really? Because sometimes I think that's *exactly* what you want to do."

Isaac's words drop like a guillotine. Triumphant, he smirks and closes his eyes, and it reminds me of playing hide-and-go-seek with my sisters. When Sarah was a toddler, she would stand in the middle of the living room with her meaty fists over her face. Because if she couldn't see you, you couldn't see her. It hasn't been easy looking after my half sisters, and it hasn't always been fun. Actually, it's never fun. And sure, there have been moments when I wonder what it would be like to just look after me. My mom died when I was in middle school, and both Sarah and Eliana were too young to remember what it was like when their mom lived under the same roof as us. But the toughest moments always pass; some are just faster than others.

"You going to say anything?"

"I'll get you your money, Isaac. No need to be a dick."

"You better. Because if I thought you were *using* what I give you instead of selling it, I'd have to make a call to child protective services."

I press my hands into my thighs to stop myself from curling them into fists. Isaac is hell-bent on making his point, and I don't risk looking at the envelope again and revealing my curiosity. I don't know why I submitted the application in the first place, but after my conversation with Sassi, I couldn't get college out of my head. Maybe a part of me wanted to prove her wrong, or right. Maybe I should never have gotten involved with Andrew or his wannabe Girl Scouts. I should have known better. I should have listened to my own advice and kept my head down. Kept to myself. I—

"One more thing," Isaac says. "You know that Chimaera we had in?"

"Mr. Richards's car?"

Isaac nods, rising to his feet. "Finally got the thing back to functional. Whoever messed with it did some real damage, though. You wouldn't happen to know anything about that, would you?"

"Didn't you say it was a rival school?"

"I did." Isaac picks his nose. "And Michael sure as heck gave the team over at Trapelo a talking-to. But . . . there are only so many people in this town who know their way around an engine like that. And the more I think about it . . . I don't think any of those boys are damn near smart enough."

Isaac holds my gaze with his steel-gray eyes. My father's eyes.

"You have until June," Isaac says, holding out the envelope in the air between us. I don't reach for it, and he drops it on the couch. But as soon as he walks out of the room, I rip it open with both hands. Although I really, really wish I hadn't.

Because suddenly I have a lot more to lose.

27

dreams

SASSI DeLUCA

When I was a freshman, I started falling in love in my dreams.

And no. I don't mean that metaphorically.

I could never remember where or when or why the dream took place, but I woke up each morning with the unmistakable tug under my sternum. The twins in my French class, my English lit partner, my tatted-up fifth-grade bus driver. We could be fighting on a battlefield or riding our bikes around a hyperrealistic Candy Land. Most of the time, it was someone I had never even spoken to before. Which made things superawkward going to school the next day and dragging around a crush that had no business existing. We can blame it on the hormones. Probably.

But now, I dream of the only person I've been dreaming about all year.

Troy Richards.

The dream always starts someplace in the middle. The two of us are waiting in a classroom, although it doesn't look like any of the classrooms I've seen at Hancock. There's something brighter about it, the colors more saturated, the light softer and wider and much more forgiving than I've ever been or will be. It's lovely. But I don't know what we're waiting for. Supposedly you only dream about people you've seen in real life, and I wonder why it's not the same with places. Anyway, the room shifts when I gain awareness of it, and Troy opens one of the windows. He's learned how to fly and he wants to teach me. But I can't risk it. Ignoring me and my fear, he steps up an invisible ladder into the sky, laughing. Then he's gone. And I'm naked.

Hey. It's a dream.

It doesn't have to mean anything.

I lie under my covers, staring at the popcorn ceiling. The weather is finally getting to be warm in the evenings, and I roll over to stick out one foot from my blankets. Then the other. Based on the purple tinge at my window, it must be after dinnertime. I didn't sleep at all last night, and today I crashed as soon as I got home from Blockbuster.

And I freakin' hate naps.

I hear my computer ding. Still groggy and drowning in nap fog, I have to summon an unusual amount of strength to lift my head off the pillows. My desktop blinks at me across the room, and even if I wanted to fall back asleep, the opportunity is long gone. Besides, I'm hungry. My stomach growls at the heavy smell of pot roast, and I stand up to swap my sweatshirt for a T-shirt. I didn't bother doing my hair or makeup today, and when I check my reflection I realize that the shirt inexplicably has the words *I BEAT PEOPLE WITH A STICK* printed on the front.

Kyle's shirt, I realize.

He gave it to me on New Year's Eve.

I sit down at my computer, and I groan when I see that the messages are from Andrew. And Naomi. I squint across the driveway to the Garcia house, and I spy both Andrew's car and his mom's where they have been parked all day. Because in addition to blowing the three of us off earlier today at Blockbuster, Andrew has since been inside avoiding me at home, too.

LAXative_22: we need to talk
LAXative_22: all of us
xxteenwolfxx: k but I can't stay up late
xxteenwolfxx: my bedtime is @ 8

My eyes go to the clock: 7:52 p.m. Sighing, I switch my status from Away to Online. I guess I should be grateful that Andrew's not trying to sweet-talk his way past my stepmom and upstairs to badger me in person, but still.

A little groveling is the least he could do.

pinktiaragirl: nice to hear from you, laxative
xxteenwolfxx: lol
xxteenwolfxx: i just got the joke
pinktiaragirl: what's going on?
LAXative_22: Troy came to my house today
LAXative_22: he confronted me about the car
LAXative_22: and the jerseys
xxteenwolfxx: omg
pinktiaragirl: wtf!
LAXative_22: has anyone heard from Tatum?

Chewing on my lower lip, I scroll to the very bottom of my contacts. Tatum's Away status is currently set to the ever-creative *WITH UR MOM*.

LAXative_22: if she hadn't fucked up his car...
pinktiaragirl: hey
pinktiaragirl: YOU asked Tatum for help in the first place
xxteenwolfxx: wait
xxteenwolfxx: does Troy know about US?
LAXative_22: no. your safe
xxteenwolfxx: for now
pinktiaragirl: *youre
xxteenwolfxx: what do we do now?
LAXative_22: nothing, we're done
pinktiaragirl: what?!!?!??!
pinktiaragirl: we're so close!
LAXative_22: close to what, exactly?
LAXative_22: NOTHING we've done has made a difference
xxteenwolfxx: wait! tatum's on
xxteenwolfxx: let me invite her
popopopopoptart joined the chat.
popopopopoptart: hullo?
xxteenwolfxx: Troy's on the warpath
popopopopoptart: he knows?
LAXative_22: he knows

I'm spinning myself too fast to follow the rest of Andrew and Tatum's cantankerous back-and-forth, and I catch myself on the edge of my desk just before I lose control. With my momentum, I accidentally tip over a stack of textbooks balanced near my elbow. I bend over to gather them and a bookmark slips out. No, not a bookmark, I realize. It's one of the brochures that Ms. Jeffers gave me, this one with a photo of two girls posing in front of London Bridge. Fake smiles on full display.

I exhale loudly through my mouth.

I've been so distracted with the Troy stuff that I nearly allowed myself to stop thinking about the college stuff. My dad and my stepmom are another story. I don't know what caused them to finally gain parental sentience, but each week that goes by without a letter from Harvard, acceptance or otherwise, they become more and more invested in every minute of my daily life. Ergo, my mail. On April 1, I came home to Deborah trying to read through an envelope addressed to me. And even if it was just a bill from my gyno, it's the principal of the matter that bothered me.

Also, legit a petty felony.

I roll the tacky brochure into a tight, tight tube and go to stash it in my desk drawer. I shove the notebooks aside, and I accidentally unearth two postcards with the same California return address. My mom's. She moved across the country shortly after the big bad Divorce, and although she's invited me too many times to count, I've never visited. But it's not like she can ever be bothered to pick up the phone when I call, so I consider us even.

Under the postcards I dig out a strip of images from the photo booth at last year's lock-in. In it, Troy and I are pouting, tongue-sticking-outing, finger-gunning. In the bottom photo, my hand will be forever flattened on Troy's pecs in that casual and possessive way that girls do. And he's forever smiling. Laughing.

At me.

popopopopopoptart: i say we go for it
popopopopopoptart: we've come this far, haven't we?

xxteenwolfxx: what's the worst thing that could happen?
popopopopoptart: that's the spirit!
xxteenwolfxx: no... im asking for real
xxteenwolfxx: what's the worst thing that Troy could do to us?
popopopopoptart: ...

Troy can do and has done everything with that smile. It opens doors for him, convinces people to share umbrellas with him, turns girls against their best girlfriends for him, and, on more than one occasion, convinced the objectively hot substitute teacher from Wayland to give him a ride home in exchange for an ice cream cone at Baskin-Robbins. Troy gets everything he wants before he could even need to want it. All because he's tall, and hot, and sure, can probably bench-press me. But if there's anything I learned from dating Troy, it's that he's not a Nice Guy. He's dumb. He's boring and simple and lazy enough that we all just project what we want to see onto him.

He's not what he looks like.

He's so much less.

LAXative_22: suspension
popopopopoptart: juvie
xxteenwolfxx: social suicide

My whole life, my whole freakin' life, I thought I was supposed to follow the rules. I don't think anyone explicitly told me to, I just did, and I noticed that adults appreciated me more for it. When my dad said to go to bed, I did. When my mom said to sit up straight, I did. In fact, in my earliest memory, I'm at a preschool birthday party for a girl with two first names, Mary

Anne, and there is a piñata hanging from one of the trees in her backyard. But when Mary Anne delivered the final walloping blow, I was the very last kid to rush forward for the candy. Because I thought we all had to wait our turns. As a result, I didn't even get a Tootsie Roll.

I did my homework on time.
I only spoke when spoken to.
I brushed my teeth.
I even flossed, every freakin' night.
I was perfect.
And *Troy Richards* gets *my* dream?

LAXative_22: Sassi?
LAXative_22: you're awfully quiet
LAXative_22: what do you think?

It's not fair.
It's not acceptable.
And *I* refuse to accept it.

I chuck the photos of Troy and me at the trash can, not bothering to see if I make it. As much as it might pain me to admit, Andrew is right. To an extent. Everything we've done so far this semester has just made Troy stronger. There's no point in continuing down the same path. Maybe, if I keep to myself and stay out of trouble, I can finish the rest of my time at Hancock in peace. Grow up. Move on. Never look back at what could have been, and forget about what Troy Richards did to every version of me. Past. Present. Future.

I know all this and more.
I could.

I should.

Which is why, when I find Ms. Jeffers's contact sheet for Harvard stuck inside the brochures, I decide to do the exact opposite of what I'm supposed to. For probably the first time in my life.

> **pinktiaragirl:** I said it before and I'll say it again
> **pinktiaragirl:** lacrosse is the only thing Troy has ever cared about
> **pinktiaragirl:** if we can take that away from him ... we win
> *xxteenwolfxx signed off at 7:59:05 PM.*

now

28

i want you to want me

JENNIFER LEE

There are only two things that come to mind in the silence following Naomi's foolhardy declaration of love. The first: I realize that she wasn't pointing at Andrew. She was pointing at me.

The second: Why now?

A hush makes its way across the bleachers, like a wave. Not the ocean kind, but rather the human wave that happens at Fenway Park between the sixth and seventh innings, when people jump to their feet and immediately look to see how their neighbor will respond. Everyone is whispering. Chloe. Zoey. The lax bros. The laxtitutes. The moms. The teachers. The hypnotist.

No—that's not entirely true.

There is one person who can't bring himself to look at me.

Andrew is still clinging to my hand, as if to show that there is nothing worth reacting to. But I don't know who he's trying to convince. Or protect. And more than anything—I just wish I was wearing more clothes. Chloe talked me into wearing one of her tube tops while the three of us were getting ready for tonight.

Chloe's and Zoey's bedrooms are connected by a narrow bathroom with two identical sinks, and each of their bedrooms is the perfect mirror of the other, minus the color schemes: Chloe's, lavender purple; Zoey's, bubble-gum pink. Even though Zoey has hated pink ever since they turned thirteen. All this week Chloe has been upset because she got dumped by her college boyfriend over spring break, and while I was crimping her hair I suggested we wear matching outfits to cheer her up. Now, however, with all the eyes on me and around me, I wish I had somewhere to hide.

"... Jennifer Lee ... ?"

"... her face ..."

"... *his* face ..."

I ignore the curious and greedy stares and force myself to keep my gaze on the court. Because Naomi is still looking at me—except, not really. Her eyes have the same glassy look that all the other volunteers' eyes have. I wonder if she's even aware of what she said. I wonder if she can hear the awful things people are whispering about her. I wonder if she'll remember any of it.

The only thing I don't wonder about is if it's true.

"Okay ... well ... thank you, Naomi ..." Jonathan the Not-So-Great clears his throat. He at least has the decency to realize that he has officially crossed the line, and he ushers Naomi and Mrs. Garcia back to their places. "Take a seat, please ..."

"... knew it ..."

"—*Mel's* sister?"

"—dyke!"

The laughter starts silently at first and expands to fill the gymnasium. Like air. Like wildfire. The ugliest attention remains on Naomi, but I catch more than a few fingers pointed in my direction.

"You okay?" Andrew whispers.

I nod, but I gently shimmy to sit on both of my hands. I don't trust myself to hide the fact that they are shaking.

"Okay, folks. Going to snap my fingers one last time . . ." Jonathan the Not-So-Great says, visibly relieved when he gets the nod from Principal Clancy. *"Wake up!"*

He snaps.

Like magic, all the volunteers rise to their feet, wide-eyed and shell-shocked. The magic is over. Mrs. Garcia and Kyle share an awkward glance, and Chloe and Zoey run to hug each other. Meanwhile, Moose shoots the lax bros a sheepish smile, scratching at his balls with both hands.

Then—Naomi bolts out the door.

"Naomi . . ." I whisper. Her reaction only causes the room to devolve into pandemonium, and Principal Clancy jumps to her feet. Eager to reclaim her place at the center of the basketball court.

"Let's hear a round of applause for Jonathan," she cheers, exaggeratedly clapping both hands above her head. "We have a ten-minute break before the next performance. Please remember to check in with your homeroom teacher so your attendance is counted, and feel free to stretch your legs. But don't go too far!"

The crowd splinters as people stand and peel off to chatter with friends, and I shakily rise to my feet. But before I can decide whether I should go after Naomi, Andrew pulls me after him onto the basketball court. The crowd spools out onto the floor around us, and Andrew attempts to elbow his way to the exit like he's cutting through underbrush. Over his shoulder I spot Principal Clancy disappearing into the hallway, apparently not one to listen to her own advice.

"C'mon. While everyone is distracted—"

"Where are we going?"

Before he can respond, Sassi materializes. I feel like everyone is trying to avoid looking me directly in the eye—whether out of respect or embarrassment, who knows—but she doesn't have the same concern. In fact, Sassi glares at me, her green eyes spitting flames. Although the meaning is clear, it still surprises me. She blames me.

"I'll grab Tatum, and the two of us will go after Naomi," Sassi mutters, all business. "It's not safe for her to be wandering around—"

"How can we—"

"Let's regroup at the yearbook office in ten minutes," Andrew suggests. "Once the chaperones realize Troy didn't check in, everyone is going to be looking for him."

Sassi disappears with a curt nod, and Andrew and I turn to leave—only to find our path barred by Chloe and Zoey standing in front of us.

"Jennifer!"

"You poor, poor thing—"

"Did you know?"

"Sorry, guys. I can't talk right now."

"*What?*"

"Where are you going?"

"I'll explain later," I say, and Andrew tugs me away before I can make any more promises that I don't have the ability to keep.

"I say we start with Clancy, see if she has an alibi," Andrew explains, tugging me toward the doors where I saw Principal Clancy exiting. "Troy made her life a living hell for the last four years. Maybe we can find something in her office."

I chew on my lower lip, desperately wishing I could borrow Zoey's gloss right about now. Once we get to the hallway our footsteps quicken, and the cacophony from inside the gym makes it sound like we're underwater.

"Did . . . uh . . ."

My eyes shoot to Andrew, and he stumbles over his words.

"Did you know . . . that . . . uh . . ."

I know what he's trying to ask, but I'm not going to make it any easier for him. I'm not stupid. Even worse, I know why it's so hard for him to ask. Because he's afraid of the answer. Something about it makes me irrationally angry—or maybe rationally so. I dig my nails into my palms, leaving half-moons on the softest part of my skin.

"What?" I ask, my voice low. "You want to know if I knew that Naomi's gay?"

The word makes him cringe.

"Yeah, I did. I thought it was obvious."

"Oh . . . well . . . I'm sorry."

"For what?" I ask. We pass by a window looking out into the parking lot, and the streetlights illuminate both of our frowns. "Does it bother you?"

"No. I mean, of course not. But . . ." Andrew gives me a critical look. "Wait. Do you . . . ?"

I start walking faster. But I don't know if it's because of secondhand embarrassment, or humiliation, or rage—or something else entirely.

The administration office is at the very front of the school, with a perfect view of the athletic fields in one direction and a direct shot to Principal Clancy's parking spot in the other. But as we creep along the trophy case lining the opposite wall, I feel like the nameless faces of Hancock's storied past are watching us. Watching me.

Unless it's not them doing the watching.

"Did you see that?" I murmur, stopping where I am. Andrew nearly walks right into me. "I thought I saw a shadow. Or . . . something . . ."

Andrew sighs. "It's late. Your brain is playing tricks on you. Don't worry. You're safe with me."

"Okay . . ."

The door to Principal Clancy's office is wide open, and I watch as the logo on her computer boomerangs from one corner of the screen to the next. But Principal Clancy herself is nowhere to be seen. On the wall next to us are several class photos, each one taken on the lacrosse field with the senior class wrangled to stand in the shape of their respective graduation year. They are in descending order from top to bottom: 1998 . . . 1997 . . . 1996 . . .

My eyes slide down the wall—and there, waiting for us on the corner of Clancy's desk, is a phone.

"What are you doing?" Andrew hisses, watching as I make a beeline across the room. "I thought we agreed not to . . ."

He trails off when he sees the look on my face. Because as soon as I lift the receiver, I can hear it. A complete and resounding—nothing.

"The line is dead," I say. My voice sounds like it's coming from one end of the tin-can phones that my dad used to make me out of empty SpaghettiOs cans. Neither Andrew or I move an inch. Then again, it's not like there's anywhere for us to go.

"Maybe the power outage did something to it?"

"Maybe . . ." I put the phone back in the cradle. "I don't like this—"

"Can I help you two with something?"

Andrew and I spin around, and Principal Clancy is in the doorway. She flicks on the overhead lights, one by one, and after blinking away the brightness I realize that Jonathan the Not-So-Great is two steps behind her. He half bows when we make eye contact.

"Well?" Principal Clancy asks. "Mind explaining what you two are doing in my office?"

"We were looking for you, actually," Andrew says. Which isn't a lie.

"I see. Is everything . . . okay?"

"Oh, yeah. We just—"

"We wanted to check the lost and found," I jump in. "I can't find my student ID. Do you keep everything in here?"

Principal Clancy nods and crosses the room, and both Andrew and I take a giant step away to give her more space. She bends behind her desk and slides a milk crate from underneath—the official home for all items lost, found, or confiscated at Hancock. The crate is filled with an assortment of loose clothing and textbooks, and at a glance nothing about it seems particularly ominous. Unsure what to do next, I poke through the crate in silence, my mind racing a mile a minute. I'm more than aware that everyone is watching me, and I can feel the boob sweat through my top.

"Have you kids been having fun tonight?" asks Principal Clancy.

"Oh yeah, loads. Have you?"

"I have. Even though it's been busier than past years."

"Really?" I say. I can feel Andrew trying to catch my gaze, but I ignore him. "Busy how?"

"Oh, nothing too exciting. One of our volunteers called in sick, so I've been running the photo booth since we started," Principal Clancy explains. She grabs a checkbook from inside her desk and tears off the top page for Jonathan the Not-So-Great. While she's looking the other way, I risk grabbing Tatum's familiar-looking pipe out of the lost and found. "Be sure to stop by and visit before the night is over."

"And you've been doing that the whole night?" I ask.

"Yes."

"And there are people who can confirm that they saw you there?"

"Yes . . . ?"

I stand up straight, abandoning the milk crate. "It's not here."

"Maybe we should try the locker room," Andrew suggests, his voice high. "Thanks, Principal Clancy."

Principal Clancy purses her lips but doesn't try to stop us. Andrew and I slide past Jonathan the Not-So-Great, and once we are completely out of sight, Andrew holds open the door to the south-side stairwell.

"Do you think we can believe—"

Suddenly, I walk directly into someone coming the other way. Not just someone—a ghost. Because I would know those shoulders anywhere. Those arms. The familiar dopey droop of a big head on a long neck. The hands that, even now, are stretched toward me, because he always does everything with two hands. Just like he's holding a lacrosse stick. Just in case.

But no—it's not Troy, I realize.

It's his father.

"Jennifer?" Mr. Richards steps to the side, and in the confusion he doesn't notice Andrew duck between the open door and the wall. "Sorry, I didn't hear you coming."

"It's okay. It's my bad," I say. Once again I feel exposed, and I shiver once—then twice when Mr. Richards gives me a long look.

Troy never officially introduced me to his dad, and the one time we met was by accident. Troy and I were buying liquor for a party, and we bumped into Mr. Richards in the freezer aisle. If it had been my dad, I'd be dead. But Troy's just laughed and told us to have fun. Instead of his uniform, tonight he's wearing civvies and a baseball cap—which is probably to hide the bald spot I know he has.

"I didn't realize you were chaperoning," I admit, hoping he doesn't hear how breathless I am. Andrew remains hidden behind the door.

"It was last-minute." Mr. Richards shrugs off my words. "There was a breakout at the jail. Two convicted felons on the loose, one with a rap sheet as long as my arm. I'm here for extra security."

"Really?"

"Fuck no." Mr. Richards snorts. "I'm pulling your leg, kid. Relax. Have you seen Troy?"

"Oh . . . yeah. Maybe . . . five minutes ago?" I lie, even though I don't know what I'm hoping to gain with it. "Everyone is in the gym."

Mr. Richards quirks an eyebrow at me.

"Except for you?"

"Yep. Except for me."

Mr. Richards nods like he understands, and when he lurches forward, I'm so surprised by the smell of malt liquor that I don't automatically step away. He's drunk. Actually, it wouldn't surprise me at all if he's the one who helped Moose sneak in a keg. According to Troy, his dad was the captain of his own lacrosse team back in his day, and Mr. Richards has always been a favorite with the boys. He even taught the team how to take pickleback shots—which, when Troy told me, I knew I was supposed to be impressed by. But Troy was fifteen at the time.

"How are you doing, Jennifer?"

Instead of responding, I take two very big steps backward, letting the stairwell door close. When it does, I'm startled to see that Andrew has vanished entirely. But I know that if I were in any real danger, he'd come running to my rescue.

Wouldn't he?

"I was watching the show," Mr. Richards continues, his head swinging toward the gym. "I'm sorry about what happened at the end there. That girl is sick in the head. I'd don't know what I'd do if that was my kid."

I forget Andrew, my entire body jolts like a snap bracelet, and I stop where I am. Now I understand how moms can lift cars off their babies. It's adrenaline and muscle—and having absolutely nothing left to lose besides themselves.

"Naomi's a friend of mine. There's nothing wrong with her."

Mr. Richards flutters his lips. Like a horse.

"You need better friends. That shit ain't natural."

I could laugh, I could cry—and I almost do. But the sound that comes out of my mouth is more like a groan. Mr. Richards ignores it, and he gives me a patronizing pat on the top of my head for good measure.

"Take care of yourself, Jennifer," he jeers, giving me a final up-down before he adjusts his cap. "You're a good girl. Would hate to see that change."

I suck in a furious breath over my dry lower lip, but Mr. Richards is already walking away from me. He can't even be bothered to look back.

And suddenly—I know what it feels like to want someone dead.

may

29

save tonight

ANDREW GARCIA

Sunday . . . game day.

If it were a normal day, in any other normal season, I'd be spending my afternoon with the team. My real team. Troy would pick me up early in his dad's convertible, Green Day booming, and if no one was around we'd either kill time doing doughnuts in the school parking lot or head straight to the weight room before the others arrived. Despite how long I've been playing lacrosse, my nerves tend to explode right before a big game, and I've always needed the additional time for a pregame poop. I know it might sound strange . . . or gross. Troy certainly loved to mock me for it. But more times than not, he'd just keep me company by bouncing around the rest of the locker room singing "Basket Case" at the top of his lungs.

But that stress is nothing compared to what I feel right . . . now.

Sassi offered to drive to the Trapelo game, and even though the field isn't far from where we live, something tells me she wants to make sure we have a quick getaway. Now more than ever I feel naked without my jersey, and I grab the puffiest jacket

I can find in the downstairs closest. I'm careful when I slide the zipper to my chin, and the simplicity of the motion brings back another memory. In this one, Troy and I are seven years old and learning to ride our dirt bikes, and after a brutal fall he helps me reclip my helmet and accidentally pinches the skin. I didn't make a sound during the fall, but the click made me cry.

Back in the present, I dip into the kitchen without bothering to turn on the lights. My mom is apparently still at her book club, and when I open the refrigerator the only things I find are a six-pack of Pepsi, a thawing chicken cutlet, and a jar of pickled red onions. I almost feel like it would be better if the fridge were empty entirely. Typically at this time of year, I should be cutting and counting my calories with the rest of my ream, and after the last few weeks I'd literally kill for a Dunkaroo. Resigned, I grab a Pepsi and close the fridge. But when I crack the can, the bubbles pour over. Par for the course. I move over to the sink, my eyes going to the rhododendron bushes in the yard. Even though there's no wind, it looks like the branches are moving, and in the dwindling light it's even more ominous than before. I also feel like I'm going to be sick.

Actually . . . I feel like someone is watching me.

"Andrew?"

I whirl around to find my mom, hands on her hips and lips puckered like she ate something sour. Although this time I don't exactly blame her.

"What are you planning on doing with my meat scissors, sweet pea?"

I glance at my right hand, realizing that I must have swiped the scissors off the counter without thinking.

"Sorry," I mutter, sheepishly returning the scissors to their place in the knife block. "You scared me."

"You're the one standing in the dark," my mom teases. She shifts from one foot to the other, and I realize it's because she, like me, is embarrassed. "I'm glad I caught you. I was thinking I could come with you to the game tonight. If that's okay?"

"Oh. I don't know . . ."

"I made snacks for the bake sale," my mom adds, revealing a large Tupperware full of cookies. The sugar cookie kind, with frosting. I must stare for a moment too long, because she laughs and shakes the container. "What's wrong? It's not like they're poisoned."

"I don't know if I'm going to stay the whole time. It might be kind of awkward."

"I know you're nervous, but don't worry. It'll be fun! Just like when you were little and we went to watch the big kids' scrimmage." She pinches my cheek. "Besides, I feel like some time together would be good for both of us. So? What do you say?"

I hesitate, picturing Sassi waiting for me outside. Slowly, it dawns on me how sad my mom looks. Her blond hair has grown out, and I can see natural spots of gray and ash at her temples. But I don't remember when she started dyeing it in the first place. She's also dressed in a perfectly chosen outfit—slacks, a sweater vest, and a charm necklace, too perfect for her to have assembled it on the first try. I find myself picturing her wriggling in and out of various clothes, complaining about her love handles. It makes me feel a pang of something sad in my gut.

"Sure. Let's bounce."

My mom cheers and grabs me in a hug. I take the cookies so

she can put her denim jacket back on, and I follow her through the front door a moment later. Neither of us locks it. But in a small town like ours, we never do.

Outside, Sassi is idling in her car. Her hair is half up, half down, and even in the fading daylight I can tell that the lipstick she is wearing looks darker than her normal pink gloss. I don't know if she looks beautiful, but she suddenly looks . . . unfamiliar. And despite her having been the literal girl next door our entire lives, I don't know if I would recognize her out of context.

Sassi's eyes go from me to my mom, and a noiseless understanding dawns on her face. She shifts her car into reverse and has rolled away by the time my mom takes out her keys.

"Was that Sassi?" my mom asks, unlocking our doors. When I nod, she smiles to herself. "I always liked that girl, you know. She's a good influence on you."

I nod in silent agreement.

If only she knew . . .

30

come as you are

NAOMI KING

The Hancock boys lacrosse games are the hottest event in town, and the bleachers are already packed with adoring fans. Students, teachers, full-time moms, part-time dads, plus an altogether startling number of townies who can't or won't let go of their glory years. It's disturbingly patriotic. Although in this zip code, allegiance is pledged solely to Hancock High.

"To the left! No, *left*—"

"My left or the crowd's?"

"You're killing me, Chloe...."

I watch from a safe distance as Chloe and Zoey secure their latest art project on the chain-link fence that separates the bleachers from the field. Compared to their previous banners, and the sponsorship flag for Maxwell Motors hanging nearby, they certainly decided to go big and not home with this one. There are life-size headshots of all the boys on the team, and each one is covered with a concerning number of lipstick kisses. Courtesy of the twins, I assume. Beyond the fence, the lacrosse field sits in the middle of a sherbet-orange-colored track, impatiently waiting for what is to come. The turf is almost the same size as a football field but slightly wider, with metal stadium seating down both of the long ends and two identical snack shacks at the short ends, both advertising one-dollar corn dogs. When the wind changes, the smell of popcorn hits me before the cold does.

The Stern twins high-five before disappearing into the crowd, and as I linger at the main entrance I stare at Troy's doe eyes on his 8.5 x 11".

Two frazzled moms try to give me their tickets before they realize I'm not working the event, and I bury my hands as deep in my pockets as they'll go. Under my overalls, I'm wearing a sweater from the pile that Mel left behind. I can feel a loose string at my wrist, but I don't dare pull it. Instead, I roll the thread into a tiny ball between my fingers and make a mental note to fix it once I get home.

As I take in the crowd, I spot Jennifer under the bleachers closest to me, sharing a joint with Chloe and Zoey as they laugh over some inside joke. All three of them are wearing matching bucket hats, and Jennifer has Troy's practice jersey over a black long-sleeve.

She looks up suddenly and waves at someone.

"Naomi!"

I freeze.

Jennifer scrambles out from under the bleachers, cheery and slightly less ladylike than usual. Mel once told me that there are upperclassman girls who soak their tampons in vodka in order to get drunk without the teachers noticing, and I wouldn't be surprised if Jennifer's already buzzed. That alone would explain why she is smiling at me.

You know.

Like *that*.

"I've never seen you at a Hancock game! First time?"

First and last. Hopefully.

"Um, yeah, actually," I admit. I shiver when the twins glare at me.

"Well, you picked a good one! The Trapelo team beat us in the playoffs last year, and our boys are out for blood. Whoever wins tonight gets a better seeding for state," Jennifer babbles. "By the way, my mom and I watched *Pretty in Pink* last night, and she loved it. But then I stayed up late rewatching *Sailor Moon*! Hence the atrocious bags under my eyes—"

"I don't think you look atrocious," I squeak.

"Thank you! That's so sweet." Jennifer laughs, giving my arm a quick squeeze. "Who are you sitting with tonight?"

"Erm . . ."

"Do you want to squeeze in with us?"

Again, I stare at Jennifer. Silent. Stupid.

"I don't want to intrude or anything."

"Intrude? What are you talking about? I'm inviting you!"

I hesitate a moment too long, and Jennifer catches me staring at Chloe and Zoey under the bleachers. From here, neither of their faces gives anything away, and I absentmindedly stroke my braids, remembering how Zoey grabbed them and dragged me out of the bathroom.

"Chloe and Zoey are harmless, I'm telling you—"

"Zoey is hooking up with Troy," I say, unable to stop myself.

Jennifer blinks at me.

"I heard them talking about it in the bathroom," I press on, throwing caution to the wind. Sassi is going to kill me when she finds out I went off script, but Jennifer is the one person I can't lie to. Not anymore. "I don't know how long it's been going on, but—"

"He told me."

Now it's my turn to gape at Jennifer, dumbstruck.

"Troy confessed on Valentine's Day," Jennifer continues. She fiddles with her charm bracelet. "He apologized. And Zoey did too. And . . . we're making it work."

"*What?*" I screech.

"Thank you for looking out for me, Naomi," Jennifer says, giving me a quick, awkward hug. "You're a good friend."

"But you can't—"

"Enjoy the game!"

Jennifer skips off before I can stop her, and I exhale forcefully through my nose. But before I can collect myself—

"Hey."

Tatum is wearing her signature neon windbreaker and a very unexpected pair of space buns on the tip-top of her head. But her appearance is not the thing I focus on. Rather, it's the fact that she has two little girls in tow. One with Tatum's head of curls, and another with the same bad attitude. Like Tatum, both of them have their hair styled in outrageously perky buns, and the two of them are standing single-file on her skateboard, Tatum steering from behind. She's casual but in control. The littler girl is wearing a kid-sized Hancock jersey that droops past her knees, with butterfly hair clips that flap when she moves.

"Wh-who's . . . this?" I stammer.

"Introduce yourselves, ladies."

"I'm Eliana."

"I'm Sarah." The girl in the jersey puffs out her chest. "And I'm a menace."

Tatum snorts. "Couldn't have said it better myself." She gives the board a kick, pushing the girls out of hearing range but still within her line of sight. "Everything okay? You look like shit."

"Yeah, it's fine," I lie. "Why are your sisters here?"

"Sorry for the change of plans. I couldn't leave them home alone."

"How are you going to . . . you know . . . while babysitting?"

"Oh, I'm not on babysitting duty. You are." Tatum smirks. "And if anything happens to them, I *will* murder you."

"Wait, what? Tatum!"

But she doesn't waste oxygen arguing. Instead, Tatum goes to collect her sisters and returns them to me a moment later. "You girls have fun," she singsongs, tucking her skateboard into her armpit. "And remember . . . don't do anything *I* would do."

Sarah and Eliana nod, and Tatum gives us all a final look of warning. Although I don't know who she's more worried about. I wait until she merges with the crowd, and once her space buns are out of sight, I turn back to her sisters.

"So . . ." I gulp. "What . . . um . . . do you guys do for fun?"

31

tearin' up my heart

SASSI DeLUCA

Kyle's jersey is bigger on me than I expected, the sleeves flapping at my elbows like the wings of some kind of conceited tropical bird. Considering the fact that I messaged him about it this morning, even I was surprised that it only took him a whole two minutes to respond. Although it probably would have been faster if he didn't have to renounce whatever freshman wannabe he promised the honor to in the first place.

I find the laxtitutes on the away team side of the field. There are eighteen of us total, one for each boy on varsity. I remember some of the girls from when Troy and I were dating, but I don't recognize the younger ones. There's been a lot of turnover between seasons, and I've started referring to the new girls by numbers in my head. Number Twenty-Two and Number Thirteen have gone the extra mile with matching hair bows and knee-high socks. And Number Two even has a custom foam finger.

As a group, we finished making our DIY posters for the boys before the crowds arrived, and as soon as Number Four has glued down her last googly eye, I follow the jittery flock to the stands. In addition to my poster, I have my yearbook camera on a strap across my sternum, and it bonks from right to left with every step. Like a metronome.

Or a ticking clock.

"Miss DeLuca!"

Ms. Jeffers pops out of the crowd like she's being fired from a cannon, pom-poms under both arms and a corn dog in hand. Without meaning to she cuts me off from the laxtitutes, but I don't mind. I can only take their squealing in small doses.

"Good to see you, hon. Are you here with your friends?"

"Kind of. I'm Kyle Hennessy's . . ." Honestly, I don't know what I am to Kyle, and I can't bring myself to say "laxtitute" out loud. I settle for flapping my arms. ". . . friend."

Ms. Jeffers smiles in a knowing and totally insufferable way.

"I'm glad I caught you outside of school. It's been a while since you've stopped by my office." She shakes an accusatory pom-pom under my nose. "I've been worried sick!"

"You just miss the doughnuts."

"That's not true! I think of you as a friend, you know."

"Please don't take this the wrong way, Ms. Jeffers. But I don't need any more friends." I smile without showing my teeth. "I need a college advisor who can *advise* me on how to get into the college I want."

"I see. Well, as your *advisor,* can I be honest with you, hon?"

Please, god, no.

"I know how stressed you are about your future, but I promise you that life is too short for any of that. Honest. Any one of us could get hit by a bus tomorrow . . . and *splat!*"

"Splat," I echo.

"So if you're asking me—"

Which, for the record, I'm *not*.

"—I think this whole situation with Harvard might be a sign that you should take a good long pause and think about what you really want in your life. You could take a gap year and travel the world, volunteer with a cause you really care about, or even start at Framingham in the fall and plan to transfer somewhere else *next* year. It's not an all-or-nothing thing." Ms. Jeffers shakes her head, and I'm surprised that the lightning bolt earrings she's wearing don't jab her in the eye. I know that I'm tempted. "It's not a matter of life and death."

"That's the problem, Ms. Jeffers. To me . . . it is."

I don't have time to watch the smile fall off her face, and I jog to catch up with the other girls without saying goodbye.

The laxtitutes take up an entire row of bleachers closest to the fence, and I'm careful to avoid stepping on anyone as I shimmy over to join them. Just my luck, Jennifer is sitting directly next to me, her poster braced on her shins. She's written out *OWL BE BACK* in coquettish bubble letters.

"I like your poster, Jennifer."

"Thanks! Yours is also . . . nice."

She's being polite. My poster only has the number nine painted on it. Kyle's. But I do appreciate the compliment.

A buzzer sounds over the speakers, and the voices of our announcers spill out into the rapidly cooling evening. Patrick and Paul Dewey played on the Hancock team when they were in high school, as did their kids and grandkids, and the Dewey brothers have been running commentary ever since.

"*Ladies and germs! Welcome, welcome to tonight's game—*"

"—*and speaking of welcomes, please give a warm one to . . . the Trapeloooo Tartaaaaans!*"

There is a polite smattering of applause as our opponents take the field like a storm cloud. The Trapelo boys are dressed in black-and-green uniforms with plaid detailing on the seams, and the only thing more lackluster than their welcome is the fact that their mascot is a fabric swatch.

"*And now . . . it is my absolute honor to announce—*"

"*—our honor to announce—*"

"*—your Hancock Hoooooowlers!*"

Jennifer and the others stand up and stomp their feet, twice, in sync.

HooOOOOooot! HooooOOOOoot!

They stomp again, and my stomach knots when I realize that no one bothered to teach me any of their new chants.

HooOOOOooot! HooooOOOOoot!

More stomping, more shouting.

HooOOOOooot! HooooOOOOoot!

The Hancock boys charge the field in rows of two, each of them cheering almost as loud as their rabid fans. It's easy to spot Troy, even in the identical pink jerseys. There is an air of authority, and playfulness, and control, and pure freakin' animal magnetism, that shimmers in the air around him. Like a heat wave in the dead of summer. The boys take a lap, and my frown grows bigger when Troy raises a gloved hand to wave in my direction.

But when the entire crowd screams back at him, I realize he doesn't see me.

He never did.

"... so hot, right?"

I peek down the row.

Number Thirteen and Number Six are deep in conversation, Number Six covering her mouth with her hand. My stomach clenches when the girls shriek, but I can't hear what they say next. I begin to sit down once the entire team is on the field, but I stop when I see that the other girls are still standing.

Number Three whispers something to Number Twelve.

"Um . . ." Jennifer titters. "Sorry. We all stand until the guys score their first point."

"Oh . . . *right*," I say, my voice strained. I rise to copy her.

The players from both teams begin warming up on their respective sides of the field, and my eyes go to the unassuming metal bench on the Hancock side. It's the spot where all the boys keep their gym bags and water bottles.

Including Troy.

"I want to say good luck to Kyle," I tell Jennifer, turning away. And just in case she doubts my steadfast commitment to my new boo-thing, I indicate my camera, just to really sell it. "I also need a few photos for the yearbook."

She nods, and I flee.

I wiggle out of the bleachers the same way I came in, but this time I take a hard right around the fence, away from the friends and families. I've swapped my usual heels for a pair of my stepmom's nicest running sneakers, which, for the record, aren't that nice, and the track feels spongy under my toes. Almost like the playgrounds I used to frequent as a little kid. No one looks twice at me, and even though I have the safety of my laxtitute disguise, I'm more inclined to use my yearbook credentials.

Because no one will question you if you just ask them to *smile.*

I walk directly to the Hancock bench and nod at the team manager, a pimply sophomore named Darren, or Derek, maybe, whose sole job is to make sure that the team has everything they need. He glances at me, my camera, and I take my place behind the gym bags.

Specifically, the bag labeled RICHARDS.

I snap a picture as Troy throws a practice toss to Kyle.

Moose fires a snot rocket.

Todd Gordon pops his knuckles.

Parker Reid stretches his quads.

And Troy blows his fans a wet kiss.

When Darren scoots off, I squat down to retie my perfectly double-knotted laces. With my back to the crowd, I remove a tiny plastic baggy from where I hid it in my socks. Apparently, Tatum keeps a healthy supply of caffeine pills on hand for the kids who claim that Adderall alone isn't strong enough, and each eggshell-colored pill is two hundred times the amount of caffeine a normal person should have each day. So before leaving home, I crushed three into a fine powder with the mortar and pestle that my stepmom uses for her homemade guac.

Just to be safe.

Seizing the moment, in every sense of the word, I grab the shaker bottle from the outside pocket of Troy's bag and screw off the lid. Then I tip the dust inside as cleanly as I can, mixing it seamlessly with Troy's favorite vanilla pre-workout. Once I'm done, I want nothing more than to sprint back to the safety of the bleachers, but I force myself to linger and take pictures.

Then, as the boys drill practice shots on their own net, I sling my camera over my shoulder and head back the way I came.

"*Sassi!*"

His voice hooks me through the throat. The ribs. The heart. And even though I want to ignore it, I do, I stop where I am. Because Troy Richards is screaming my name.

"*Saaaaaassiiiiiii!*"

I turn around, slowly, to see Troy jogging over. I try to keep my face impassive. His red helmet almost seems to glow under the stadium lights, and even when he gets closer I can't see his expression underneath. But I realize it's not because of the shadows. It's the black face paint drawn in lopsided triangles on his cheeks.

My heart rockets into my mouth when I see him holding the shaker bottle.

There's no use trying to outrun him. If anything, my safest bet is staying right where I am. With witnesses. Once he's close enough that I can smell him, Troy spits out his mouth guard. It's connected to his helmet by a rubber cord, but a glob of phlegm lands on the front of my jersey.

Ugh.

"*Ugh,*" I say out loud, and I wipe at the spot with genuine disgust. "Can I help you?"

"Yeah. For starters, you can tell me why you're wearing that stupid jersey." Troy snorts, pointing at my boobs. "You'd never wear mine, and *I* was number one."

I gape at him and look down at Kyle's jersey as if realizing that I'm wearing it for the first time. When Troy and I were dating, I went to every single home game, but it's true that I refused to wear his jersey in public. I wanted to be with him, but I didn't want to be his property. I wanted to be *me* dating *him*, and he said he didn't mind as long as there was an *us*.

I didn't realize it'd still be a sore spot a year later. Or that he ever cared.

"People change," I manage.

"Did you?"

"No. Not that much."

Smirking, Troy lifts his bottle and unceremoniously waterfalls his pre-workout through the front of his helmet. I hold my breath, but he just guzzles another squirt. And another. From the corner of my eye, I can tell that people in the stands are starting to stare at us, clearly wondering what's keeping their star player from the rest of his team.

"So are you and Kyle dating or what?"

"Don't tell me that's what you wanted to—"

"Don't hurt him. He's one of the good ones."

Again, I gawk at Troy.

"I'm serious, Sassi. If you're trying to get back at me, leave him out of it."

"Wow. Everything has to revolve around you, doesn't it? I can't even . . . Troy. Are you *flexing* right now?"

Troy shrugs, resting his lacrosse stick along his shoulders. And, yes. Flexing. I can't help but ogle the cords of muscle between his elbow pads and the top of his gloves.

"What? Can you blame me for being concerned? You're clearly trying to replace me."

"What if I actually like Kyle?"

"Well? Do you?"

I hesitate just long enough that Troy takes it as an invitation. He steps closer, the energy changing between us. Fast. There is sweat on his brow and his eyes glow dark. Blue and wild, like the ocean.

Or a black, black hole.

The night that Kyle and I first kissed, I had gone to Hilary Maxwell's party simply to get out of my house. I wasn't looking for anything but an escape from my stepmom and her lackluster charcuterie boards. I drove myself because I didn't plan on drinking. I never do. And I didn't. Which means I can't claim any of the normal excuses for what happened next. Kyle found me in the kitchen at the beginning of the party as I made myself a mocktail. Soda water, ginger beer, two slices of lime, one slice of lemon. When I finished it, he made me another one. Without having to ask. And it was perfect, down to every last detail. I didn't realize he was watching me. Then, unlike Troy, Kyle asked if he could kiss me at midnight.

But I kissed him first.

"Hey, it's okay. I won't tell Kyle that you still have feelings for me," Troy says suddenly.

I flinch and take a step back. I wish he did too.

"I certainly don't—"

"You didn't have to say anything. Your eyes did," Troy murmurs, his voice low. "And just so you know . . . whatever you still feel for me . . . I feel it more."

My cheeks flame red with mortification, but Troy just salutes me with his water bottle and trots away, blowing another kiss to the crowd.

And for the life of me, I don't know which of us is right.

32

all star

TATUM STEIN

I move through the crowd at a lazy and leisurely and sluggy pace. Just fast enough that my board doesn't stop. I usually avoid functions like this, and I'm gobsmacked by how many people I actually recognize. There's the touch-starved soccer mom who started taking Ativan when her youngest signed up for piano lessons, the dad who likes to pack shrooms when he goes camping with his mistress, even the geriatric husband-wife duo who asked for sildenafil and no further questions. I might not remember first names, but I sure as shit know their prescriptions, and their dogs.

Who are Pippin, Charlie, and Fenway, respectively.

Because I'm distracted, I bump into a man in front of me. He's younger than his white hair would lead you to believe, and he's dressed in a black jacket and pants, plus a black baseball cap. None of his clothes have logos on them, which makes him hard to place. But if I had to guess, he's a townie that got away and then inexplicably got dragged back in.

It almost makes me feel bad for him.

"Sorry about that," I say, tipping an invisible hat in his direction. I continue on foot and head to the very end of the stands, where the Hancock guys are finishing their warm-up, and I lean my skateboard against a trash barrel before ducking under the bleachers. Because of the shadows, at first I think I'm alone, but then I see two bodies sloppily groping each other nearby.

"Hey. *Hey!* Scram."

"Narc," one of them mutters.

"Narc? Do you *know* who I am, you horny weirdo?"

They don't respond, and I irritably shoo them away with both hands.

Alone at last, I reach into my bra and pull out my last cigarette and my Simpsons lighter. But on second thought I put the lighter away and settle for simply pinching the cigarette between my teeth. Then I lie on my belly in the dirt. Above me, I can see the feet of people in the stands, but what's even more telling is the space between bodies. I can tell who is huddling for warmth, and who clearly wants to be. I even spot Sarah in the nosebleeds, her light-up sneakers popping pink and purple as she shimmies excitedly in place.

Naomi has her work cut out for her.

A referee blows his whistle, and the Hancock team lays their lacrosse sticks on the sideline closest to me before they run to line up across from Trapelo and touch gloves. Unfortunately for us, Troy is never without his lacrosse stick. Which is alarming, and unsanitary. Furthermore, Andrew warned us that the officials check every player's equipment at the beginning of each game to make sure it's up to regulation standards.

Meaning I'll only have one minute and thirty-one seconds before the start of the game to make my move.

"*Now introducing Darcy Lamott to sing our national anthem...*"

There is a loud shifting above me. For a moment, I wonder if the bleachers will cave in. Meanwhile, on the field, the lax bros stand shoulder to shoulder, arms linked behind them, and they all turn their backs on me to face the flag.

"*O say can you see...*"

Darcy starts singing, and the poor girl is awful. But thankfully I don't have time to sit and listen. I identify Troy's stick based on the rubber ducky duct tape around the basket, and I pull it toward me as far as I dare. With my free hand, I take a pocketknife out of my windbreaker, and from the end I pull out a tiny pair of needle-nose pliers. I also produce a roll of matching tape. My dad and I used to go camping every fall before my sisters were born, and he showed me how he used his pocketknife to cut cigars. My dad said he would give me his knife on my eighteenth birthday. But seeing as he wasn't around, I took the liberty and literally gave it to myself.

"*... rockets' red glare...!*"

I work fast and delicately but deliberately, clipping the plastic around the head of the stick and covering the damage with a matching piece of tape. It's weakened, but you can't tell by looking at it. Once I'm done, I slide the entire stick back exactly where I found it among the others. No one the wiser.

"Get shafted, you ass," I mutter under my breath.

"*... home of the braaaaave!*"

The audience applauds, and I can't tell if people are more excited for the game to start or the preshow to end. I crawl back out the way I came, and as soon as I grab my board I hear someone shout my name.

"No skating, Ms. Stein!"

Principal Clancy descends on me. She's wearing a cardigan knit with the Hancock colors and a pair of dangling earrings that look suspiciously like lacrosse sticks. But she's moving too much for me to be certain.

"Evening, Lisa."

"Pockets, Ms. Stein."

I stare at her without moving. Principal Clancy clears her throat, and clears it again when I don't move.

"Want a cough drop? I might have something that can help with that—"

"Someone tried to sneak in alcohol before the game. You wouldn't happen to know anything about that, would you?"

"Not this time."

"Then, please, empty your pockets."

I grumble, but I do as she asks, presenting a Dum-Dum wrapper and my purple pipe.

"I won't be having any funny business tonight. This is an important night."

"You're telling me . . ."

Unmoved by my attitude, Principal Clancy snatches the pipe from me before I can defend my civil liberties. She's never given me the benefit of the doubt, and I wonder if she'd look at me any differently if I told her I was accepted to Framingham, or if she knew how many of her teachers are on quaaludes. As she walks away, there is more than a small part of me that wants to go after her.

And if we didn't have more important things to do tonight, maybe I would.

33

whoomp! (there it is)

ANDREW GARCIA

Once Darcy Lamott is applauded off the field, she is replaced within seconds by a referee who has an objectively impressive goatee and a zero-tolerance policy for bullshit. Because unlike other sports that choose sides with a coin toss, lacrosse has its own unique starting sequence.

The face-off.

Each side selects a player to battle one-on-one for possession of the ball. Some teams even have athletes who specialize in the face-off, like how football teams have kickers. Usually, the duty goes to the person who is too short to play lacrosse in college but who is still absolutely brutal. Tonight, Hancock is represented by a senior named Sam Klein. He's short but scrappy, and he got jacked last summer, which may or may not have been his response to a rumor that he once put peanut butter on his dick and let his dog lick it off. Sam crouches on the midline opposite the Trapelo brute, the ball between them and their teams around them. All of them waiting. Hungry. Poised.

The referee blows a whistle and the boys launch into each other.

The game is on.

Hancock scores effortlessly in the first forty-five seconds, but no one is surprised. It's Hancock, after all. The boys move the ball up and down the field, rapid-fire, and from afar it looks like ballet at high speed. Contact ballet. There can be no doubt in anyone's mind that lacrosse is a ruthless sport, and each time the players collide, the blow ricochets through me as if I'm the one getting thwacked.

Troy scores the first two goals, and with each point he takes a victory lap, the dutiful laxtitutes cheering him on at full volume.

"HooOOOOooot! HooooOOOOooot!"

"Another stuuuuupendous throw by Troy Richards . . . !"

I can't remember the last time I was a spectator at a game, not a player, and I force myself to watch every agonizing second. The ball zips from one end to the other, Tinkerbell-like, and the crowd oohs and aahs on cue. There are ten players for each team on the field at one time: one goalie, three defenders, three midfielders, and three attackmen. The midfielders are the only ones who can run the entire length of the turf—the attack can't cross the midfield line toward their own goal, and vice versa for defense. Like in hockey, the players can move behind the goal, and to score, they have to shoot the ball into the six-by-six-foot cage without crossing the line. Otherwise, it's a turnover.

"The goal is gooooood!"

There's an assist. Another goal. Cup checks. A clever toss around the world. A pretentious swish behind the back. Troy dives. Kyle ducks. Moose takes a ball to the ribs. They make it look easy. Because for them, it is.

Even without . . . me.

"You sure you're not cold, sweet pea?"

I blink, and blink again when I realize how dry my eyes are. I nearly forgot that my mom is squished into the bleachers next to me. While I've been mesmerized by the field, she is happily scoping out the crowd. Neither of us said a word during the drive over, and now that we're here, it's even harder to look her in the eye.

"I'm fine."

"You sure? Do you want a hot chocolate or something?"

"Maybe later," I say. I turn my entire body to watch Kyle chuck in the ball from the sidelines, hoping my mom will get the message.

She doesn't.

"I think it's really healthy for you to be out here cheering for your friends. I'm proud of you. I know it can't be easy."

I don't know what to say in response, but she doesn't give me the time to.

"Is that Kyle Hennessy's mom?"

"I don't know."

My mom hums something to herself.

"Oh my gosh, is that Mrs. Mahoney? I haven't seen her since her youngest went off to Catholic school."

"I don't know, Mom. Probably?"

"Andrew, you could at least pretend to look."

HooOOOOoooot! HooooOOOOoot!

Troy skips through another victory lap, and I finally turn to follow my mom's gaze. But instead of Kyle's mom or Mrs. Mahoney, my eyes lock on a reedy-looking man wearing all black. He has a shock of white hair and wears a bright red lanyard tucked into the front of his down vest, but I can't see what's on it.

Even so . . . something about him seems weirdly familiar.

"Where's Mrs. Mahoney?" I ask my mom. I hesitate when I see that her entire face has gone slack, her eyes the size of saucers. "Mom . . . ? Is everything okay?"

"Hmm? Oh, yes. Sorry. I thought I saw someone I used to know."

I shiver through my sweatshirt and don't push her on it. It's weird picturing my mom having her own life before being, well . . . my mom. What I do know is a random assortment of fun facts and faceless anecdotes. She was the first girl at Hancock to wear a miniskirt to class, a bright red pleather number that she still keeps in our basement. She once told me about a teacher who posted grades in the hallway after she flunked a test, and how he became her favorite teacher because of it. She asked my dad out on their first date by telling him a dirty joke, though to this day I don't know what the joke was. Not that I want to. I don't know what's harder to picture: the innocent, test-failing version of my mom . . . or the miniskirt-wearing one.

"*Out of bounds!*"

Despite the fact that everyone's attention is on the field, I look around for the man with white hair. I don't see him, but I do spot Tatum sitting with Naomi in the nosebleeds. Tatum feels me watching and gives a quick nod. When I look straight ahead, I see Sassi with the laxtitutes, fake-laughing at something one of them must have said.

Everyone is where they are supposed to be.

And now . . . all we can do is wait.

"*Gooooooaal . . . !*"

Eventually Trapelo calls a time-out, and during the lull I spot the man with the lanyard as he walks toward the bathrooms. Something about seeing him in motion puts it all together. Because even though his face wasn't enough, I'd recognize his gait anywhere.

"Where you going, sweet pea?"

"Bathroom."

Leaving my mom with a bemused look on her face, I follow the man as fast as I can without breaking into an all-out sprint. I'm not fully lying to her: I shadow him all the way into the men's bathroom. We're the only ones inside, and I take the urinal next to him before I can think of anything better to do.

Finally, he catches me staring.

"Can I help you, son?"

"Coach Lancaster?"

The Harvard coach blinks at me, recognition dawning on his face one degree at a time. We only met a handful of times when he was scouting Troy, but I'll never forget that Coach Lancaster compared Troy and me to the Gait brothers from Syracuse University, two of our sport's living legends. Two brothers. Two bodies playing as one. And even though we all knew my grades wouldn't make me a good candidate for Harvard, Coach Lancaster said to keep in touch.

"Andrew Garcia." He zips up. "Why aren't you on the field, son?"

"I'm taking the spring off. To focus on my grades."

"Well, I certainly hope to see you back next year. You have passion, kid. And a mean streak."

"Thanks, Coach," I say. As ridiculous as it sounds, it only dawns on me now that this might not be the best conversation to have at the urinals. "If you don't mind me asking . . . why are you here? Are you still recruiting for your freshman class?"

"Ah, no. Tonight is more pleasure than business." Coach Lancaster shrugs. "I got an email with free tickets, and I thought, why not? At the very least, it would be good to check up on Mr. Richards, make sure he's living up to his reputation."

"Oh . . . who sent you the email?"

"Someone with the team, I think. A Ms. DeLuca, if I remember correctly."

Sassi.

Coach Lancaster excuses himself and leaves without washing his hands. I stand perfectly still, my mind reeling as the sounds of the game bounce off the tile floor.

The girls and I went over every detail of our plan for tonight: the caffeine pills, the lacrosse stick, everything. But not this. I had no idea Sassi was going to invite the Harvard coach, and I doubt that's the kind of thing she just forgot to mention. I don't know what she's planning. I don't know why she wouldn't tell me.

But . . . I do know I don't ever want to be on her bad side.

34

this is how we do it

TATUM STEIN

At halftime, the scoreboard is stuck at a striking 8–6, Hancock in the lead.

Despite my best and better judgment, I agree to buy my sisters hot dogs. And it seems like everyone else must have the same idea, because by the time we arrive at the snack shack, the line is moving at a snail's pace. As for my sisters, they've strangely taken to Naomi, and as we stand in line, Sarah dangles off Naomi's arm like it's her own personal jungle gym. I don't know what surprises me more, that the weight doesn't knock Naomi over, or that she doesn't seem to mind.

"Would you rather drink a gallon of pickle juice or a gallon of mayonnaise?" Sara asks.

Naomi considers it.

"Mayonnaise."

"Would you rather go without shampoo for the rest of your life or toothpaste for the rest of your life?"

"Shampoo."

Sarah and Eliana squeal. I roll my eyes, and when it's finally our turn, I slide a ten to the kid at the counter.

"One slice of pepperoni and three hot dogs, please."

My sisters cheer. We shuffle to stand by the pickup window, and I'm surprised to find Andrew waiting alongside a blond woman in a denim jacket. He doesn't introduce us, and a look passes from Andrew to Naomi to me without anyone noticing.

"Hancock, showing us how it's done!"

None of us can see the field from here, but judging by the announcers, the third quarter starts just as explosively as the first. With lacrosse, the teams swap sides every quarter, meaning Hancock is back where they started at the beginning of the game. Our hot dogs appear after another minute or two, and Naomi blushes scarlet when I hand her the extra one. She mumbles a thank-you, but my eyes are on Sarah as she impatiently reaches for her own paper plate.

"Sarah, wait—"

Ignoring me, Sarah grabs her food and promptly drops it when she realizes how hot it is, spilling it everywhere. She doesn't cry out loud, but she turns her wet eyes to me.

"Can I get another?"

I shake my head. "Serves you right. I told you to wait."

"Please, Tate?"

Sarah juts her bottom lip out, manipulative little creature.

At that moment a steaming tray of nachos appears on the counter, and the woman next to Andrew steps around us to grab it. When she disappears toward the condiments table, Andrew takes the opportunity to come over to us.

"How are you guys doing?"

"Okay," Naomi says. "Is that your mom?"

Andrew nods.

"How much longer do you think this is going to take?" I mutter, checking my watch. "Shouldn't something have happened by now?"

Andrew looks at my sisters, but when I shrug off his concern, he keeps talking.

"The caffeine pills should only take thirty minutes to kick in . . . so any minute now. Maybe? Are you sure you broke the right stick?"

"Yes."

"You're sure—"

"*Yes*, Andrew." I sigh and look around, not at all surprised to see that Sarah has disappeared in the brief time that we were speaking. Naomi reads my mind.

"I think I know where she went." She looks from me to Eliana, doing the math. "Want me to grab her while you wait for your pizza?"

"Please."

Naomi nods. She heads back to the line and nearly bumps into Mr. Levitan coming in the opposite direction. Naomi mumbles an apology before she disappears, but Mr. Levitan's not looking at her. Or any of us.

"Katie?"

I do a double take at the obvious pain in his voice, then turn to follow his gaze. Andrew's mom is carrying her nachos with both hands, a glob of synthetic cheese on the front of her jacket. Her eyes are as wide as lacrosse balls.

"*Sam?*"

Andrew and I clock the tension that passes between them. But whatever history Mrs. Garcia and the chemistry teacher share, something tells me it isn't romantic.

"It's good to see you."

"You too. How have you been since . . . ?"

"Fine. Yourself?"

"Fine."

"Enjoying the game?"

"Yes."

Andrew clears his throat, obnoxiously but successfully reminding both adults that they aren't alone. Mr. Levitan nods at us and hurries away, and only once he's gone do I realize that he didn't even bother waiting around for his food. Mrs. Garcia stares after his retreating tweed coat.

"Mom? How do you know Mr. Levitan?"

"Sam was a few years ahead of me in school. Years ago . . . a lifetime ago . . ."

"Really? I didn't know he was from Hancock."

"He's always kept to himself." Mrs. Garcia shakes her head. "To be honest, I haven't seen him since his daughter died."

Andrew and I stand up straighter. Beside me, Eliana is too busy blowing on her hot dog to pay attention to what we're talking about.

"What happened to her?"

Mrs. Garcia tears off a hunk of nacho chips and chews slowly, looking for her words in the awkward silence that follows.

"Kimberly Levitan was one of the seniors who died in that car accident ten years ago. The police said she was driving drunk, but Sam believed there was also someone she swerved to avoid. He claimed there was a paint scratch on her car that he didn't recognize, but no one was able to prove it. He was simply out of his mind with grief . . . as were we all."

"What color was the paint?" I ask.

Andrew shoots me a curious look.

"Red, I think. But you'd have to ask him."

"Did he ever find out who the second driver was?"

"For some reason, Sam always thought it was Michael Richards . . . Troy Richards's father. It was an open secret at the time that Michael had a drinking problem, but he stopped soon after the accident. I thought it was a coincidence, but Sam thought it was proof of a guilty conscience."

Andrew and I share a glance. But before either of us can ask any more questions, there is an unmistakable roar of anguish from the bleachers. Based on the sound alone, something important is happening on the field. Big enough that someone is screaming.

And that someone sounds an awful lot like our Sassi.

35

hey jealousy

SASSI DeLUCA

"HooOOOoooot! HooooOOOOoot!"

The second half begins with even more stomping, even more cheering.

"HooOOOoooot! HooooOOOOoot!"

The laxtitutes have a chant for everything these days. Every time Hancock scores. Every time Trapelo scores. And every time one of the guys gets pummeled by the defense. I'm too embarrassed to ask Jennifer to explain them all, and each time the girls start singing I'm brutally reminded that I sure as hell don't belong here. I only agreed to this insane plan because I knew it would be invaluable to have someone on the inside.

"Hancock, showing us how it's done!"

This time the laxtitutes start gyrating in place, and I can feel the bleachers bend up and down with their movements.

"Nine-*nine*, you're so *fine*! Nine-*nine*, you're so—"

Kyle is on a breakaway, and a moment later he scores. Like Troy, he chest-bumps his teammates and takes a jubilant lap around the field, but he slows when he gets to the chain-link fence in front of us.

And then he stops.

"Sassi!" Kyle bellows, joyful. He presses his entire body against the fence, and although the entire crowd is screaming at him to get back on the field, he only has eyes for me.

"Kyle . . . ?"

"Are you having fun?"

I stare at Kyle, stunned. And painfully aware that the laxtitutes have a similar look on their faces.

"Shouldn't you be . . . Aren't you a little busy right now?" I ask.

Kyle shrugs, grinning from ear to ear.

"Yeah, I'm having fun," I say finally. "Thank you."

"Oh no. Thank *you*. You're my lucky charm!"

I smile despite myself. Kyle's enthusiasm is many things. Obnoxious. Ineffective. But right now, it's also contagious.

Someone whistles from the center of the field, and Kyle and I both turn to see Troy waving. He whistles again at Kyle. Like a dog.

"You should probably go."

"Probably," Kyle admits. But he stands his ground. "Can we make a bet before I go?"

"What kind of bet?"

"If we win, I get to take you on a real date."

"And if you lose?"

Kyle shrugs again, beaming from ear to ear. "I won't."

"Fine. Just . . . go play," I say. Kyle winks at me, trotting back to his place with a literal skip in his step. I sit back down, twisting my camera strap between my hands.

Jennifer smiles at me, a weird mixture of satisfaction and delight on her face.

"That was cute—"

"*Don't.*" I cut her off.

I follow Kyle with my viewfinder as he takes his place at midfield, waving his apologies to the referee with the nasty-looking goatee. My eyes go to Troy, and I try not to react when I realize he is watching me. It isn't possible to hear Troy from here, but when he points his stick in my direction, then at Kyle, his meaning is clear.

It's a warning.

Trapelo takes possession on the next face-off. And this time the tempo of the game is fast, faster than it was before. The referee dives out of the way as Kyle steals the ball, passing it to Troy without looking. Troy runs it down the field and—

The ref blows his whistle.

"Oh no, folks! That one is offsides..."

"Our ref is a real pickle..."

Troy storms up to the referee. No one can hear him over the booing crowd, but it's obvious that he's furious. Ferocious. In fact, I don't think I've ever seen Troy argue with an official before. Not like this. The back of his neck is almost as red as his helmet, and whatever he's saying, it isn't friendly. Not by a long shot. Kyle tries to pull Troy away by force, but Troy shakes him off.

"What is he doing?" Jennifer murmurs next to me. "He's going to get a penalty if he isn't careful..."

I look around to see if Andrew and the others are watching, but suddenly they are nowhere to be seen. Begrudgingly, Troy returns to his position. Thanks to the referee, Trapelo restarts with possession of the ball, and their attackman manages to run it down the field before two Hancock defenders check him in the gut. Someone passes back to Troy, and he sails to the goal. But as the other team closes in, Troy is still too far away to make the shot.

And although he makes his next decision in an instant, something tells me it was a long time coming.

Troy lobs the ball high. Higher than it's been moving all quarter. I watch as it arcs across the night sky toward Kyle in what seems like slow motion. Because even though Kyle catches it, the ball is moving too slowly, and he's primed to get walloped by the defense. Which he does.

We all see it coming.

So does Troy.

And even if I don't know a lot about lacrosse, I remember what that play is called.

A mother-freakin' murder pass.

"Oh no, folks! Number nine is down—"

"*TROY!*" I roar, hands cupped around my mouth, nearly drowning out the announcer, "BACK THE FUCK OFF!"

Jennifer and the laxtitutes gape at me. But there's no time to apologize. On the field, Kyle holds on to his leg with both hands. And for more than a moment, I worry that he might have broken it. Troy tries to help Kyle up, but Kyle shoves the hand away. Troy laughs and nudges Kyle's shoulder. And Kyle tackles him around the knees.

Next thing anyone knows, the two of them are all-out brawling.

"Crazy stuff! In-fighting on Hancock—"

"—gotta be girl drama, Paul—"

"*—what would you know about girl drama—?*"

"TROY!" I bellow. Again. Jennifer has to physically pull me back from scaling the chain-link fence. Kyle's head snaps at an angle and the referee rushes forward as quickly as he dares. It's utter chaos on the field and in the bleachers. Finally, a referee manages to get between Troy and Kyle, throwing them off each other with brute force.

Then the referee points to the penalty box.

36

livin' la vida loca

NAOMI KING

At the top of the quarter the game is tied. At a lucky, or unlucky, 13–13.

The referee sentences Troy to the sidelines, and he watches, *fuming*, as the game continues without him. Ten players against nine. And in the brief duration that Troy is out of play, Trapelo manages to score.

Twice.

We were hoping to trigger some level of 'roid rage with Tatum's caffeine pills, but even I didn't think we'd be this successful. Troy never sits down while he's in the penalty box, but he paces back and forth, talking to himself under his breath. It reminds me of going to the zoo as a kid and visiting the big cat exhibit. The tigers always scared me senseless, but Mel was fascinated with them, and somehow we always ended up at their enclosure just in time for feeding. Usually, the zookeeper would toss in hamburger patties, which surprised me and disappointed her. But one time we caught them chucking in cow bones. My dad explained that the bones were to keep the predators stimulated.

That's Troy now, I realize. Understimulated. Bored.

Hungry for blood.

After I left Tatum and Andrew at the snack shack, I found Sarah in one-woman silent protest under the bleachers, and I convinced her to come back to our seats in exchange for my hot dog. Now I sit with all three of the Stein girls at the very top, and even though I know I should be watching the game, it's nice seeing how much Tatum loves her sisters and they love her.

By the end of the quarter, Sassi appears, sheepish, in our row.

"Hey, ladies."

"Sassafras? Why aren't you with the laxtitutes?"

"They said I should take a walk. Cool off. Can you believe that?" Sassi plops down next to me. "I'll tell you this, those pills are working. Only problem? Troy's turning all his rage onto Kyle."

"We saw. How's lover boy doing?"

"He's *not* my—"

"Dude. Let it go. I don't know who you're trying to fool at this point." Tatum snorts, cradling the back of her head with both hands. "Don't you agree, Naomi? Methinks the lady doth protest too much."

Sassi gapes at Tatum, then me.

"Naomi?"

"Um . . ."

I'm saved from answering by Troy's less-than-triumphant return to the game. Even from where we're sitting, it's obvious that his teammates are trying to give him a wide berth. And when the team manager runs out to give Troy his water, Troy chucks the shaker bottle over the fence as hard as he can.

"All right, folks, our boy Troy Richards is back in play!"

"I'll be more impressed if he can stay in play, Paul..."

With the minutes counting down, Hancock wins back possession of the ball. Sam Klein considers passing it to Kyle, who is open, but settles for throwing to Troy. Too intimidated to do anything but what Troy tells him to do. Troy takes the ball and swerves around the Trapelo thugs. He's going to shoot. He does.

The game is back to 14–15.

Until Troy promptly projectile vomits.

Everywhere.

"*Dude.* How much did you dose him with?" Tatum whistles. I can feel Sassi shrug next to me.

"All of it?"

Troy braces himself on his knees, pale, watery vomit dripping through the bars on the front of his helmet. I can't bring myself to watch and close my eyes, but I can hear Sassi greedily snapping photos next to me.

CLICK.

CLICK.

CLICK.

"We got him!" she squeals. I barely manage to hum a response.

Hancock calls a time-out.

"Do you guys see Andrew anywhere?" I ask, and I risk opening my eyes. I'm just in time to see Troy rip off his helmet with both hands, and I close them again.

"He's with his mom. Get this! Apparently Mrs. Garcia went to school with—"

TWEE!

Before Tatum can begin her story, the referee blows his whistle.

The fourth quarter unfolds almost identical to the ones before it, and even I have to give Troy credit for playing in his current state. And in the same helmet. With the Howlers down by a single point, the team's chance of securing a good ranking for playoffs is on the line, and despite any of our ulterior motives, Sassi, Tatum, and I all fall silent in the final three minutes of the game.

3:00...

2:55...

2:50...

Troy is lining up a shot when his lacrosse stick breaks into two pieces. Next to me, Sassi slowly lifts her camera to capture the temper tantrum on film.

CLICK.

"I'm telling you, Paul, if Richards can't get his act together, the team might be down their star player."

"I haven't seen a temper like that since '92..."

For a split second Troy just stands still. Empty-handed. An eerie calm washing over him. And before the referee can respond, Troy rips the stick away from his nearest teammate, scoops the rogue ball from where it dropped, and scores the winning point.

But not until he twists the stick from his right hand to his left and back again.

Left. Right. Left.

Left. Right. Left.

My eyes widen.

I've seen that move before. It's the same trick he did with my Game Boy. Except now I understand what it means.

"Did you see that?" I say, grabbing Sassi by the elbow.

"Yeah, bozo." Tatum snorts. "Everyone did."

I shake my head, tightening my grip on Sassi.

"Um, ow—?"

"He scored with his *left hand*," I mutter. "Not his right. Which means Troy isn't a righty. He's both. And if Andrew was lying about that . . ."

". . . then Troy *did* punch him in the face at Hilary's party," Tatum finishes. "Why wouldn't Andrew tell us?"

"Only one way to find out," I murmur.

Sassi's eyes narrow as the crowd goes hog wild. Because the lax bros are carrying Troy down the field on their shoulders. With the final point, the game is back to a tie, which means they're headed into sudden death. Because of him.

Their hero.

"Naomi, can you grab Andrew?" Tatum says. "We'll put my sisters in Sassi's car. Meet us in the parking lot."

"Totally . . ."

While Sassi and Tatum hustle Tatum's sisters out of our row, I make my way to where Andrew is sitting with his mom. He doesn't see me approaching until I'm right next to him, and he jumps an inch in the air when I touch his shoulder.

"Naomi?"

"Jennifer is looking for you," I say, the lie dry and flaky on my tongue. "Come with me."

Andrew nods and does exactly that, just as I knew he would. Mrs. Garcia gives me a curious look but doesn't say anything to stop him, and Andrew follows me out of the stadium.

By the time we've climbed the hill to the parking lot and Andrew sees Tatum and Sassi waiting for us, he's merely confused.

"Where's Jennifer?"

"Freakin' lax bros..." Sassi mutters.

Realizing something is amiss, Andrew spins to me, a wounded look on his face. "Naomi...?"

"Did you see Troy score just now?"

"Yeah. I was with my mo—"

"Oh. Kay," Sassi interrupts. "So you saw him score with his left hand?"

"Yes...?"

"Cool. So I guess you just forgot to share with us that he can play both ways. Just like you didn't tell us that he's the one who *hit* you on New Year's Eve. Isn't that right?"

Andrew freezes.

"Why didn't you tell us, Andrew? Why didn't you tell me?"

"It's not my story to tell."

"What's that supposed to mean?"

"I'm sorry, okay! You're right. I should have told you guys everything." Andrew runs both hands through his hair until it stands on end. "We're in this together, aren't we?"

"I mean, *we* thought we were," Tatum tuts. "But I suddenly get the feeling that you're lying to us about what really happened that night. And *why* we're doing any of this to Troy in the first place."

She gestures to the lacrosse field, and at that moment a shriek of joy drifts up from the crowd. Andrew hesitates, rubbing his arm.

"Fine. The truth is... I was there. At Hilary Maxwell's house party. That part of the story is true."

"Yeah. Got that. Next?"

"And . . . the reason Troy hit me . . ."

"Was it because Jennifer kissed you?" I guess. But Andrew just shakes his head.

"No. *She* didn't . . ."

new year's eve

37

kiss me at midnight

ANDREW GARCIA

Say what you will about Hilary Maxwell, the girl can throw a party. Keg and Bagel Bites included.

I'm not surprised that I'm one of the last to arrive, and when I do there are cars parked all the way down the driveway. If I had to guess, I'd say it's barely thirty degrees outside, without the windchill, and my mom made me take one of my dad's old ski jackets before I could leave the house. Wearing it makes me feel like a little kid, the sleeves hanging over my fists.

The front door to the Maxwell house is unlocked, and I let myself into the warmth as quickly as I can. Inside, people are laughing, drinking, dancing, small-talking, all the way up the spiral main stairs to the third floor. But our host is nowhere to be seen. There are quite a few older kids that I don't recognize, which surprises me, but I have to assume they are college strays that Hilary brought home with her for the holidays. I was only a sophomore when Hilary graduated, but she knew me because I was on the lacrosse team. Because she knew Troy. Then again, everyone does.

I find Troy in the living room, one elbow perched on the mantel next to a row of Maxwell family photos, all of which were taken outside the Maxwell dealership. He grins when he sees me but doesn't say anything, holding a conspiratorial finger to his lips. Next to him, Kyle is in the middle of telling a story to two college girls, and Troy's eyes are laughing. But I can't tell if he's laughing at Kyle or with him.

"The hamster was never the same after that—"

"Garciaaaaaaa!" Troy roars, pulling me into the party with a one-armed hug. "What took you so long?"

"Sorry, I was waiting for my mom to fall asleep," I lie, even though I don't know why I feel the need to lie. Suddenly, there's nothing more embarrassing than the way my mom kissed me on the cheek before I left the house. "I didn't think she'd make it as long as she did."

Troy tuts with faux concern and uses both hands to spin me around like a windup toy, turning me to face the older girls.

"Ladies, this is Andrew."

"Hello," I say. The girls just stare at me. Unimpressed.

"Okay, hotshot." Troy snorts. "Let's get you a drink."

Troy throws a lazy arm around my shoulders, and the two of us head for the basement. I spot a group of people playing strip pool from the top of the stairs, Moose among them. He waves when he sees me.

"'Sup, Garcia!"

I try to wave at Moose without looking at him or his dick.

Troy leads the way down the carpeted stairs, and when we reach the basement I realize it's even more crowded than I thought. Not that I'd expect anything less. People are loaded up on the leather couches facing the plasma TV that is twice the size of my parents', but just like my parents they are watching a broadcast of First Night in downtown Boston. The camera cuts to an eagle-eye view of the crowd, and everyone in the city is wearing a twisting balloon-animal type of hat. As Troy stops to say hello to someone, I'm shocked to clock Sassi DeLuca perched on the farthest edge of the couch. We're neighbors, it's true, but she's so busy with all her extracurriculars that I rarely see her in person.

Also, she doesn't drink. So this isn't exactly her scene.

"Hey, Sassi."

Sassi doesn't respond. Instead, she takes one look at Troy and stands, marching up the stairs in the direction we just came from. Oh well. I never figured out why the two of them broke up, but she clearly hasn't gotten over it. Troy catches me watching Sassi and laughs.

"Drinks are outside. C'mon."

We open the sliding glass door to the porch and step into the cold a moment later. I almost slip on a patch of black ice, but Troy steadies me. I want to complain about the temperature but don't, forcing myself to burrow deeper into my dad's jacket. Not that it helps. There are a half-dozen coolers to peruse, and Troy kicks open the one nearest us, handing me a beer from within. It's so cold my fingertips threaten to stick to the side.

"Any resolutions for the new year?" Troy asks, cracking a PBR for himself. I can tell he's a few drinks ahead of me, but I don't mind.

Like in lacrosse, I'll just have to work a little harder to catch up with him.

Troy waits for me to respond and I take a sip of my beer, trying to ignore the fact that it's Jennifer's face that flashes in my mind's eye. The two of them have officially been unofficially dating for two months now, and I have no right to be jealous. Troy asked her first.

"No, I don't think so."

"Really?"

"Really, really," I insist, forcing another sip. The beer is so cold I can't even taste it. "I already have everything I could ever want. Life is good in my playbook."

Troy rolls his eyes, not buying it. He leans on the railing, facing away from the festivities, and although I think about suggesting that we head back inside, I don't. I stand next to him, my elbows going numb through my jacket when they touch the railing. There isn't a lot of snow in the Maxwells' backyard, and what little dusting there is won't last. All in all, it gives the entire world a simple, frozen-dinner quality. Peaceful.

"Aren't you going to ask me . . . ?"

"Right, sorry. What about you? What are your resolutions?"

"I want to *destroy* Trapelo this season." Troy hums, staring out into the black. "This is my last spring on the Hancock team. I want to go out with a bang."

"Boom . . ." I whisper. Troy elbows me, and I elbow him right back. "Aren't you ready to get out of this town? I bet if you asked nicely, those college girls would love to take you back to campus with them."

"I guess. But I also wish things could just stay this way," Troy admits, a startling layer of earnestness in his voice. He gestures to the frost, and me, and the party. "This is perfect."

Now it's my turn to laugh.

"Sassi was eyeballing you earlier, you know," he continues. "Are you gonna kiss her at midnight?"

"Ew. No. Sassi is like a sister," I say, making a face.

"A hot sister—"

"*Dude.*" I laugh and turn around, still leaning on the railing but now facing the party. The glass doors are fogged from within, and I doubt anyone can see us out here. "Besides, you guys dated."

"No hard feelings. You should go for it, if you want to."

"Oh yeah?" I say, taking another sip. "What happened there, anyway?"

"I guess I just realized . . . she wasn't my type."

"Come on. Sassi is everyone's type." I shake my head. "If not perfect, what are you looking for?"

Troy is silent, thinking hard, and I don't have the heart to tell him I didn't mean the question literally. It's so cold that I can feel my nose and brain going numb, and when he shifts I can sense his body heat through his flannel. I also realize he's not wearing a jacket, which means he's probably more than a few PBRs ahead of me.

"Hey. Aren't you cold?" I ask suddenly.

There is a round of applause in the basement, and when I look at the doors I can see the colors and shapes of happy people smooching in the Boston Commons. The new year has arrived, and the lax bros sing along to the TV, loudly and off-key. I laugh at the chaos of it all, but I realize Troy hasn't made a sound. Suddenly, his face goes slack, and it looks like he's about to say something. Instead, he leans toward me.

Troy's lips taste like beer and Burt's Bees.

I'm too surprised to move.

He pulls back.

And I'm no longer laughing.

"Troy..."

"Does that answer your question?"

"You've had too much to drink," I mutter. My utter shock makes it hard to feel much, and the only thing I do feel is embarrassment. But I don't even know who I'm more embarrassed for, me or him. "You don't know what you're doing."

"I know exactly what I'm doing."

And that's when I realize... he does.

But before I can say anything, whatever it is that I'm supposed to say, or want to say, the sliding door opens for the second time. Noise pours out of the basement, breaking the silence around us.

"Troy?"

Jennifer is grossly underdressed for the weather in a bright pink dress and heels, and she looks between the two of us with just as much pink in her cheeks. But she's more confused than accusatory, and she closes the door before speaking again.

"What's going on?"

"Nothing," Troy snaps.

"That didn't look like nothing—"

Troy whips around fast, one fist raised, and I step in front of Jennifer out of sheer instinct. I don't know what he's going to do, but I can't risk it.

"What?" Troy hisses at me. "You think I'd hurt her? Come on, Garcia. You know me."

"I thought I did! But that was before..."

Troy's eyes shutter.

"Before what?"

I don't know why I said it, or why I said it as loudly as I did, but I quickly realized it was the wrong thing to say. Troy reacts without blinking, without thinking, and when I take a step toward him, he punches me squarely in the face. Jennifer gasps, and when I stumble into the side of the house she drops to her knees in the slush next to me.

"If you tell anyone about this, you're dead," Troy says to me, and only me. He doesn't even bother looking at Jennifer, and his voice is suddenly robotic, expressionless. Terrifying.

He means it.

Jennifer pulls me into her arms, but it's not until Troy goes inside that she starts to cry. I rest my chin on top of her head, looking over her shoulder into the party. From here, the confetti on the TV looks like a silent blizzard. Troy takes his place among the crowd, but not quite. Because even from here I can tell he's watching me through the foggy glass. Waiting to see what I'll do next.

Neither of us smiles.

Meanwhile, inside, on TV . . . the new year begins.

sudden death, overtime

38

wannabe

ANDREW GARCIA

The girls wait in silence for me to finish my story.

Sassi, for the first time in her life, is at a complete and utter loss for words. Meanwhile, Tatum looks like she swallowed something spiky. As for Naomi . . . well. If she found a way to scrunch up her eyebrows any more, she'd actually have the unibrow that people tease her for. While I'm speaking, their eyes never leave my face.

"Look . . . I'm sorry I didn't tell you everything from the beginning. But I couldn't risk it. Because as much as I hate Troy for what he's done—"

"You wanted to *protect* him," Sassi says, incensed. "After everything he did, to you, to us . . . you were still worried what would happen to Troy if people found out."

"I mean . . . yeah."

Tatum sticks a finger down her throat, which I ignore.

"I dunno . . . maybe Andrew's right. It wasn't his secret to tell. If Troy's dad is as bad as everyone says . . ." Naomi hesitates. "I don't forgive you, Andrew, but I understand."

"I don't," Tatum grumbles. "I don't buy it either. You've been best friends with the guy for *how* long, and you didn't know he's into dudes?"

"What? Sassi dated him—"

"It's a *spectrum*, you prudes," Sassi fires back. "Besides, Naomi's right. Mr. Richards would blow a freakin' gasket. We all know what Troy's dad is like."

"I don't—"

"One time, Troy's dad got cut off when he was driving us to practice," I interrupt Naomi, "and in return, he took a tire iron to the guy's bumper at the next red light. But because he's a cop, there were never any charges. None that made it to court, anyway..."

"Let's just say the rotten apple doesn't fall far from the tree." Sassi shudders. "I can't picture what Mr. Richards would do if he knew."

"Exactly," I say, taking a step closer to her. But Sassi draws away from me, unwilling to yield the high ground. "I never lied to you or anything like that. I really did want to punish Troy, and I still do... but I didn't want to permanently ruin his life either."

"So you let him ruin yours?" Tatum challenges.

Before I can respond, a family with several squealing kids walks directly between us, shattering our bubble and my focus. It's only when I see the entire crowd spewing out of the bleachers in the distance that I realize the game is officially over.

Based on the revelry... we won.

"Maybe this is a good thing, right?" Tatum muses. "Now we have the intel we need to take Troy down once and for—"

"I'm not outing someone," Naomi says, her voice flat.

"Jesus, Naomi. Where was your nobility when you were douching him with toxic chemicals?"

"I agree with Tatum," Sassi says, just as bitter as the rest of us.

"And we're sure that Jennifer knows?"

"I mean, she knows that Troy was hooking up with Zoey before Valentine's Day," Naomi says, shrugging. "I told her about it earlier tonight, and she barely batted an eye."

"You *what?*" Sassi screeches. "What are you talking about?"

I open my mouth to answer, when three things happen at once.

First, Sassi's eyes go wide enough that I can see the white eyeliner drawn on her lower lids. Second, a vicious blur of red and pink tackles me around the waist. And third, my ex–best friend screams bloody fucking murder at the top of his lungs.

"GARCIAAAAAA!"

I'm barely a match for Troy on a normal day, and right now, thanks to us, the guy is juiced out of his skull. Tatum's caffeine pills have effectively turned Troy into a real-life Incredible Hulk, and he smashes both of us into the concrete. Hard. I bite my tongue and my mouth floods with the tang of blood.

Sassi and the others must scream, but I can't hear them over the ringing in my ears.

"Troy!"

"It was you, wasn't it?" Troy spits, rolling on top of my chest and forcing the air out of my lungs. "You sabotaged my gear, you piece of shit—"

"I didn't!"

Troy slugs me in the jaw without any regard for who sees, and although Tatum and Sassi try to drag him off, there's no point. I doubt he even feels their hands on his back.

"I'm going to get help!" Naomi wails. She disappears before anyone can stop her, and Troy laughs when he realizes where she's going.

"Once a snitch, always a *bitch*—"

"Don't call her that!" I shout, lunging for him. Troy doesn't expect me to fight back, and with our combined momentum we go rolling down the hill next to the parking lot. One after the other, over and over. We must look fucking bizarre. Stranger still, it reminds me of when we were younger and would race down the hill behind Troy's house, before crash-landing into a pile of leaves that we'd spent all afternoon raking up.

But any nostalgia I feel is promptly squashed when I choke on a mouthful of mulch.

Eventually, I roll to a stop. But the taste of dead plants lingers. Sassi and Tatum come sprinting after us as fast as they can, careful not to fall over themselves in the process. Troy gestures to the girls.

"Since when are you all friends?"

"Leave them out of this," I mutter, pushing myself up on my elbows. "This is between you and me."

"Good point." Troy snickers. He kicks me hard in the stomach and I curl around his foot. He's still wearing his cleats, and when he comes in for a second blow, the spikes drag across my side. "Then again, if that were the case, am I supposed to think it was a coincidence Coach Lancaster showed up tonight?"

"I didn't invite him!"

This time I'm telling the truth. Not that he cares.

"Do you know what he said?" Troy demands. He kicks me again, but this time I latch on to his calf. Using his weight against him, I pull Troy back to the grass, and we are vying for control when Tatum and Sassi reach us. "Coach Lancaster was disappointed by my lack of *sportsmanship*," Troy sneers, throwing his elbow at my stomach. "And he said that if we don't win state, he might have to reconsider my spot on the Harvard team. But you know what's really not sportsmanlike? Trying to ruin your best friend's chance at—"

"It wasn't Andrew!" Sassi yells. "I invited the coach! It was me, Troy!"

Troy's surprise causes him to hesitate, and Tatum seizes the opportunity to leap onto his back. She wraps around Troy like a koala, and Sassi plants herself in front of me like a human shield.

"Sassi—"

"Calm down!" Sassi barks. "Both of you!"

Troy hocks a loogie, and it gives me no pleasure to see there is blood in his spit. I must have managed to land a punch or two, and there is an open gash across one of his eyebrows from our fall. Without stitches, he might scar in the exact same place I did.

"Do you have anything to say for yourself, Garcia?" Troy steps closer to me, and it's as if neither of the girls exists. "I could press charges, you know. Then you won't just be off the team, you'll be kicked out of school. You'll be fucking done. After that, you'll be lucky to get a job picking up trash along the freeway. You'll be just like Tatum's deadbeat daddy. Don't you have anything to say for yourself? Don't you want to apologize? Beg for my forgiveness?"

"Dude. *Shut up*, already," Tatum mutters.

Troy merely swats her off his back and advances on Sassi

and me. His footfalls are heavy. Leaden. He doesn't seem to notice that our audience has grown, a dozen curious spectators drifting over from the lacrosse field.

"Hey! Watch it—"

"Why would you do this, Andrew?" Troy demands, his voice thick. "You're my friend. My brother. My teammate. I've looked up to you my entire life, and I've always wanted to be like you. You've always had everything I wanted. I love you—"

"Ha! Oh, we know . . ."

Troy bristles, his attention sliding to Tatum. She has the decency to catch her mistake, and gulps, but that same reaction only confirms the obvious. She knows.

Troy turns back to me, slowly.

"You told them?" he hisses.

Troy lunges at Tatum before I can say anything, but Sassi gets there first. She throws a knee at Troy, directly in the dick, and when he goes down he only takes her with him. I heave myself forward as Sassi cries out in pain, but a second blur of pink beats me to it. Kyle is still wearing his lacrosse gear, and when he tackles Troy at full force the sound reverberates through my bones.

"Kyle! Be careful!"

It's unclear whether Sassi means to be careful about hitting Troy or injuring himself, and Kyle instinctively turns to her. Troy plants a lucky strike on his jaw, and when Kyle stumbles back I take his place.

"You broke my nose!" Kyle shouts. "What the fuck, Troy!"

Reenergized and bloodthirsty, Troy pounces on me. One hundred seventy pounds of solid muscle slams into my chest, and his hands wrap around my throat. It feels like my lungs are on fire, and when I rear against him the pain hits my lower ribs. If I'm lucky, it's a fracture. I'm too distracted to notice that the mass exodus from the lacrosse field is almost complete and a circle has formed around us. Every single person there hears what I say next.

"I'll kill you, Troy!"

Troy's face darkens.

Because for the first and last time . . . he believes me.

Everyone does.

I roll to one side and spot Sassi on her knees, desperately trying to help Kyle with his bleeding nose. She holds my gaze over his head, just as horrified as everyone else. But not by Troy, I realize. By me. Tatum crouches behind her, still breathing heavily, one hand pressed to her mouth. When she moves it, I see that her bottom lip is bleeding too.

Otherwise, no one moves. No one says a word. Until . . .

"Andrew Garcia!"

I turn to see Principal Clancy barreling toward us, my mom and Naomi in her wake. Clancy shoves her way through the curious onlookers with a ferocious strength that would be comical in any other circumstance.

"My office."

"But—"

"Now."

now

39

i love you always forever

JENNIFER LEE

"Andrew...?"

There's no response—not from him, the shadows, or anything else in this stupid school. Bracing myself, I take the stairs two at a time until I'm back on the third floor. Even though Mr. Richards is long gone, I'm careful not to let the door slam behind me. Precious seconds later, I find Sassi, Naomi, and Tatum exactly where they're supposed to be.

In the very last place any of us wants to go back to.

Naomi is sitting on the floor of the yearbook office—crying. I try not to stare at the booger that connects from one of her nostrils to the corner of her mouth. She has her knees pulled into her stomach, and Tatum squats across from her on her heels. Sassi, on the other hand, stands in one corner of the room, eyeing a low table I didn't notice before. There are several glossy photos spread across the top, and from here it looks like a working layout for the *Howler*.

Sassi sighs. "Nice of you to join us."

Because I'm looking at Naomi, it takes me a moment to

realize that Troy is no longer hanging from the ceiling. The jump rope suspending his body seems to have exploded into pieces while we were gone—*hundreds* of pieces. Because now his corpse is flopped in an unceremonious pile on the floor, and the plastic beads have scattered everywhere, under chairs and into the farthest corners of the yearbook office. Something tells me the odds of finding my charm bracelet have officially jumped from narrow to paper-thin.

"Naomi . . . are you okay?"

She answers my question with her own.

"Did you hear what people were saying? They were so . . . *mean.*"

"I'm sorry," I say. I extend a hand, then think better of it and ball my fingers into a fist. "Don't let them get to you. They're morons."

"Actually, they're assholes." Tatum turns to glare at me. "And don't tell her how to feel. You literally did the least you could to help."

"What are you talking about?"

"You know what I'm talking about. You're the queen bee of this school, princess. Tell your hive to stop buzzing."

Naomi covers her face with both hands.

"I'm so ashamed—"

"Don't be," I insist. "You have nothing to be ashamed of."

"No one liked me before. And now . . . !"

Tatum promptly smacks the back of Naomi's head.

"*Ow!*"

"Do you think I'd still be here if I didn't like you guys?" Tatum gestures to Sassi. "Don't make me say it out loud, Naomi. You're weird and nerdy and objectively creepy, but you're an awesome baker and have a bizarre little encyclopedia for a brain. Even my sisters love you! Honestly, I wish I'd been more like you when I was your age and stopped trying to impress other people."

"But what about—"

"Your awful taste in girls?"

I blush scarlet, and Naomi shrugs.

"I kept the secret for so long. . . . I didn't know if anyone would care," she admits. "I wasn't ready to find out. I tried telling Mel before she left for college."

"What did she say?"

"It's not the life she'd choose."

Tatum grimaces.

"I'm telling you, Naomi, one day this is all going to be so, so boring." I flap my arms lamely at my sides. "Who you love will never be the most interesting thing about you. In a good way. I promise."

"I dunno . . ."

"You're so young," Tatum adds, shockingly sincere. "You have your whole life ahead of you, and so, so many more idiots to fall in love with."

Naomi sighs and averts her eyes.

"Kind of depends how the rest of tonight goes . . . doesn't it?"

No one has a response to that. Tatum catches my eye over Naomi's head, and together we pull Naomi to her feet.

"This is for you," I say, handing Tatum's pipe back to her.

"Thanks," she huffs. "Now what do we do?"

"Andrew was supposed to meet us here," Sassi says, thumbing through the photos in front of her. Something tells me she's trying to prevent herself from staring at the body, and I don't blame her. "Wasn't he with you, Jennifer?"

"He was, but—"

"These are quite good," Tatum interrupts. She's moved to stand beside Sassi, and she paws through the images with both hands. Curious, I step closer. It's not a layout for the yearbook, like I thought, but a dozen newly colorized photographs of Hancock student-athletes from over the decades.

"Thanks, Tatum."

"My uncle has this one in his shop," Tatum continues, moving one photo in particular to the very top. I recognize it immediately from the trophy case downstairs. "He and Mr. Richards were on the same lacrosse team. I've never seen the color version before."

"No one has. That's the point."

"I just saw Mr. Richards," I say, every single hair rising on the back of my neck. "He's here, in the school."

"Troy's dad is *here*? Why?"

"I don't know," I admit, anxiously reaching for my charm bracelet before I remember it's gone. "I bumped into him as Andrew and I were leaving Clancy's office. I tried using her phone, but the lines are down. Something really, really weird is going on. . . ."

Naomi whimpers.

"What was that, Naomi?"

"It's just . . . earlier? I thought I saw something in the hallway. A shadow . . . or . . ."

I bristle as I remember the same inexpressible feeling of being watched.

"You're imagining things."

"What if whoever killed Troy got to . . . ?"

"Let's focus on one lax bro at a time," Sassi says, her voice steely. She's about to say something else when Tatum shushes her. But there's no point—because we can all hear it now.

Footsteps.

"Someone's coming," Tatum hisses.

"Maybe it's Andrew . . . ?"

As the footsteps in the hallway get louder—and louder—Sassi risks cracking the door for a better look. I automatically move to stand by the person closest to me—Naomi—and when I see the fear in her eyes, I link my arm with hers. She leans into me for support, and I can't help but notice that she smells like vanilla. A man's voice comes to us from somewhere around the corner. He's close but still too far away to identify.

"Hello . . . ?"

"Is it the janitor?" I ask.

"Does it matter?" Tatum hisses. "If anyone finds us with Troy's body, we're dead."

We all turn to glare at her.

"Metaphorically . . . speaking."

Sassi closes the door as slowly and quietly as she can. "Whoever's out there, it looks like they're doing room checks. I could see a flashlight."

"Which means it's only a matter of time until they search in here. . . ." Naomi trails off.

"I told you they'd be looking for Troy!"

"Yeah, but I didn't think it would happen this fast!"

"Guys, focus . . ." I plead.

Sassi frowns, considering every inch of the yearbook office before she responds. Like me, I'm sure she's realized there's no place in here big enough to hide a 170-pound corpse.

"We need to move the body."

I cringe at Sassi's suggestion, but it seems like I'm the only one.

"Where to? If they're checking all the classrooms—"

"Lockers." Tatum snaps her fingers. "Leave it to me."

"Hello...?"

"It's Mr. Levitan," whispers Naomi, the first of us to recognize his voice. "We need to stall him!"

Suddenly, Tatum stands up perfectly straight.

"Holy shit."

"What?" I ask.

Tatum hurries back to the table of color photos.

"Tatum, care to explain—"

"What's the one thing Mr. Levitan wants most in this world?" she asks. She grabs one of the largest images, drops it in her excitement, and picks it up again.

"Uh...?"

Tatum turns the photo to face us. It's the first one that I recognized—with a young Michael Richards and his boys hoisting the state trophy on top of his car. Mr. Richards sits behind the wheel, and the rest of the team is flexing and laughing in all their splendor.

"Proof of his daughter's killer," Tatum says, pleased.

We all stare at her.

"Andrew's mom told us that Mr. Levitan always suspected a second car ran his daughter off the road," she explains, "because there was paint on her car that he didn't recognize. *Red* paint."

"So?"

"So?" Tatum says, incredulous. "Look!"

Gleefully, she moves the colorized photograph closer to us. Because there, in bright screaming color, is Mr. Richard's car.

A blood-red Chevy Nova.

june

40

everybody (backstreet's back)

ANDREW GARCIA

The yearbook office smells suspiciously like cinnamon buns.

Unlike the first time we met in the beginning of February, today the door is open when I arrive. But instead of feeling welcome, I unconsciously linger on the threshold. From here, I can see Sassi standing at the windows as she mindlessly blows the steam off her Dunkin' Donuts cup. Meanwhile, Naomi fiddles with the keyboard at one of the computer stations, knees pulled to her chin and both jelly shoes wedged uncomfortably on the seat beneath her. The girls have their backs to me, and even from here it's obvious that they're not speaking to each other. I begin to wonder if it's at all possible to leave before they notice me, even though I'm the one who suggested meeting in the first place.

"Boo."

Tatum's voice is tart, and I turn to find her directly behind me. Too close to me. She's wearing a tiny pair of rectangular sunglasses, despite the fact that we are inside, and when she takes a step forward I reluctantly slouch into the office. Something tells me she does it on purpose.

But neither Sassi nor Naomi says hello.

"Don't get too comfortable," Sassi mutters, still looking out the window. At what, I'm not sure. Classes are over for the day, and the parking lot is steadily emptying out, with the last school bus having left fifteen minutes ago. "Clancy's officially removed me from the editorial board of the *Howler*."

"I can't stay very long either," Naomi pipes up. Like Sassi, she's careful to avoid eye contact. Once I'm close enough, I can see that she's brought a Tupperware of homemade cinnamon buns, which explains the objectively homey smell. But something about seeing the heavy frosting up close makes my stomach queasy, and for once no one seems eager to give them a try. "My parents think I'm at work."

"This will be quick," I promise.

"Cool. And what is *this*, exactly?" Tatum gestures to the space between us. She sets her skateboard down in front of one of the rolling TVs, and all three girls look at me.

It's been a little over one week since the Hancock-Trapelo game. Troy stopped fighting as soon as Principal Clancy appeared in the parking lot, but something tells me that the only reason why was because my mom came with us to Clancy's office. Once we were away from the crowds, Principal Clancy announced that she's benching Troy for the next two games and that I'm suspended from class until further notice. Not only that, but for the rest of the semester I have to do community service with the janitorial crew. Sean is already enjoying wielding his power over me. Troy seized his chance to tell Principal Clancy that he suspected the girls were helping me prank him, and over the course of the last week they've each been called down to the front office. Sassi lost the *Howler*, Naomi received a second demerit on her record, and if Tatum had bothered to show up to any of her classes, I suspect she would have been expelled.

But the worst part is that even after the game, and the fight, my mom still insisted on driving Troy home.

"I want to start by saying I'm sorry about what happened last weekend," I begin. "Next time—"

"Hang on. There isn't going to be a next time, Andrew. We're done." Sassi shakes her head with such force that her ponytail smacks into her eyes. "*I'm* done. I thought that part was obvious."

"But—"

"Dude, give it up." Tatum scowls. "Nothing we've tried to do this year has made a shit of difference. And now the four of us have an even bigger Troy-shaped target on our backs than we did before. I won't throw good money after bad."

"Tatum's right," Sassi adds. "I *knew* this was a bad idea. I should have listened to my gut. And we should just be thankful it wasn't worse."

"I hear you, Sassi. I know things are hard right now . . . I do. But we agreed to work together because we all hate Troy—"

"That's not why I said yes."

Sassi, Tatum, and I look at Naomi. She pushes herself away from the computers, cinnamon buns forgotten.

"What do you mean?"

"It wasn't just about Troy," Naomi explains, shoving her hands in her pockets. Today she is sans pigtails, her braids hanging loose around her face, but she somehow looks even younger than usual. "I've never been the kind of person to stand up for myself. With Troy, sure, but also with my parents . . . or my sister. I choose to be quiet not because I'm afraid but because I don't want to bother anyone. Most of the time it's not worth it. But I thought teaming up with you guys could be my chance to prove to everyone I'm not a pushover. To prove it to *myself*." Naomi drops her eyes to her feet. "Except now that Troy knows what we did . . . what we were trying to do . . . it won't stop with him. It'll just get worse. If I'm lucky, people will forget about me. They usually do . . ."

Sassi softens at the resignation in her voice.

"Naomi . . ."

"Jennifer told me the truth."

Sassi braces herself as Naomi whirls on her, suddenly . . . angry. Angier than I've ever seen her. Even Sassi takes a step back.

"About . . . what?"

"You've been lying to us this entire time. Jennifer told me that *you* broke up with Troy! So why are you really here? What were you really hoping to get out of this?"

Sassi gapes at Naomi, now her turn to be at a loss for words. The manicured hand holding her coffee cup droops to one side, threatening to leak the contents onto the tile floor. Somehow, Sassi's silence is even more unnerving than Naomi's unexpected wrath. The calm before the storm. Tatum looks from them to me, but neither of us tries to intervene.

"Jennifer told you that?" Sassi mutters.

Naomi hesitates, then nods.

"Well . . . that would explain why everyone on the team

stopped talking to me." Sassi looks at me next. "Is that what Troy told you? That I broke up with him?"

"He might have suggested . . ."

Sassi forces a laugh. But this time I don't know who she thinks she's fooling.

"I should have known Troy would be too cowardly to tell people the truth. Fine. You want to know what really happened? Simple. He stopped making an effort. He treated me like shit. He said we were never really dating. And me? Even worse. I *loved* him. I would have kept trying to make it work. But *he* broke up with *me* so he could hook up with Kat Hicks at postprom. Trust me, I wish I had broken up with him. But the truth is that I stayed as long as I could. For all my talk, I was just as stupid as the next girl."

"You're not stupid, Sassi," Tatum murmurs. "You loved him."

Sassi slams her coffee down on the nearest table, causing the rest of us to jump.

"I didn't get involved with this perverse group project because Troy broke my heart." She makes a face. "Like I told Andrew, I found out that Harvard only takes one incoming freshman from Hancock every year, and Troy stole that spot from me when he committed to the lacrosse team last semester."

"Sassi . . ."

"Save it." Sassi flicks her hair over her shoulder, and only now do I realize she's not wearing her usual Harvard crimson. She really has given up. "Everyone knows that Harvard is my dream. But what you might not know is that it's because my mom went there, and I wanted to be like her. Stupid, right? Especially since she can't even be bothered to return my calls."

"Speaking of college . . ."

Tatum takes a folded piece of paper out of her back pocket and hands it to Sassi. I can feel the conversation spiraling away from me, but for the life of me I can't figure out how or when to jump back in.

"What is this?"

"Read it yourself."

Sassi hesitates but does just that, her mouth twitching as she reads silently. Tatum doesn't wait for her to finish before addressing the rest of us.

"Sassi convinced me to apply to Framingham University. And . . . I actually got in." Tatum jabs her thumbs through the belt loops of her jeans, but there's not a single drop of pride in her announcement. "Not that it matters anymore, thanks to Troy."

"Did Clancy finally expel you?"

"Worse." Tatum shakes her head, removing her sunglasses. Her eyes look bloodshot, but I honestly can't tell if it's from smoking or crying. "I've lost so much money because of Troy, my uncle won't let me go. He's made it very clear I need to stick around and provide for my sisters. Otherwise, he'll take them away."

"Tatum—"

"And, hey, while we're doing the group therapy thing, when was *anyone* going to tell me that Troy's dad is a cop?" Tatum interrupts. "Did no one think that would be important information?"

"Why does that matter?"

"Because, Sassafras. The asshole arrested my dad!"

Sassi inhales so sharply that we all hear it. As for Naomi, she steps closer to rest a hand on Tatum's shoulder. Tatum quickly shakes her off.

"I don't need your pity."

"Is there anything I can do to . . . ?"

"I'll handle it," Tatum snaps, glaring at me. "I always do."

At that the yearbook office goes silent, and the only sound any of us can hear is the hum from the computers. As the girls look at one another, I realize they are right. I thought that, with their help, I would be able to do something that mattered. We would be able to give Troy a taste of his own medicine and free the school from his tyranny in the process. But we have nothing to show for our efforts. What's more, we're all worse off than we were before. The plan, my plan, was stupid. Short-sighted.

And even if they don't say it out loud . . . it's all my fault.

"I'm sorry," I murmur. The apology is all I have to offer, and it doesn't help anyone.

"Save it, Andrew," Tatum snaps. "The only thing that would make any of this better is if Troy was *gone*. That's the only way my uncle might forgive me."

Sassi and Naomi share a glance.

"But what if—"

"No, Andrew," Sassi says. "I only agreed to meet today as a courtesy. So I could tell you to your face . . . I'm out."

Naomi is the first one to move, and for a moment I think she's going to come to my defense. Instead, she grabs the cinnamon buns and storms out of the office, taking the smell of sugar with her. Tatum shoves her sunglasses back onto her nose and follows at a distance.

Which just leaves Sassi . . . and me.

"Sassi..." I hesitate, then stop myself entirely. There's no use in asking her to change her mind, so I settle for a sigh. "Do... you want to walk home?"

Sassi chucks the rest of her coffee in the trash can.

"I still have work to do here," she says, gesturing to the table of images she has been colorizing all semester.

"I can wait for you...?"

"No need. Kyle is giving me a ride."

"Oh."

"Bye, Andrew."

She stares at me, pointedly, until the message is received. Officially dismissed, I trudge out of the yearbook office, leaving Sassi to finish whatever she needs to do for the *Howler*. I find myself heading in the direction of the library, although I'm halfway downstairs before I realize that my feet are leading me to the locker room. At that moment, someone taps me on the shoulder, and I half expect to see Naomi fluttering behind me. Just like our first day back, when she tried to warn me about Troy.

Half expecting... maybe even half hoping.

"Hi, Andrew."

"Jennifer...?"

Jennifer and I stare at one another, hushed. The air in the stairwell suddenly pushing in from all sides. Jennifer is wearing her letter jacket, her hair in a messy bun, and unlike me, she looks surprisingly refreshed. I haven't spoken to her since the Trapelo game, but only because I knew better than to try.

"I've been trying to talk to you all week. I'm so sorry about—"

"It's okay," I say, taking one step up so we are at the same eye level. "What happened at the game wasn't your fault."

"That's not what I wanted to apologize for," Jennifer admits, biting her lower lip. "I'm sorry about everything. New Year's Eve. This entire semester. I'm sorry I wasn't brave enough to tell people the truth before things got even more out of hand. I just . . . I didn't want Troy to get in trouble. I was afraid . . . of him, and for him."

"I understand," I say, and even though it's the truth, the apology isn't enough. I search Jennifer's face, although for what, I'm not sure. Her eyes are just as beautiful as they've always been. Just as sad, too.

"Are you still dating Troy?" I ask, unable to help myself. Because I already know, and fear, the answer.

"Yes."

"And . . . you knew that he and Zoey were hooking up? The whole time?"

"Yes."

"Jesus, Jennifer . . . why are you still with the guy? What do you see in him?"

"Please don't look at me like that."

"Like what?" I ask, hearing the desperation in my own voice. "Do you love him?"

Jennifer balks ever so slightly.

"It's my life, Andrew."

"But—"

"No. That's my answer, Andrew. *Because* it's my life," Jennifer says again. "Because it's not just Troy I would lose if I broke up with him. I'd lose the team. My friends. I've been playing on the girls lacrosse team for two seasons, but no one took me seriously before. No one cared or even noticed me. It's not worth it to—"

"But don't you realize you're losing yourself living this way? You think *that's* worth it?"

Jennifer frowns and takes a step, putting herself one stair firmly above me.

"Why do you care?"

"Isn't it obvious?" I groan. "Because I like you, Jennifer."

"Andrew—"

"I *like* you," I say again. "And sometimes I more than like you. *More* than sometimes."

For a moment Jennifer doesn't react, and I realize I'm holding my breath. We both are. The only reason I said it is because I officially have nothing left to lose, and a twisted part of me doesn't think there's anything to gain. But I need to be sure. I want and need to rip off every Band-Aid. Now or never. That said, as I wait for her to respond, Jennifer breaks into a cautious smile. It's like the sun coming through clouds on a rainy day. The storm hasn't quite passed, but there's a promise that it will. When she doesn't move, I take a second step so we're back at the same level, and Jennifer tips her face to me, waiting for me to do something. Anything. So I kiss her.

And Jennifer Lee kisses me back.

now

41

gettin' jiggy wit it

JENNIFER LEE

"Hello?... Anyone here?"

After a quick debate and an even quicker game of rock-paper-scissors, I stand guard at the door to the yearbook office as Sassi goes left—toward Mr. Levitan—and Tatum and Naomi go right—toward the library. Even though I'm supposed to be keeping watch, I squeeze my eyes shut, straining to use my other senses. I can't hear what Sassi is saying, but knowing her, it's convincing.

"... Ms. Deluca...?"

"... Hi..."

A lifetime later, Tatum and Naomi return, each carrying one end of the massive senior banner the Stern twins hung outside the library. Even I'm not able to hide my disappointment.

"We can't move him with that! What if he bleeds through it or—"

"Chillax! It's not like he's bleeding... anymore."

"Fine. So who's going to... you know...?"

Naomi gestures toward the center of the room, and I look at

Troy before I remember that I'm trying not to. Tatum sighs and kneels alongside his body. For a moment, I think she's going to start praying, and I absentmindedly clasp my hands over my heart. My family has never been particularly religious, but when my grandparents were alive we'd go to church on Christmas Eve. I always liked the singing.

"Tatum . . . do you want any help?" I whisper. I don't bother hiding my relief when she shakes her head no.

Tatum begins by rolling down Troy's jersey so his torso isn't exposed. She slides as much of the banner as she can under his legs, picking up his feet one sneaker at a time. Then his shoulders. Once the body is on top of the banner, Tatum begins to roll it from one end to the other—like it's a Fruit Roll-Up. Troy's left arm flops onto the ground at an unruly angle, and Tatum gags before tucking it securely inside. Once she's done, I see my hands jerk out and grab one corner of the banner before she needs to ask me for help. As a unit, Tatum, Naomi, and I pick up the banner and penguin-waddle into the hallway, in the opposite direction from Sassi's voice. Tatum shoots me a triumphant smile as we turn the corner, but I remain focused on my hands. Sassi and Mr. Levitan might be out of sight, but they're not exactly out of mind—especially given the fact that we're standing a mere five feet away.

Once we are safely around the next corner, the three of us look down at Troy's corpse.

Then at the wall of lockers.

"I'm on it," Tatum mutters. We rest the banner on the ground, and once her hands are free she heads for the locker closest to us. I quickly bow out of the way as Tatum rests her ear against the metal door.

"Anything I can do?" Naomi squeaks.

"Sure. Stop mouth breathing."

Naomi presses her lips shut, and I watch as Tatum clears the lock by spinning the dial clockwise, three times, past zero. Then, still clockwise, until she hits the first number. Which I don't think she exactly sees as much as she hears. Next, counterclockwise, past the first number, until the second—and finally, even slower, clockwise, until she reaches the last number. Otherwise, it's just as hard as it sounds. Literally.

Tatum pushes up and the locker opens on the first try. Naomi exhales a massive sigh of relief, and I realize she might have taken Tatum's words a bit too literally.

"Nice work, Tatum."

"*Psh.* No biggie."

The inside of the locker is a freshman girl's messy fever dream—complete with *NSYNC posters, gel pens, puffy stickers, and even a lone Tamagotchi. I take an armful of textbooks to hide in the trash, and Naomi clears out a plastic container that smells alarmingly like last week's Meatless Monday special.

Then it's time to move Troy.

"Fuck me. He's a biiiiiiig boy," Tatum huffs.

Troy's body was hard enough to move the first time, and now I realize how rigid he's become. Like a Ken doll. Once, when I was five or six, I went down to Rhode Island to visit my grandfather at his beach house. My parents took us to walk along the breakwater, and for some reason I thought it'd be fun to chuck my favorite Ken at the rocks. Which I did—over and over. I don't know what exactly inspired me; maybe it was just that I was proud of how strong I could be. Besides, it wasn't until I saw Ken's head pop off that I realized my actions were permanent. Now, as Tatum and Naomi awkwardly fold Troy's limbs to fit him in the locker, I try to hold the image of Ken's headless torso in my mind's eye. Nothing more than plastic. Nothing left to do but cry.

Mercifully, the door closes on the first try.

Naomi, Tatum, and I take a moment to rest, each of us silently and intently watching the others to see what they'll do first. We're all a little out of breath, although I don't know if that's from the physical exertion or the lingering panic of almost getting caught by Mr. Levitan.

The door to the stairs slams in the distance, causing all of us to flinch. Sassi appears a moment later.

"Success?"

"You could say that." She makes a face. "He took the photo and went to find Mr. Richards."

"To do what, exactly?"

"Not our problem."

"But what did he say?" Tatum presses. Her enthusiasm is nearly palpable. "Was I right? Will it be enough proof?"

"Yeah. He said . . . *Thank you.*"

That sobers Tatum real fast. She takes a step forward, toward the yearbook office, then immediately stops where she is.

"Ew. I stepped in something."

"Is that . . . blood?"

We all stare in horror at the dark substance smeared from Tatum's boots to the bottom of the locker. But instead of responding, Tatum swipes her thumb over her Docs, and before I realize what she's doing—before I can stop her—she sniffs it.

Then she pops her finger in her mouth.

"Tatum!"

"Chillax. It's not blood," she hisses. "It tastes like chocolate syrup."

With all of us watching, Tatum hastily opens the locker a second time, and Troy's body spills out onto the floor. One foot bends at a wonky angle, and I immediately close my eyes. I simultaneously have the urge to puke and to cry, and the only thing keeping me from doing either is fear—the same kind of fear that pumps adrenaline into your veins moments after a head-on collision, when you know, technically, you're still alive, but you're all too aware of how close you were to being otherwise. When I finally manage to look again, I see Troy lying on his stomach, the back of his jersey rolled up around his midriff.

Sassi mutters to herself, seeing something that I don't.

"It's fake blood?" Naomi asks.

"Yep."

"The drama department used fake blood in their preshow," Sassi muses, twisting her ponytail. She drops to her knees, rolling Troy from his belly to his backside.

"You're telling me the theater kids did this?"

"No. But I think someone tried awfully hard to cover up how and where Troy died."

We all look at one another, perplexed.

Then—the body.

Without the banner to cover it, we can all see Troy's corpse up close and personal for the first time. My eyes travel to Troy's mouth, where there is a slick coating of saliva, and something that looks more green than white in the semidarkness.

"Was he . . . poisoned?" I ask.

None of the girls respond to that.

With all of them watching me, I kneel alongside Troy. My attention goes from the strange discoloration at his mouth down to the side where Troy's jersey is bunched up at his ribs. I didn't dare get this close before, but now that I am, I risk checking his pockets for good measure.

"What are you looking for?" Sassi asks, terse.

"My bracelet," I explain, suddenly unable to meet their gazes. "I . . . broke up with Troy at the beginning of the night. And I gave his bracelet back." I frown, sitting back on my heels. "But it's not here. I didn't see it in the yearbook office either."

"You didn't think that was important for us to know?"

"I told Andrew," I say, frowning. "Besides, I didn't think it mattered. I would never hurt Troy."

"But if Troy had it when he was alive, and he doesn't have it now . . ." Sassi trails off, staring at the fake blood. "I bet if we find the bracelet, we'll find where he was actually killed."

I set my mouth in a thin line, and I'm about to stand up when something else catches my attention. I didn't notice it earlier because Tatum had pulled down Troy's jersey, but now I can see there is a distinct impression on Troy's skin, a smattering of dirt—no, gravel. It almost looks like a turf burn. But judging by the blood at the edges, Troy was dragged over the gravel before rigor mortis set in. Which supports Sassi's theory that he didn't die in the yearbook office.

"What are you thinking, Jennifer?" Sassi asks, scrutinizing my every move.

"I think . . . I think he was killed outside. Maybe in the parking lot?"

"There's no way he got in and out of the building without a chaperone noticing."

"The roof," Naomi says, realizing. "Andrew told me that he and Troy used to . . ."

Sassi moves first, completely disregarding Troy's body as she pivots and heads for the stairs. Tatum, Naomi, and I hastily lift his body and position Troy inside the locker as best we can, and a moment later we follow her at a distance. Sassi is many things, but she's not an athlete, and we manage to catch her in the south-side stairwell. When she tries the door to the roof, Sassi finds it unlocked—but the door catches when it's open just an inch. Too narrow for any of us to squeeze through.

"I think it's barricaded with something."

"Any ideas?"

"Yeah, one." Tatum snorts. *"Push."*

Tatum, Naomi, and Sassi throw their shoulders at the door, and with their combined power it bursts open with little protest.

Inexplicably, a lacrosse stick falls out of the way.

It's still early enough that the sky is pitch-black, the only light coming from the slice of an early moon and the rotary in the distance. The four of us walk outside single file, like elementary schoolers, and I squint at the outline of an industrial AC unit. But I don't need to be able to see clearly to hear the ballasted roof crack underfoot, its thin coating of gravel stretching from one edge of the roof to the next, with several flattened beer cans, cigarettes, and Doritos bags thrown into the mix. I know that upperclassmen like to sneak up here during their free periods, but I've never seen it for myself. And now, searching the ground on his hands and knees is—

"Andrew?"

Andrew stops what he's doing, stupefied, and pops to his feet as fast as he can. But it's not fast enough.

"What are you guys—"

"We could ask you the same thing," Tatum mutters. "Needed some fresh air?"

This time Andrew doesn't say a word. His hair is sticking straight up, and he's breathing so heavily that I can see his chest moving. I steel myself and step forward, determined to defuse the tension regardless of my own bewilderment.

"Andrew, we examined Troy's body," I say. "He was poisoned."

"What?" Andrew snaps. But he doesn't sound horrified, just bewildered. "You're sure?"

"Yes! There was foam and—"

"How's that possible? He seemed totally fine when I saw him."

"Hang on." Tatum glowers, the apprehension on her face a mirror to my own. "You told us that you hadn't seen Troy all night."

Andrew goes rigid as Sassi, Naomi, and Tatum share a glance, but this time the girls stay silent. Almost as if the three of them are privy to some secret that I don't know. Not yet. Again, my instinct is to rush to Andrew's defense, but I falter when his hand falls open at his side. A flash of silver between his fingers.

"Is that . . . my bracelet?" I murmur. But we all know the answer to the question.

He balls his hand into a fist.

"Andrew . . ." Sassi begins. Her voice is soft, positively homicidal. "When did you last see Troy?"

four hours ago

42

good riddance (time of your life)
TROY RICHARDS

"I didn't think you'd show."

Andrew doesn't respond. But if you knew the kid as well as I do, you'd know that *that* is more than enough of a response.

I'm still not used to seeing him out of his lax uniform. His second skin. And he looks . . . smaller. Tonight, he's dressed down in a black hoodie with a band logo that I don't recognize and, even more unusually, *jeans*. It's almost impossible to see his face in the rapidly darkening evening, but even from a distance I can recognize Andrew by the way he walks. Hands in his pockets, chin jutted out, like he's always moving toward something and can't wait to get there. He scans the roof and I resist the urge to wave, knowing he won't be able to see me. I'm sitting with my back to the AC unit, and from here, I can see everything.

The school, the parking lot, even the lacrosse field in the distance.

Our lock-in officially started about an hour ago, and people are already determined to have a good time. The DJ hasn't started the dance party just yet, but when I escaped up here they were gearing up for a battle of the bands–style contest with several of the wannabe groups from my grade.

It was necessary to sneak out. Or up, in this case.

Eventually, Andrew spots me and stops where he is. His shoulders tighten—the poor kid is always thinking too much. After a long debate with the imaginary angel on his shoulder, Andrew sits next to me. But he makes a point of keeping a gap between us.

Maybe he thinks it will give him the upper hand.

"Yeah, well. I'm here now." Andrew leans forward with his elbows on his knees, hands clasped.

I smile humorlessly. The two of us haven't spoken since the Trapelo game—due mostly to Clancy's strict warning that if either of us tries anything, we'll *both* be expelled. Unlike Andrew, I'm still wearing my jersey. And if you ask me, it's a perfect spring night. We can even hear crickets from the cemetery on the other side of the main road.

Otherwise, we're entirely alone.

"What going on, Troy?"

I reach into the shadows next to me, pulling out a red-and-white cooler with a fading Hootie sticker slapped on the side. It used to belong to my dad when he was a Howler, and it was impossible to get the smell of beer out of it. So I stopped trying. The last time we used it, Andrew and I went to Cape Cod with the rest of our team. I was talking to Sassi at the time, and Andrew was flirting with a freshman girl whose name I never learned. All the guys had sock tans from our uniforms, and by the end of the trip the tans became sunburns. For the Fourth of July weekend, we stayed at someone's place in Falmouth. I grilled. We never drink during the lacrosse season, but summers are a different beast. That said, my absolute favorite part of the trip was the drive to and from the Cape, Andrew at shotgun. Before we got on the road, I realized that I had forgotten to grab the cooler out of my dad's garage, at which point Andrew just laughed and revealed he had already chucked it in the back. Because Andrew is the guy who always remembers things like that. Always the one looking out for other people.

I open the cooler, revealing a six-pack of PBR on ice.

"*That's* the emergency?"

"I also have weed if you prefer," I admit. "C'mon. These beers aren't going to drink themselves."

Andrew sighs. He shimmies closer and we look out at the streetlights like we're stargazing. From here the lacrosse field seems bigger, emptier. It used to be grass when we started playing but was replaced with turf when I was a sophomore—the kind with plastic bits that rub your skin and get stuck in your shoes, making the long practices even longer.

The mood isn't friendly between Andrew and me, but neither of us has the energy to fight. Not anymore.

"I've always hated this stuff," Andrew admits, but he takes another sip. "For your sake, I hope they serve better beer at college. You think someone is going to find us drinking on school grounds?"

I smile and chug the rest of my beer. It's not my first, and I already feel a little nauseous. I blame the bake sale.

"What are they going to do? Graduation is *tomorrow*. I'm as good as gone."

Andrew is silent.

"Remember the first time we played Eddy Forty Hands?" I

nudge him. "You couldn't drink liquor, so we did it with that shit wine instead."

"I remember *not* remembering."

"Or what about after my junior prom, when Kyle's dog ate our pot brownies? His parents thought we killed the poor guy, but he was just stoned out of his fucking mind."

This time Andrew snickers, and we laugh until we stop.

Another silence descends on us.

"You ruined my life, you know," Andrew says.

"Your life? That's rich, Garcia. At worst I ruined high school. Cry me a fucking river. If people found out about . . . if *my dad* did . . . well. My actual life would be over. Maybe one day people will understand, or even better, not care, but right now they do. And he *always* will."

Andrew goes silent and drinks. He doesn't stop until the can is empty, and I hand him a second. I can feel his body warmth but I'm hypercareful not to touch him. Which he notices.

"Troy . . . I'm sorry."

"For what?"

"I don't know. It's hard to keep track."

We both laugh at that. I down the rest of my beer to match him. Again, something twinges in my gut, but I ignore it. And burp loudly.

"Why did you invite me up here?"

"No reason. I guess I was just feeling nostalgic. It's my last night before graduation . . . I wanted to spend it with my best friend. Bury the hatchet. Say goodbye."

"*Are* we friends?"

"Jesus. Just shut up, Garcia." I run a hand over my skull. My hair is still painfully, disgustingly short, but it'll grow back. "I'm trying to be nice."

"Maybe you could talk to your dad about—"

"That's something that even you can't fix."

"Maybe it won't be as bad as you think! It's the nineties." Andrew shrugs. "More importantly, he's your dad. He just wants you to be happy—"

"That's not enough."

Andrew rests his hand on my shoulder. And we both know I misread the gesture.

Or rather, I want to.

"You got me. There is another reason I wanted you to meet me here," I say, rising to my feet.

"You want another apology?"

"No." I waggle my eyebrows. "I want a rematch."

Andrew looks confused. Then I take two lacrosse sticks from where I stashed them at the edge of the roof. Mine feels heavier than it usually does, but I have to imagine it's the significance of the moment. The memory in the making.

"Troy, this is your lucky—"

"Exactly. I want you to have it. The school is going to need your bloodlust once I'm gone." I sigh when he raises his eyebrows in surprise. "I asked Clancy, and she said she'd let you try out for the team again in the fall. If you want."

"Troy . . ."

I offer Andrew a hand, yanking him to his feet.

"One more game. For old times' sake."

"But I don't have my helmet or—"

"What? You scared?"

Andrew smiles.

Challenge accepted.

I empty my pockets of anything that might slow me down, setting my wallet and Jennifer's charm bracelet on the ground behind the AC. I stand up so fast that for a moment my vision blurs, and I take an extra step to ready myself. Then, with me cradling the ball to start, Andrew and I line up directly across from one another. Ten feet apart, at most. Careful not to step on any of the exposed piping on the rooftop. The gravel shifts underfoot a bit more than I'd like, but I ignore it. That's what I get for drinking on an almost empty stomach.

I remember when Andrew and I first met. Because he was little, but he was fast. And he's only gotten faster over the years. We became friends in a blink, and then he became my best friend. Then something more. But after tonight, I will leave him here. He'll be a part of this place and my memory. A part of me and my story.

Again my stomach rumbles, louder than ever, and again I ignore it.

"What are we playing?"

"One v. one," I shout, not bothering to keep my voice down. No one is looking for us. In fact, I dare them to come find us. "I'll count it down, okay?"

"Okay."

"Three . . . two—"

Andrew surprises me again and bursts early. I laugh. I run, giddy, ready, even though I'm not in my cleats. The ground bounces back under me. My muscles snap awake. My ribs expand with my inhale. Every inch of my body loves this. *I* love this. Andrew does too. I can see it, see him, feel it all. Even when my vision contracts, I push through it, blaming the PBR. When we collide at the center of the roof we are evenly, perfectly, *forever* matched. And whatever happens tonight, whatever happens tomorrow, there is comfort in the realization that I'll always have this.

My school.
My moment.
My best friend.
CRACK!

five minutes ago

43

man! i feel like a woman!

JENNIFER LEE

"It was an accident."

I stand in a line with the other girls, facing Andrew. Four v. one. We've all crossed our arms, and if it weren't for the seriousness of the moment, I'd say we look alarmingly like the poster for a new girl band. Andrew doesn't know where to look, but our attention remains riveted precisely on him. His story—his confession.

He continues.

"When Troy didn't get up, at first I thought he was joking . . . I thought he must have been. He *had* to be. I mean, I heard the hit. I felt it. But I didn't see him drop. I broke away with the ball, and even when I realized he wasn't chasing me, I kept going. When I saw Troy on the ground, he was just . . . flat. He was here, and then he wasn't. And when I realized what happened, I blamed myself. Of course I did . . . and I knew everyone else would too."

Andrew pauses to run both hands through his hair, oddly excited. Suddenly, I can't bring myself to look at him, and instead I choose to stare at the ground. The beer cans, the lacrosse sticks—it all seems too obvious. There is even a single drop of blood from where Troy hit his head, but in the watery moonlight it looks more like a piece of dried gum. Because Andrew was too busy moving Troy's body to clean up the actual crime scene—until now.

"But don't you see? If he was poisoned, Troy was always going to die," Andrew says. "It wasn't my fault after all."

"But you thought it was," Sassi mutters, not sharing his enthusiasm. "And you staged the body so we'd think there was another killer in the school. You tricked us, Andrew. You told us we were friends. You *begged* for our help! And the whole time you were hoping . . . what?"

"We *are* friends. Sassi. I just, I panicked—"

"No. You knew exactly what you were doing, and you decided to *use* us. Just like Troy. But at least he had the decency to own how much of an asshole he was." She shakes her head. "The only thing worse than a lax bro is a *liar*."

"But why?" Tatum presses. "Why go to the trouble?"

Andrew gapes like a fish out of water, his eyes going to me next.

"Jennifer—"

"Don't look at her like that," Naomi cuts in, the first of us to uncross her arms. "You brought her to the yearbook office on purpose, didn't you? So someone else would find the body and sound the alarm. You wanted to use Jennifer as your shield."

Andrew takes a nervous step forward.

"I'm not saying what I did was right. I thought if I could convince you guys there was a murderer in the school, then the teachers would believe it too," Andrew says, gaining steam. "But Troy had to have been poisoned *before* he hit his head. Which means there is an actual killer! And that someone could be . . . anyone . . ."

Suddenly, slowly, Andrew trails off. When he doesn't continue, I manage to drag my gaze to his face long enough to see what he's staring at. Naomi. Tatum. Sassi. Naomi—who admitted that she sold Troy a cookie at the beginning of the night. Tatum—who had the access and ability to slip a little something extra into Troy's stash. And Sassi—who even Chloe said she saw drinking with Troy and the other seniors. Even though . . .

"You don't drink," I say to Sassi.

"And?"

"No fucking way," Andrew mutters, stumbling back. Because he must have realized the same thing I have.

It could have been any one of them.

Or . . .

"It was *all* of you," I whisper, the words thick on my tongue. "You all poisoned Troy."

Hushed, the girls look at one another. More surprised than anything else. Because what Andrew did to Troy was an accident—at least, the first part of it was. And they all agreed to help after we found Troy's body because the way he staged the body *did* make them think there was a killer in the school.

Another killer.

The girls look at Andrew.

Then me.

Then back to one another.

"I hated Troy for what he did to me," Naomi says unhurriedly.

Her eyes are glued on Sassi and Tatum, and the glare from the security lights makes it hard to see through her glasses. "But I could have killed him for what he did to you."

"Ditto," Sassi murmurs.

"Same," Tatum adds. "And I won't tell if you don't."

A silent understanding passes between them. Because I can't be certain whether it was all of the girls or just one of them, but it doesn't matter. If I'm right, there's no reason for them to investigate further, let alone snitch on each other. The only one who might is Andrew.

And he realizes it too.

"Sassi . . . Naomi . . ." he whispers. "Tatum, please . . ."

Tatum steps forward, and Andrew instinctively scoops up one of Troy's lacrosse sticks to defend himself. For a bizarre moment I wonder if he's going to try to duel, and I pick up the second stick.

"Andrew, stop!"

"I'm sorry! Okay? You're right! What else do you want me to say?" Andrew's voice creeps higher. "I didn't know what to do. I was a coward! Is that what you want to hear?"

"Kinda, yeah," Naomi mutters.

"Save it, Andrew," Sassi chimes in. "You can't talk your way out of this one."

"And stop fucking *crying*," Tatum adds. "You're the one who hung the guy up like it was your fucking birthday party—"

"Everything we did this year, we did for *you*," Naomi continues. "For all of us. And it still wasn't enough. Because when things got hard, you were just thinking about yourself."

"That's not true . . ." Andrew trails off. His eyes land on me, but even though I can see the desperation in his face, it suddenly feels like I'm watching everything from far, far away. The lacrosse stick droops at his side, and he takes another step backward.

"Careful!" I call out.

If Andrew hears me, he doesn't show it.

"You're all crazy! All of you!" he shouts. "No one will believe you!"

A hand reaches for Andrew. It's too dark for anyone to really see whose it is. Too fast to tell if the hand is reaching to pull him in or to push him away—but it doesn't matter. Because he flinches. Andrew takes a final step, and in the process he trips over the lacrosse stick. There's nothing any of us can do.

And then he falls.

graduation day

epilogue

Saturday.

Graduation day.

The morning arrives one inch at a time. Undiscerning. It starts at the eastern edge of the horizon and softens from black to blue from the outside in. The air around Hancock High is warm and heavy, and the distinct change in humidity is the first real hint of what is to come. Summer, in most people's cases.

Or the blind hope of rising seniors, in others.

Alone, Principal Clancy unlocks the double doors at the front of the school. Right on schedule. She checks the clock on the wall above the trophy case, but when no one tries to leave, she props the exit open with a cinder block. Then she sneaks a cigarette. Because for everyone else, for now, there is no rush. People are exhausted. Sleepy. The underclassmen groan and dawdle and hug as if they will never see each other again. Meanwhile, the current seniors stand in uncomfortable half circles, many of them finally realizing that after today, they really, truly won't see each other again. Because this afternoon—graduation—is an event for families, not friends. There will be no more homerooms, no awkward birthday parties, no unrequited crushes, no painful silence while waiting for the bus. Slowly, people start to laugh and cry and make promises they don't intend to keep about staying in touch. Then, like an afterthought, yearbooks are passed around for the first and final time: 2 GOOD 2 BE FORGOTTEN, NEVER CHANGE, I WISH I COULD HAVE KNOWN YOU BETTER BUT YOU SEEM LIKE A REALLY GREAT PERSON LOL, HAGS!

Maybe that's why people don't immediately see the red-and-blue lights.

When the first police car pulls into the bus loop, confusion crackles through the crowd in starts and stops. Like Pop Rocks. More than one person suggests it's a senior prank, somebody else fears that it's part of the drama club's ambitious postshow, and poor Kyle Hennessy doesn't think anything at all, still riding the dopamine high that comes with first and last love. But all theorizing and giggling subside when Principal Clancy hustles to the back of the school. Her cigarette left on the ground.

Two ambulances arrive ten minutes later.

The sirens off.

By this time tomorrow, news of what happened during the lock-in will have reached every white picket fence in town. That is, if you can call the rumors that people are spreading *news*. But there is one thing that everyone in Hancock will agree on: When the police finally emerge from the school, the girls are with them.

Naomi King.

Sassi DeLuca.

Tatum Stein.

And Jennifer Lee.

After they arrive at the police station, Sassi will make her one and only phone call to the one and only lawyer she knows—her stepmom, Deborah DeLuca—and Deborah will answer on the first ring. While waiting to speak with the detective on duty, Tatum is the one who will tap Naomi on the shoulder, eager to point out Mr. Levitan as he appears with Mr. Richards's baseball cap in his fist, telling anyone who will listen that there's been a terrible, terrible accident. Not that any of the girls will bother correcting him. The officers will think it's a misunderstanding at first, but all too soon it will become obvious that it's the worst kind of coincidence—the kind that leads to more paperwork. Eventually, following standard questioning, the police will report that the tragic, unprecedented events of the lock-in were the fallout of a lovers' quarrel—because according to the girls, Andrew Garcia killed Troy Richards before committing suicide. A real-life Romeo and Juliet, more or less. As a result, in a weird way, Troy's legacy will achieve the one thing his life never could: the truth.

Now, I know what you must be thinking.

Who killed the other lax bro?

Was it Naomi King, whose jealousy of Andrew and Jennifer finally drove her to snap and push Andrew off the roof? Or picture-perfect Sassi DeLuca, moved to the point of rage and self-preservation after discovering Andrew's half-assed attempt to save himself? Tatum Stein certainly had something to lose, with her new college acceptance on the line, but could that force her to do something so heinous? And Jennifer Lee . . . sweet Jennifer Lee . . . Why on earth would she have gone along with any of it? Could it be as simple as choosing to side with her new friends? Stranger still, if only one of the girls was responsible for Andrew going over the edge, why would the other three stay quiet? Is it possible, like with Troy's poisoning, that we—they—could *all* be accomplices? Alibis for each other?

Sorry.

I meant to say *friends*.

A year from now, a modest scholarship will be created in Troy's memory. Two years from now, Andrew's name will be forgotten by everyone but the sticky pages of the *Hancock Howler*. Principal Clancy will retire eventually, but not before discontinuing the lock-in night altogether, at which point the drama club will find a new venue to terrorize people with their antics.

As much as it can, as much as it ever does, life at Hancock High will go back to normal. And I'm certain you've figured the rest of it out for yourself. I mean . . . the truth is obvious.

But *I'm* not telling.

She'd kill me too if I did.

acknowledgments

This book was a glitter bomb surprise.

Don't get me wrong—I've *always* wanted to be an author, a real, real-life Writer, but I had no idea that this one would be my first. Before it was a book, I wrote *Kill the Lax Bro* as a TV sample—a pandemic hobby, and my version of a "normal" high school drama, with, sure, just a dollop of my own wish fulfilment—and I have to start my list of gratitudes with the actors who participated in my virtual table read: Michelle Ann, Chandler Garcia, Jun Lee, Shaye Miller, Gloria Rodriguez, Abby Yazvac, and Lucille Vasquez. The story may have changed since then, but if it weren't for that video, this version of *Lax Bro* might not exist. The journey getting here (*gestures vaguely*) was long and winding, and is still going, but it's been an honor and a delight. I'm infinitely grateful for the opportunity to write a story that heartbroken high school me would have really wanted to read.

Up next, my family.

To my parents—all four of you—*thank you.* Mom, if you hadn't surprised me in the eighth grade by printing and binding one of my stories as a Christmas gift, I don't know when I would have realized that I could *finish* writing a book. I still think of our car rides telling "Highway Stories," and our adventures with self-publishing, and I wouldn't trade a single moment of the road. Dad, your objectively insane level of discipline (thank you, rowing) is one of the greatest things you've shared with me, and it's undoubtedly what got this book written on the five a.m. shift before my day job. Now that I think about it, you also printed an insane number of early projects for me at your office, which probably wasn't allowed—but I won't tell if you don't. Popi, I don't know who I would be if you hadn't bought me all those comic books—not to mention how you stayed out late for every Harry Potter release so I could wake up to a copy the next day. Margie, you were one of *Lax Bro*'s first beta readers, one of the classiest women I know, *and* you approved of the blow job jokes! My love and gratitude, for all of you, forever.

To my (big) little brother, Chandler. Look, dude—I just love how grown-up and cool you've become (you're welcome!). Thank you for reading every draft of *Lax Bro*, and for talking me off every ledge along the way.

To my (little) big sister, Mariah. You are the best cheerleader a girl could ask for. But don't forget that of the two of us, you were always the better writer. Seriously. It's time to write your own.

To the Milkman-Stein-Palace cohort, all my love and then some extra.

To my niece, Josie. You're waaaaay too young to read this book, but if and when you do, I hope it'll remind you to be just as brave and badass as you are right now. For context—yesterday was your fourth birthday.

To my Nanu, the woman who taught me how to read, love, and write books. This is not our story. But that one is coming, I promise.

Kill the Lax Bro would not exist if it weren't for the hard work and care of the many, many humans who helped it toward publication. Oh, and by the way—if you're an aspiring author currently skimming the acknowledgments section and looking for a blueprint of the Who/How books get made, know I was doing the exact same thing only a moment ago. The following folks are some of the best in the business.

To my literary agent, Michael Bourret, who believed in my writing before this book ever existed. Thank you for taking care of her, and me, and for answering my anxious author text messages.

To my rock star editor, Kelsey Horton, who took a one-in-a-million chance and saw *Lax Bro* for what it could be, well before anyone else did (even me!).

To the genius minds behind my cover, Casey Moses, Christine Blackburne, and Trisha Previte. This is what dreams (and manifesting) are made of!

To my production editor and copy editor, Colleen Fellingham, thank you for your incredible attention to detail and your intrepid nineties fact-checking—and making sure I didn't overdo the em dashes.

To the rest of my team at Delacorte Press and Penguin Random House: Joey Ho, Wendy Loggia, Tamar Schwartz, and the entire RHCB marketing and publicity teams, THANK YOU! Also—Emma Leynse! Extra-special thanks to you!

In addition to my family, I've been lucky to find friends who feel like family—plus an overwhelming number of girls who've threatened to commit a felony against an ex should the need arise. I'm even thinking of the people who've given me (great) unsolicited dating advice in bar bathrooms; the strangers who saw me crying in airport terminals, and bus stations, and my car, and stopped to ask if I was okay; the upperclassman who made me dinosaur chicken nuggets when I forgot to feed myself; and the long-distance friends who've Instagram stalked & blocked for me without question. I won't be able to list you all, but I will try.

To my *sisters*, Daniela Hargus and Erica Skye Schaaf. You two will never know what you mean to me, how deeply I carry the years, the laughs, the firsts, and the lasts, but I will certainly try to tell you. Repeatedly. Text me when you read this! I miss you!

To my quasi roommate turned neighbor turned Covid-19 survival buddy turned TV agent, Jillian Davis. We should have known we'd be stuck together after we showed up at a college party dressed as Anna and Elsa. Not letting you go anytime soon.

To my Big, Catherine Mazzocchi, who taught me how to drink wine and use InDesign. No, seriously—I use InDesign to pitch every project I write, including *Lax Bro*. It's a superpower, all thanks to you!

To the ladies of my first writers group in Los Angeles, who also read the earliest version of my *Lax Bro* script, Maddie Buis, Katherine O'Keefe, and Lily Olsen. I've never met anyone else who'd drop *everything* to throw a party just so I could invite one dumb boy to hang out. And to all the other girls who gave me notes (and love) over the last few years, Maggie Cannan, Hannah Evangelidis, Dani Gaj, Zina Kresin, Kylie Lewis, Eve Miller, Olivia Pecini, and Yolanda Rodriguez. Also, shout-out to my book club babes, Justin Bunka, Courtney Doyle, Monica Montoya, Margaret Starbuck, Ysabel Riina, and Hannah Pitts.

Now some miscellaneous love!

To all the authors I've met, the many of you who have answered my cold emails/DMs, Zoomed with me, had virtual coffee dates, agreed to blurb, and held my hand—I'm continually, endlessly indebted. Thank you for showing me, shoving me onto, and keeping me on the right path.

To my unofficial lax bro consultant, Sean Dewey, thank you

for answering all my questions and for making me laugh, always. I still hate how funny you are.

To the moms and sisters of my exes who still reach out (hi!).

To Professor Keith Giglio from Syracuse University, the first person to take me seriously as a screenwriter, who made me take myself seriously and who ultimately pushed me to make the jump to LA.

And to Taylor Swift (yes, that Taylor Swift), for teaching an alarming number of up-and-coming writers that if people don't want bad songs (or books) written about them, they shouldn't do bad things.

Speaking of.

In no particular order, I want to give a sincere, parting thank you to some (not all) of the boys who've broken my heart. Because if it weren't for you, I'd have a lot less to write about. So, to the one who wanted to become a DJ—and the one who broke up with me over AIM—and the one who ripped the bow off my Madeline costume in preschool—and the one who offered to come with me after my grandmother fell, and later asked me to give his girlfriend a ride home from the hospital—and the one who picked his nose and told me I'd "get over it" after I confessed that I'd "never felt this way before" (hey, you were right!)—and the one I thought was *The One* until he made it very, very clear, he wasn't—and—oh! The lax bro. Duh. Thank you all for the inspiration and for making this book, and the next, even better.

Finally, I want to acknowledge anyone and everyone reading this who has ever had their heart broken. By a lax bro or otherwise. All I can say is this: Feel it. Share it. Write it down.

And know I cannot wait to read about it.

about the author

CHARLOTTE LILLIE BALOGH is an author, a screenwriter, and a comic book writer born and raised outside Boston. She self-published her first book at sixteen years old and later graduated as a Remembrance Scholar from Syracuse University. CLB is a lifelong superhero fanatic, and she launched into the television and film industry by working at DC Entertainment on projects including *Wonder Woman 1984* and the CW's *Stargirl*. When she's not writing, CLB mentors young women through RowLA and WriteGirl, helping to create the next generation of real-life superheroes.

charlottelillie.com